IF FOUND, PLEASE RETURN TO

MAX CRUMBLY

IMPORTANT: If I'M missing, please turn this book over to the local authorities!

WARNING:

This journal contains
wacky humor,
thrilling action,
nail-biting suspense,
cool raps,
and a mind-blowing cliffhanger!

Also by
RACHEL RENÉE RUSSELL

Dork Diaries: Tales from a Not-So-Fabulous Life

Dork Diaries 2: Tales from a Not-So-Popular Party Girl

Dork Diaries 3: Tales from a Not-So-Talented Pop Star

Dork Diaries 3½: How to Dork Your Diary

Dork Diaries 4: Tales from a Not-So-Graceful Ice Princess

Dork Diaries 5: Tales from a Not-So-Smart Miss Know-It-All

Dork Diaries 6: Tales from a Not-So-Happy Heartbreaker

Dork Diaries OMG!: All About Me Diary!

Dork Diaries 7: Tales from a Not-So-Glam TV Star

Dork Diaries 8: Tales from a Not-So-Happily Ever After

Dork Diaries 9: Tales from a Not-So-Dorky Drama Queen

Dork Diaries 10: Tales from a Not-So-Perfect Pet Sitter

Dork Diaries 11: Tales from a Not-So-Friendly Frenemy

The Misadventures of Max Crumbly 1: Locker Hero

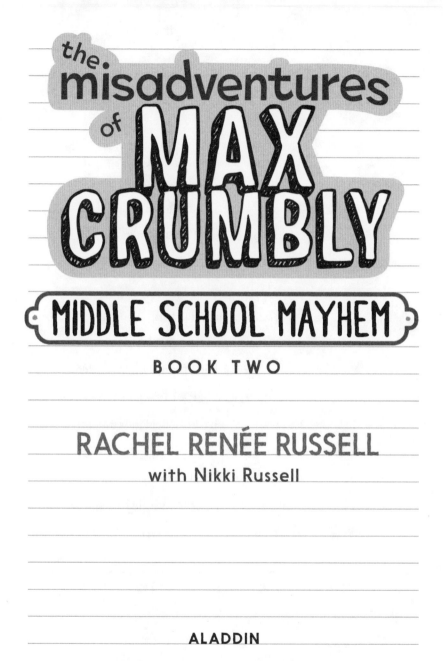

the misadventures of MAX CRUMBLY

MIDDLE SCHOOL MAYHEM

BOOK TWO

RACHEL RENÉE RUSSELL
with Nikki Russell

ALADDIN

New York   London   Toronto   Sydney   New Delhi

This book is a work of fiction. Any references to historical events, real people, or real places are used fictitiously. Other names, characters, places, and events are products of the author's imagination, and any resemblance to actual events or places or persons, living or dead, is entirely coincidental.

ALADDIN • An imprint of Simon & Schuster Children's Publishing Division 1230 Avenue of the Americas, New York, NY 10020 • First Aladdin hardcover edition June 2017 • For information about special discounts for bulk purchases, please contact Simon & Schuster Special Sales at 1-866-506-1949 or business@simonandschuster.com. • The Simon & Schuster Speakers Bureau can bring authors to your live event. For more information or to book an event contact the Simon & Schuster Speakers Bureau at 1-866-248-3049 or visit our website at www.simonspeakers.com. • Book designed by Karin Paprocki • The text of this book was set in Italo Medium Extended. • Manufactured in the United States of America 0517 FFG • 2 4 6 8 10 9 7 5 3 1 • Library of Congress Control Number 2017937154 • ISBN 978-1-4814-6003-3 (hc) • ISBN 978-1-4814-6004-0 (eBook)

To Lee "Bat Boy" Mignogna

Happy fourth birthday to a superhero-in-training
ready to vanquish baby sharks and
Pac-Man ghosts everywhere!

THE MISADVENTURES OF MAX CRUMBLY
(IMPORTANT STUFF YOU NEED TO KNOW IN THE
EVENT OF MY MYSTERIOUS DISAPPEARANCE)

1. FROM HERO BACK TO ZERO

I Knew middle school was going to be challenging, but I never expected to end up DEAD in the computer lab, wearing a SUPERHERO COSTUME, with four slices of PIZZA stuck to my BUTT!

My morning actually started out pretty normal. . . .

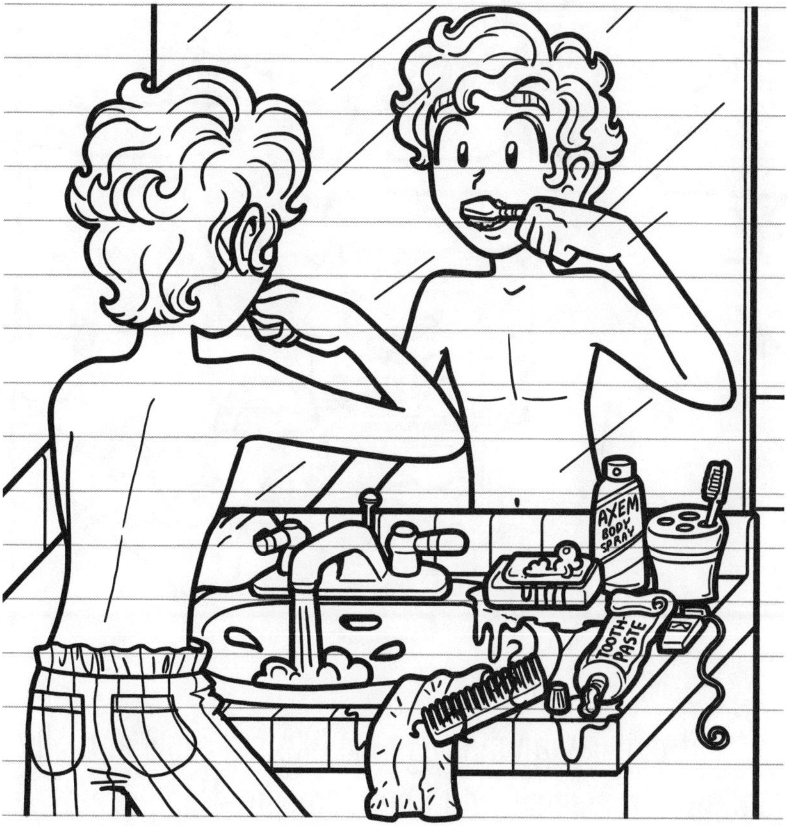
AXEM BODY SPRAY
TOOTH-PASTE

Hey, I'm NOT stupid! I KNEW I wasn't superhero material! But that never stopped me from staring in the mirror and wishing . . .

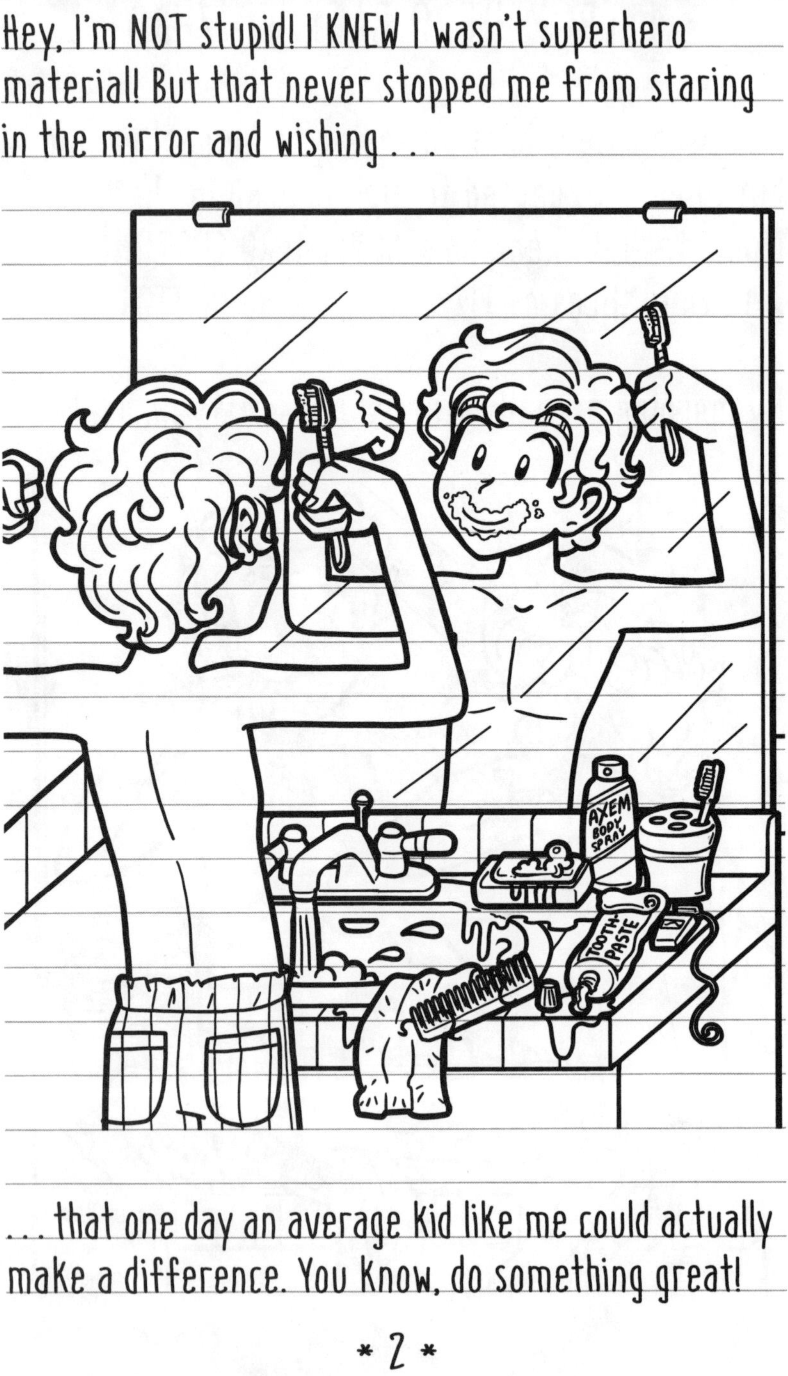
AXEM
BODY
SPRAY
TOOTH-
PASTE

. . . that one day an average kid like me could actually make a difference. You know, do something great!

Yeah, right! WHO was I Kidding?! My situation was HOPELESS! I could never change the world. . . .

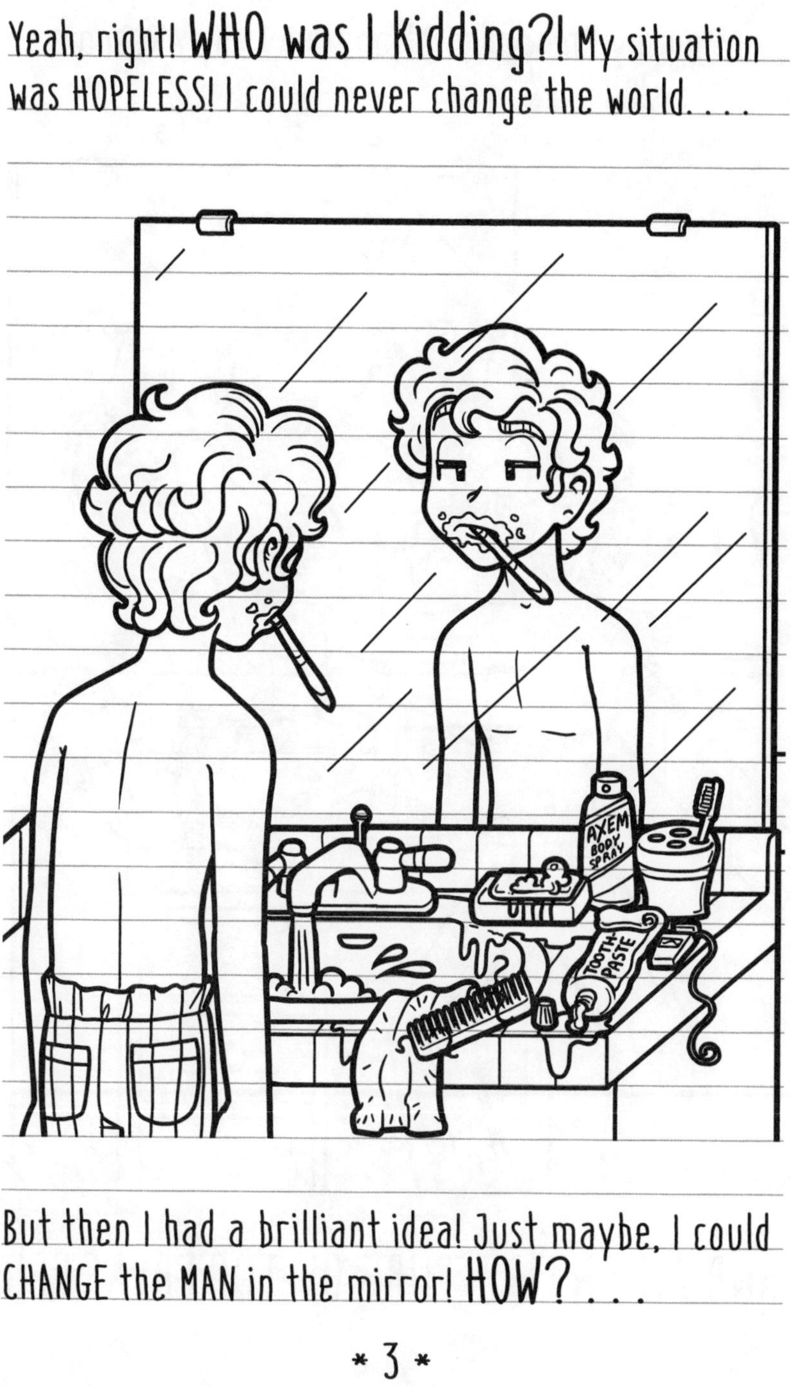

AXEM
BODY
SPRAY
TOOTH-PASTE

But then I had a brilliant idea! Just maybe, I could CHANGE the MAN in the mirror! HOW? . . .

By using my knowledge of anatomy, my awesome drawing skills . . .

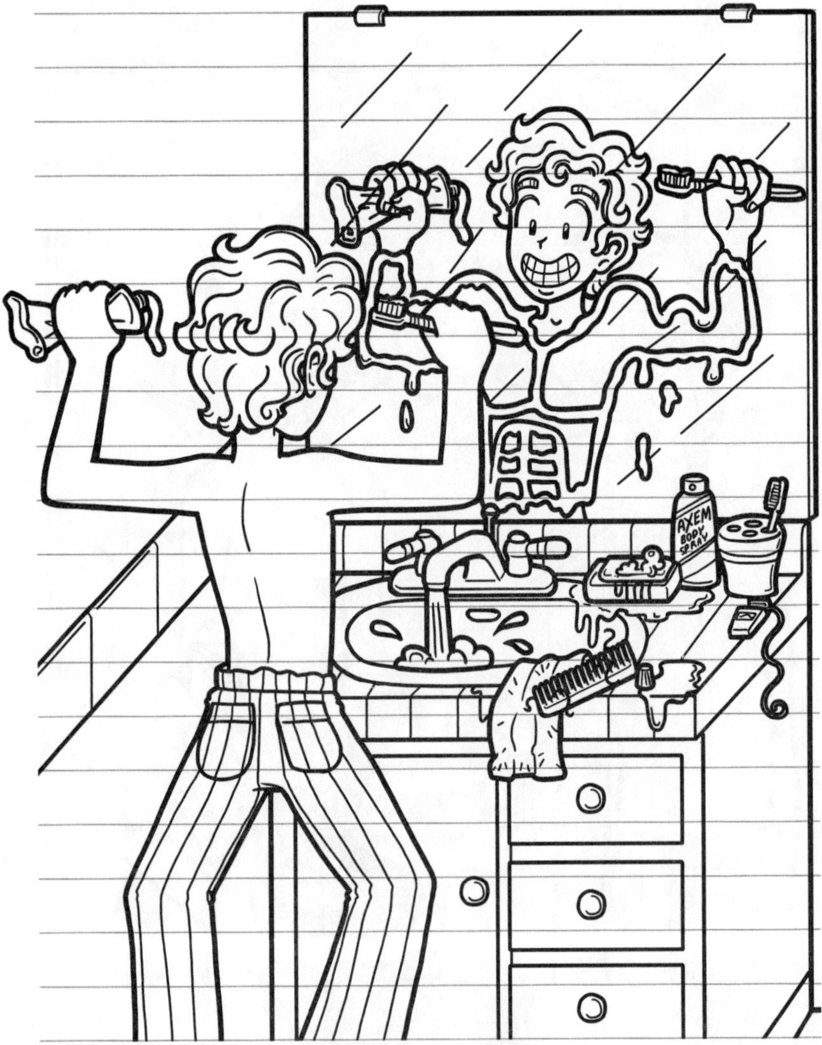
AXEM
BODY
SPRAY

AND AN ENTIRE TUBE OF TOOTHPASTE!!

Yeah, you're right. I guess you could call me kind of . . . WEIRD!

But it's all GOOD! Most of the famous superheroes and infamous villains are ALSO a little disturbed. So I like to think of it as untapped potential.

You're probably sitting there wondering HOW I managed to create such a HUMONGOUS MESS (I mean the mess at my school, NOT the mess in my bathroom).

It all started when ~~Doug~~ Thug Thurston shoved me into my LOCKER after school. Unfortunately, I was trapped inside there for HOURS!!

I'm not going to lie to you! I totally FREAKED!

But give me a break!

I was all alone. In a dark and creepy school building. Locked INSIDE my locker.

For possibly an ENTIRE THREE-DAY WEEKEND!

Honestly, dude! YOU would have freaked out too!

Anyway, after what seemed like forever, I finally managed to escape through the ventilation system.

But as I was passing the computer lab, I accidentally stumbled upon three burglars in the process of stealing the school's brand-new computers! It was SURREAL!

I started thinking about how I'm such a LOSER that kids at school call me BARF ~~because I accidentally threw up my oatmeal on Thug's shoe in PE class.~~

~~Sorry, but if you had seen those pus-filled ZITS on his face up close, you would have thrown up too!~~

Anyway, I FINALLY had the chance to completely CHANGE my pathetic life. HOW?!

By stopping the burglars and saving the school's computers ~~while at the same time impressing Erin, president of the computer club!~~

~~But don't get it TWISTED! It's not like I'm crushing on her or something! I BARELY know the girl!!~~

And then, *BOOM!!*

My rep would BLOW UP, and I'd instantly go from ZERO to HERO!

SWEET!!

This, my friends, is the very STRANGE but TRUE tale of how I fought EVIL and INJUSTICE in the DANK, DARK, DANGEROUS halls of South Ridge Middle School.

I've documented every detail in my journal, *The Misadventures of Max Crumbly,* which I keep with me wherever I go. So let's pick up right where I left off in my last entry. . . .

I had just outsmarted those bungling burglars and was BLASTING through my school like a rocket to go exchange intel by cell phone with my trusty sidekick, Erin! . . .

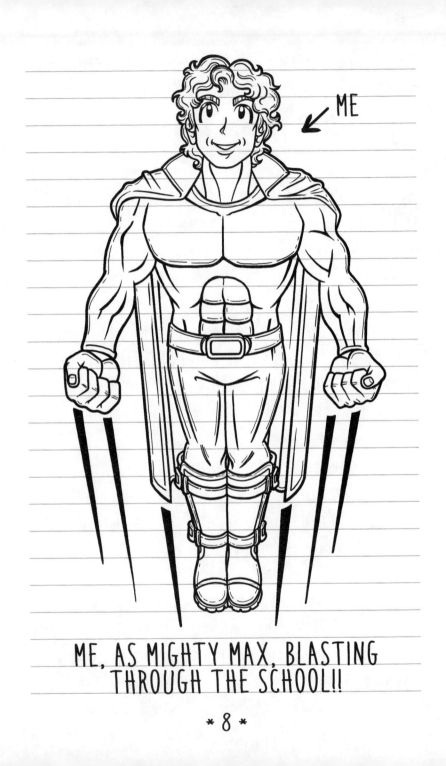

ME, AS MIGHTY MAX, BLASTING
THROUGH THE SCHOOL!!

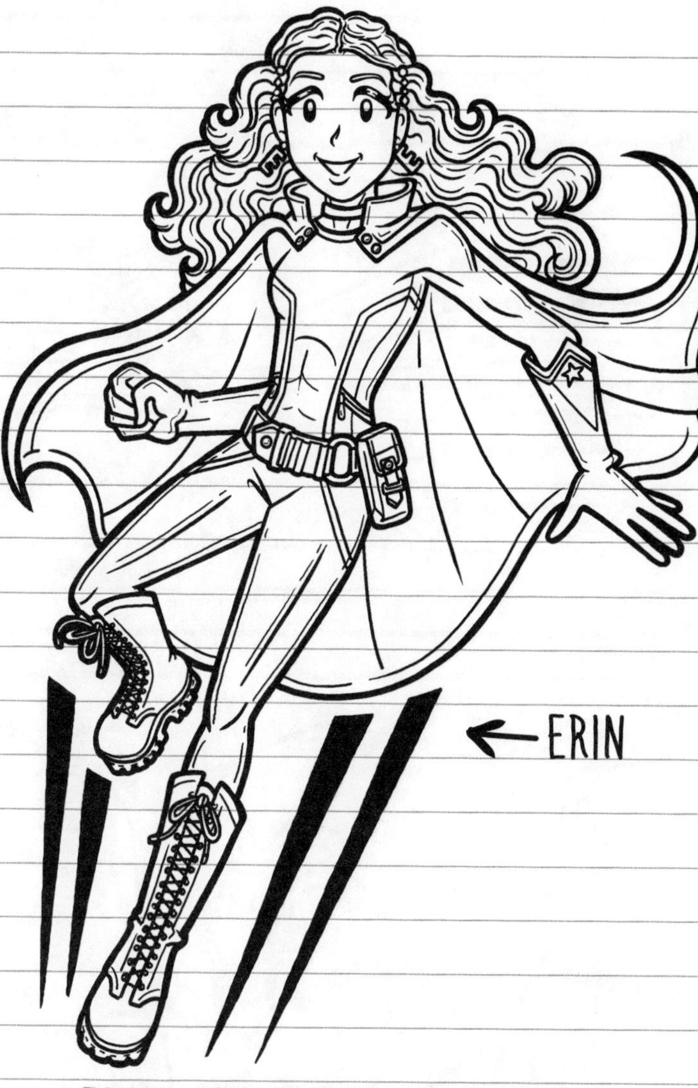
ERIN

ERIN, MY SUPERHERO BFF!

Okay, I'll admit I may have exaggerated a little. This is what REALLY happened. . . .

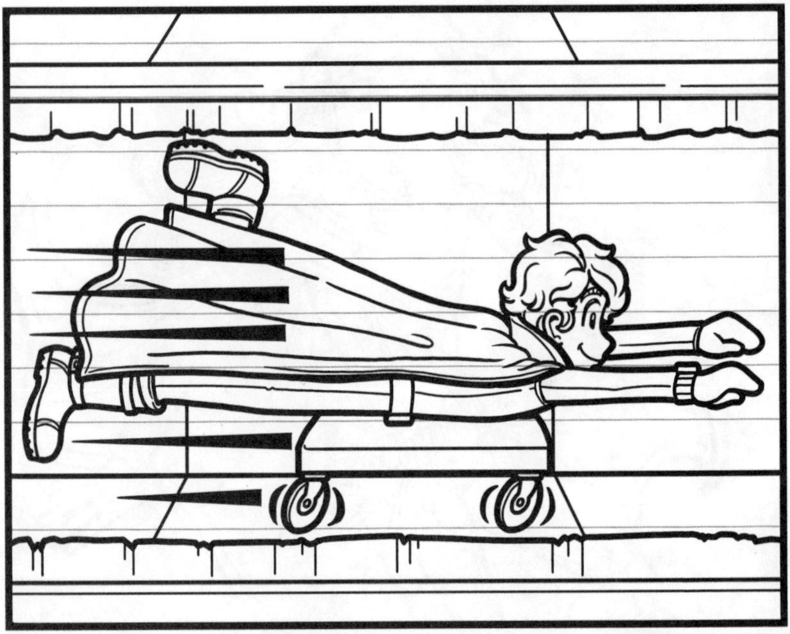

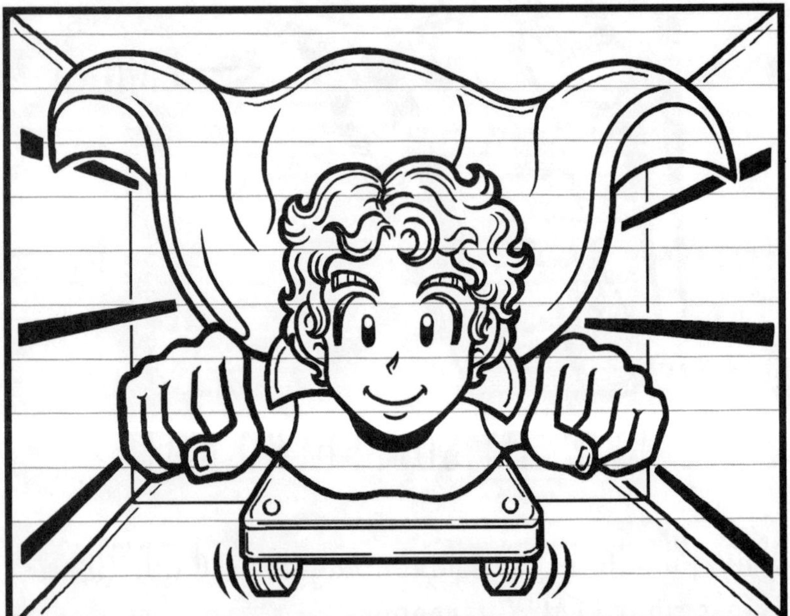

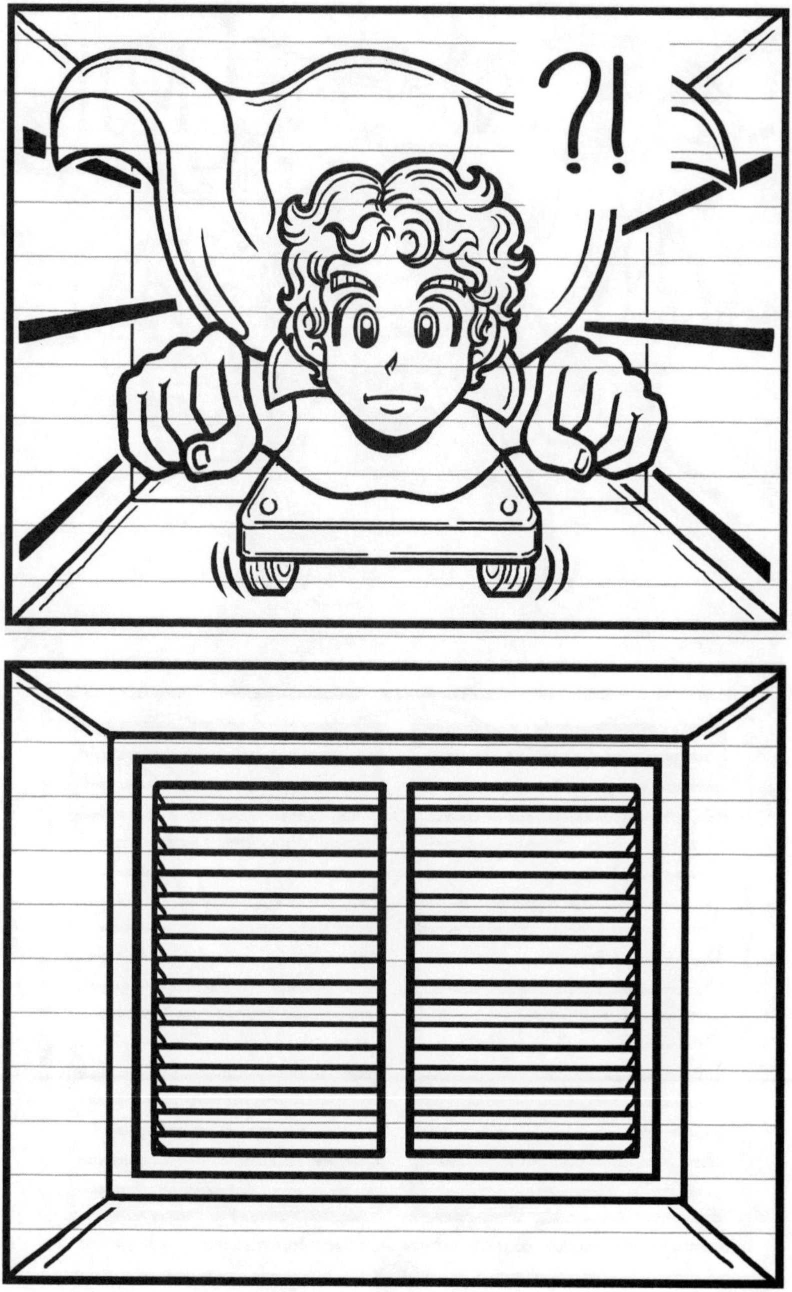

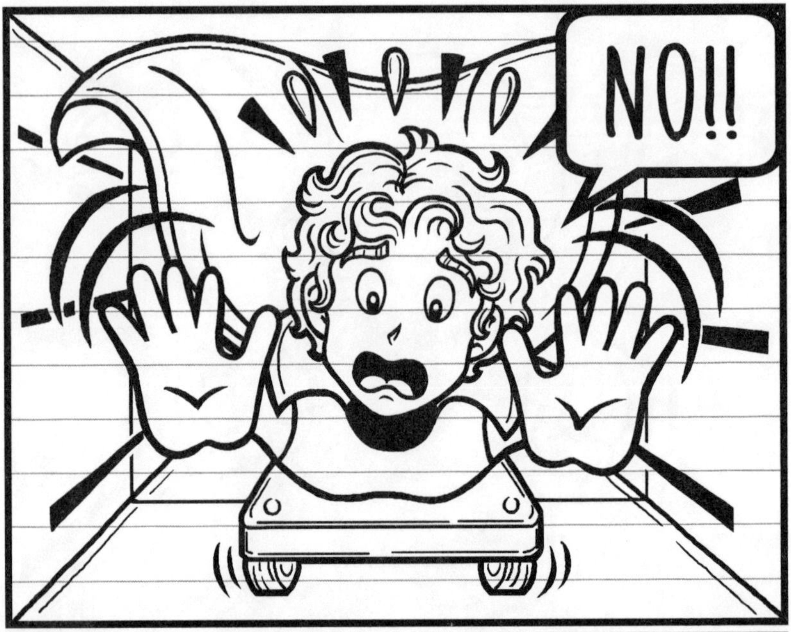
NO!!

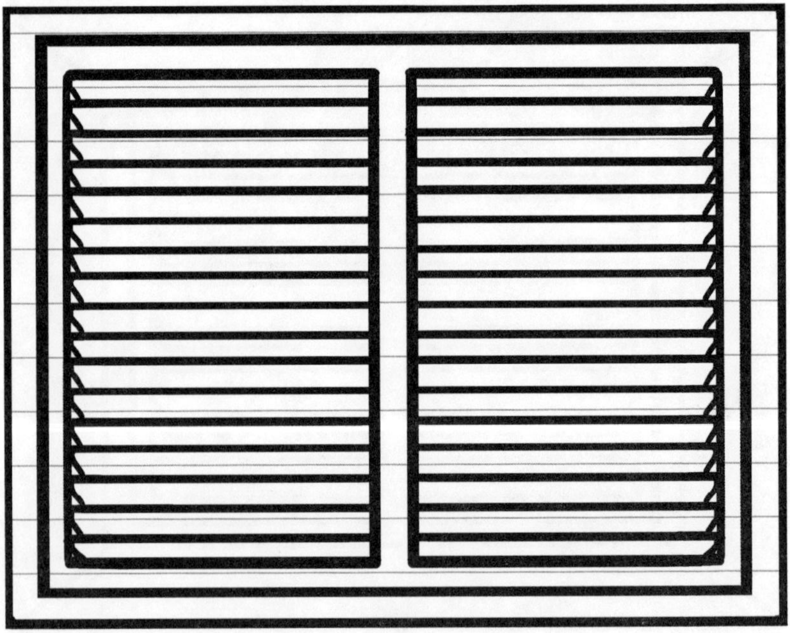

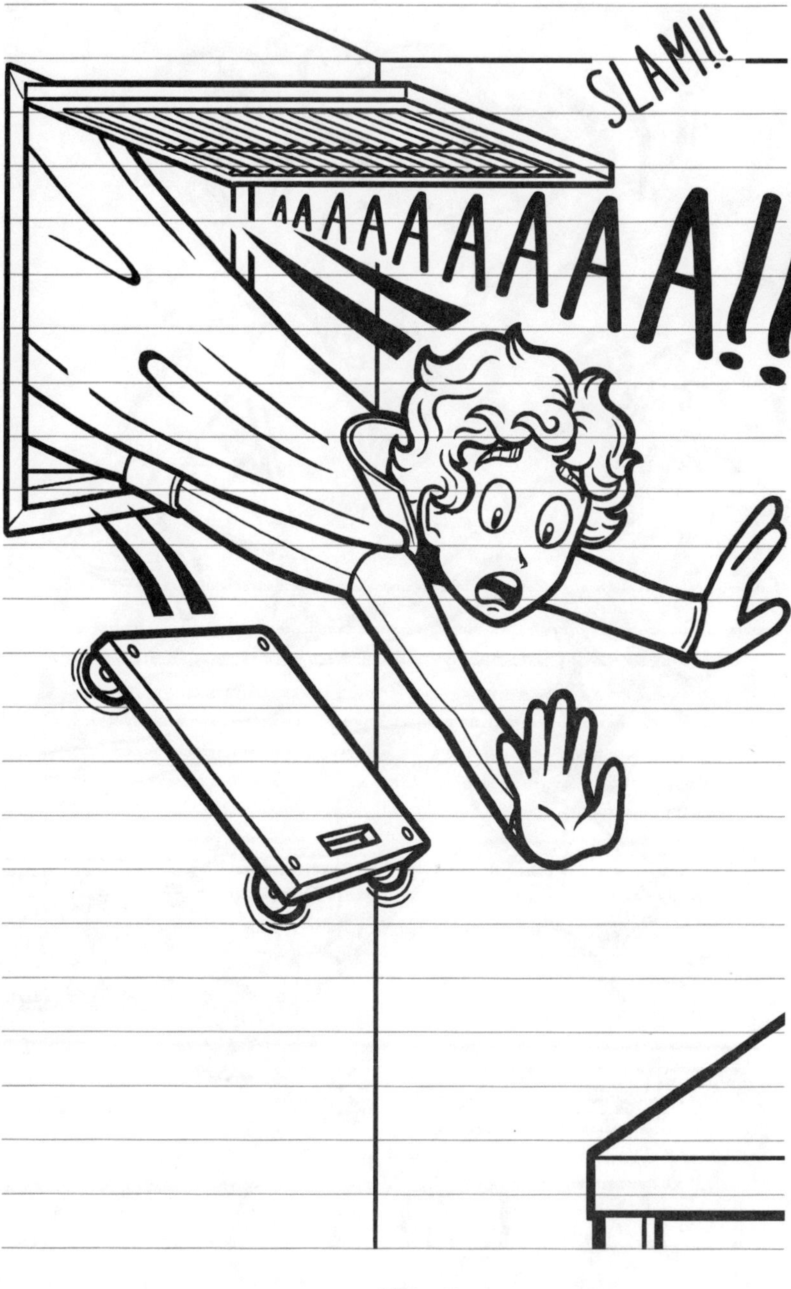
SLAM!!
AAAAAAAAAA!!

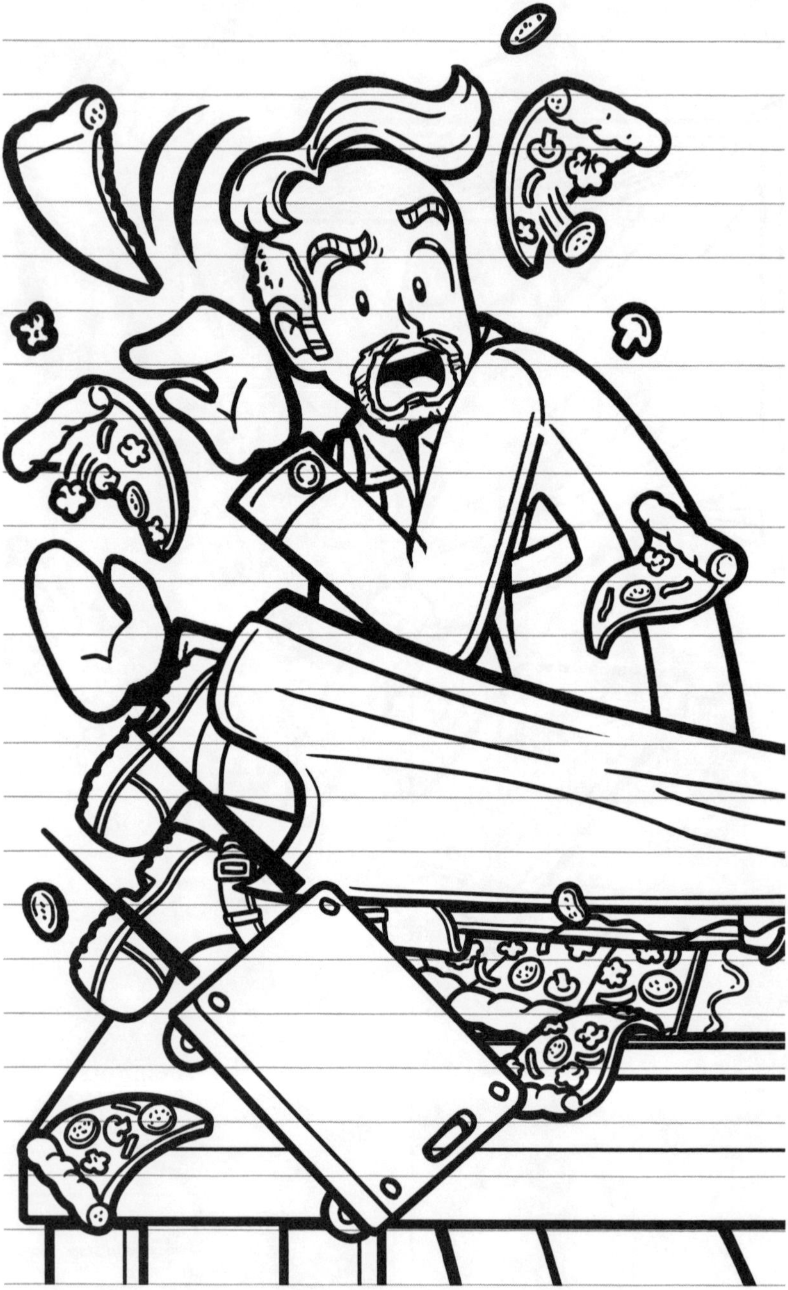

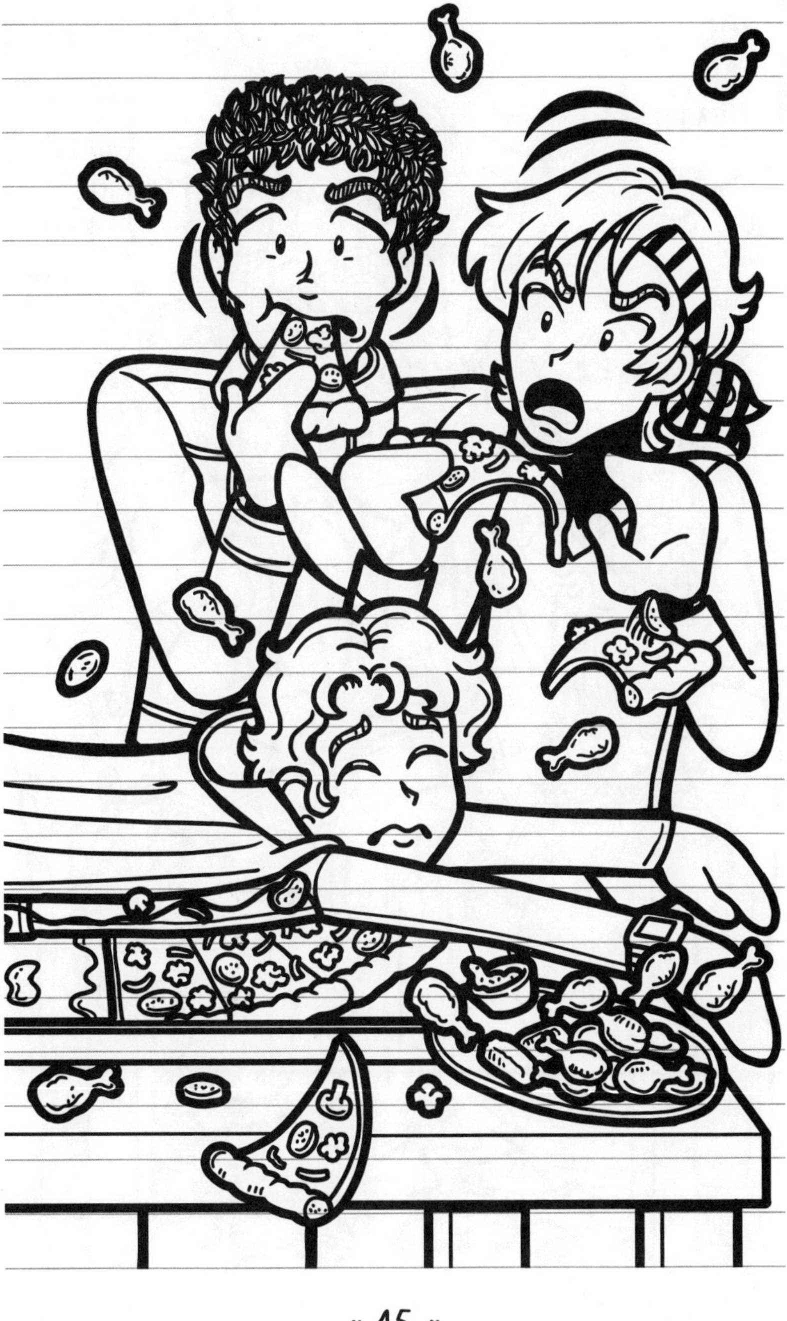

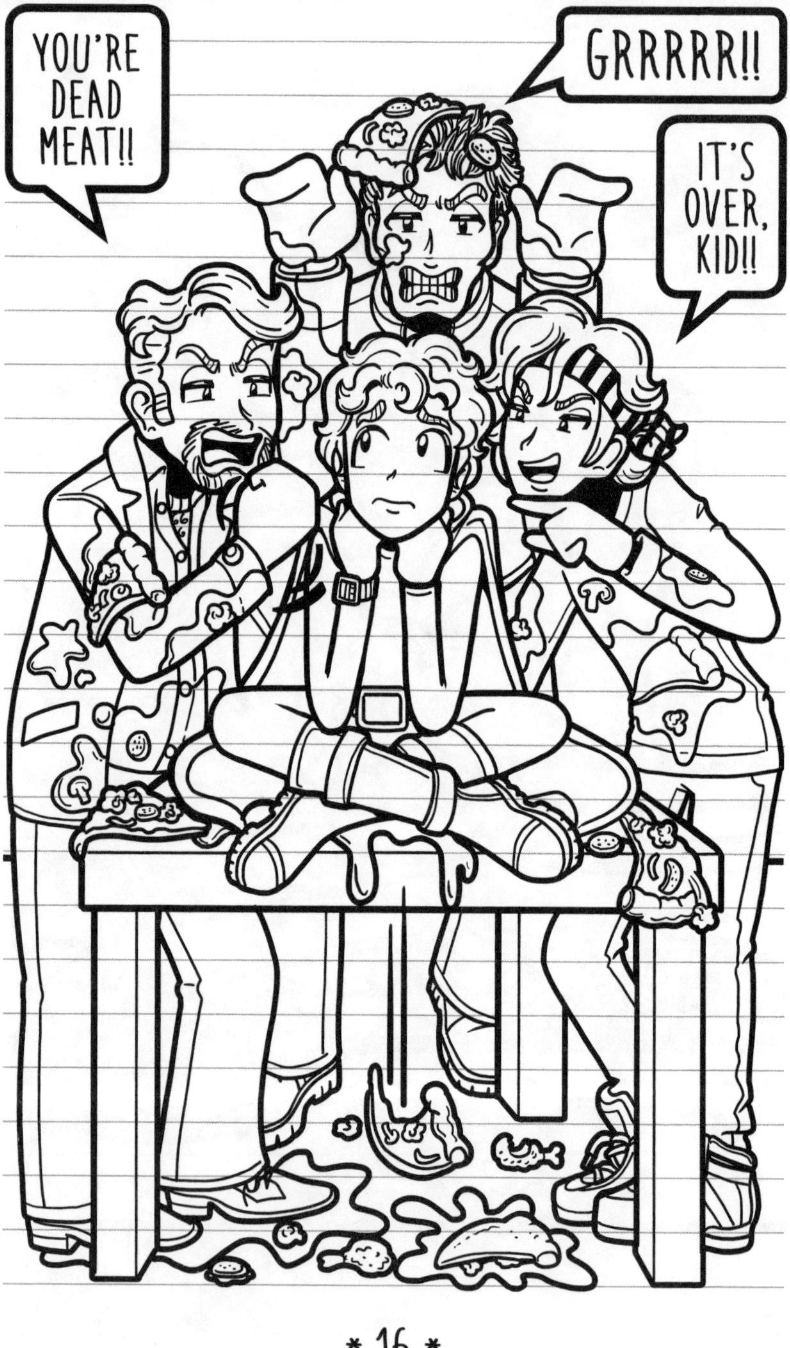
YOU'RE DEAD MEAT!!
GRRRRRR!!
IT'S OVER, KID!!

It was the . . .

WORST.
DAY.
EVER!!

2. A MIGHTY MEAT MONSTER MESS!

I just sat there on top of that stupid pizza for what seemed like FOREVER.

Those three crooks were all up in my face like bad breath, staring at me and giving me the evil eye.

The entire FIASCO was very . . . AWKWARD!

It actually inspired me to create a RAP. . . .

A MIGHTY MEAT MONSTER MESS
(A RAP WRITTEN BY COOL MAX C.)

I was rolling through the vents
one night at school.
On a tricked-out skateboard
that was super COOL!

I was zooming fast.
The ride was tight.
But I think I turned left,
when I should have gone right.

I tried to STOP,
because the DANGER was real!
I went FLYING through the AIR,
like I was Shaq O'Neal.

Crash-landing on that pizza
was BRUTAL, I swear!
That Mighty Meat Monster
SPLATTERED everywhere!

Pepperoni, anchovies,
and mushrooms are fine!
But not STUCK in a place
where the sun DON'T shine!

Greasy Queasy Cheesy.
Imagine my frustration,
trying to get outta
this MESSY situation!

My body was bruised.
My face was smashed.
My ego was crushed.
My skateboard was trashed.

What started out
an exciting THRILL,
ended with three CROOKS
ALL UP in my GRILL!

Okay, I'll say . . .
"You mad? So sad!"
"I'm really sorry, bro!"
"Hey, dude, MY BAD!"

So I'm sitting here
about to LOSE my MIND!
Pizza so HOT, I got a
RASH on my BEHIND!

Don't call me BARF.
Don't call me a ZERO.
You see, I TRIED to be
a SUPERHERO!

I might SCREW UP.
I might fall FLAT.
But Max C.'s NOT going
DOWN like THAT!!

If this scene were in one of my favorite comic books, it would be written like this:

When we last left our hapless hero, he was sitting on a Mighty Meat Monster pizza, completely surrounded by three RUTHLESS criminals about to plot his very long and painful DEATH!

Will Max be SHREDDED to bits like mozzarella cheese on the hard and crunchy PIZZA CRUST OF DOOM?

Will those hungry burglars still EAT the PIZZA Max is sitting on?

~~Even though it's as germy as week-old underwear and tastes like butt-sweat, body odor, and fear?!~~

And, most important, will brilliant computer whiz ERIN help Max get out of this MESSY situation ALIVE ~~by hacking into the school building's automated systems~~?!

Or will her computer CRASH, trapping her for an eternity behind the BLEAK yet BRUTAL blue screen of DEATH?! . . .

* 21 *

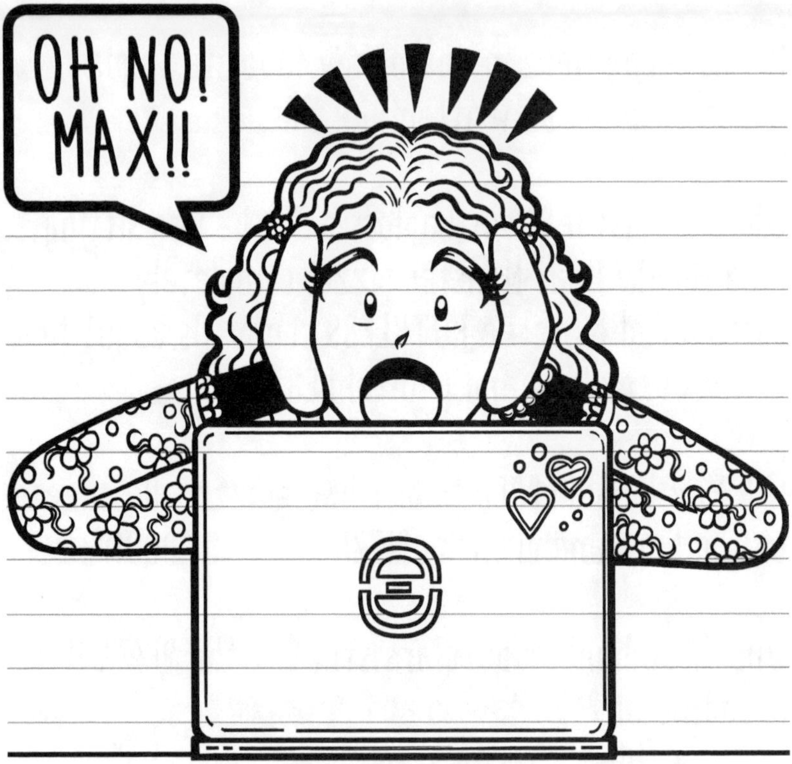
OH NO! MAX!!

ERIN, TOTALLY FREAKING OUT!

Stay tuned for the riveting answers to these exciting questions and more!

I know! You DON'T have to remind me.

I totally SCREWED UP! **AGAIN!**

This superhero stuff is a lot more difficult and dangerous than I thought it would be.

That's why I need to warn you! This story is going to end with my EXCRUCIATING DEATH or another mind-blowing CLIFFHANGER, just like a real comic book! Sorry, folks, but that's the way it is.

So if this is going to make you have a meltdown, please stop reading. **NOW!**

For those of you who are DYING to know what happens next, buckle up and get ready for a thrilling roller-coaster ride!

But BEFORE I get back to my story, I need to tell you some important things that I've learned so YOU won't make the same mistakes that I did.

Hey, if I can prevent what happened to ME from happening to YOU or another kid, then the heat rash I got on my butt from sitting on that hot pizza was totally worth it!

3. DUDE, I THINK MY LOCKER IS BUSTED!

Grown-ups are always lecturing us kids to ENJOY our childhood because it's the BEST time of our lives.

Sorry! But if THIS is supposed to be the good part, then my future is going to be just one GIANT bucket of . . .

PUKE!!

I'm the most PATHETIC superhero EVER! But it's mostly because I didn't carefully think things through and make a brilliant PLAN.

RULE #1: A SUPERHERO MUST ALWAYS BE PREPARED.

I wouldn't be in this situation if I hadn't gotten trapped inside my stupid locker to begin with.

Regardless of my superpowers, I should have had a plan for how to ESCAPE from my locker. If I had to do it all over again, I would . . .

Courageously blast through my locker with the sheer power and speed of a lightning bolt as . . .

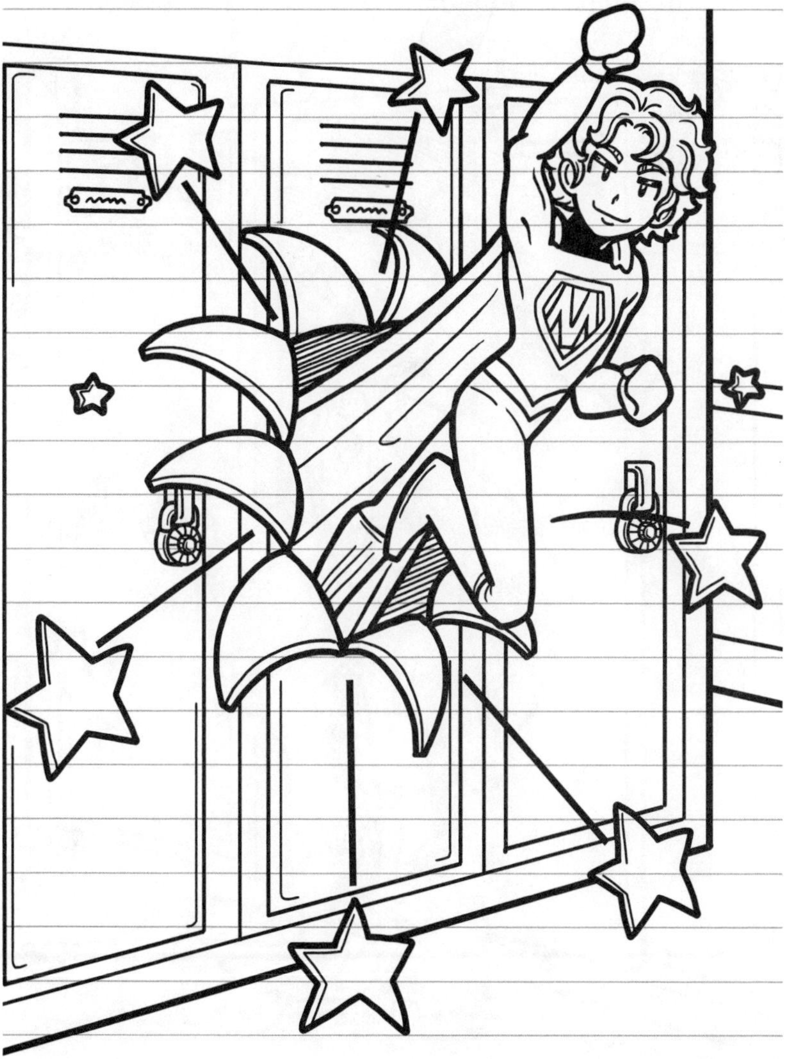

MIGHTY MAX!!

Eerily ascend from the mysterious underworld, shrouded in billows of ghostly fog, and telepathically open the locker door as . . .

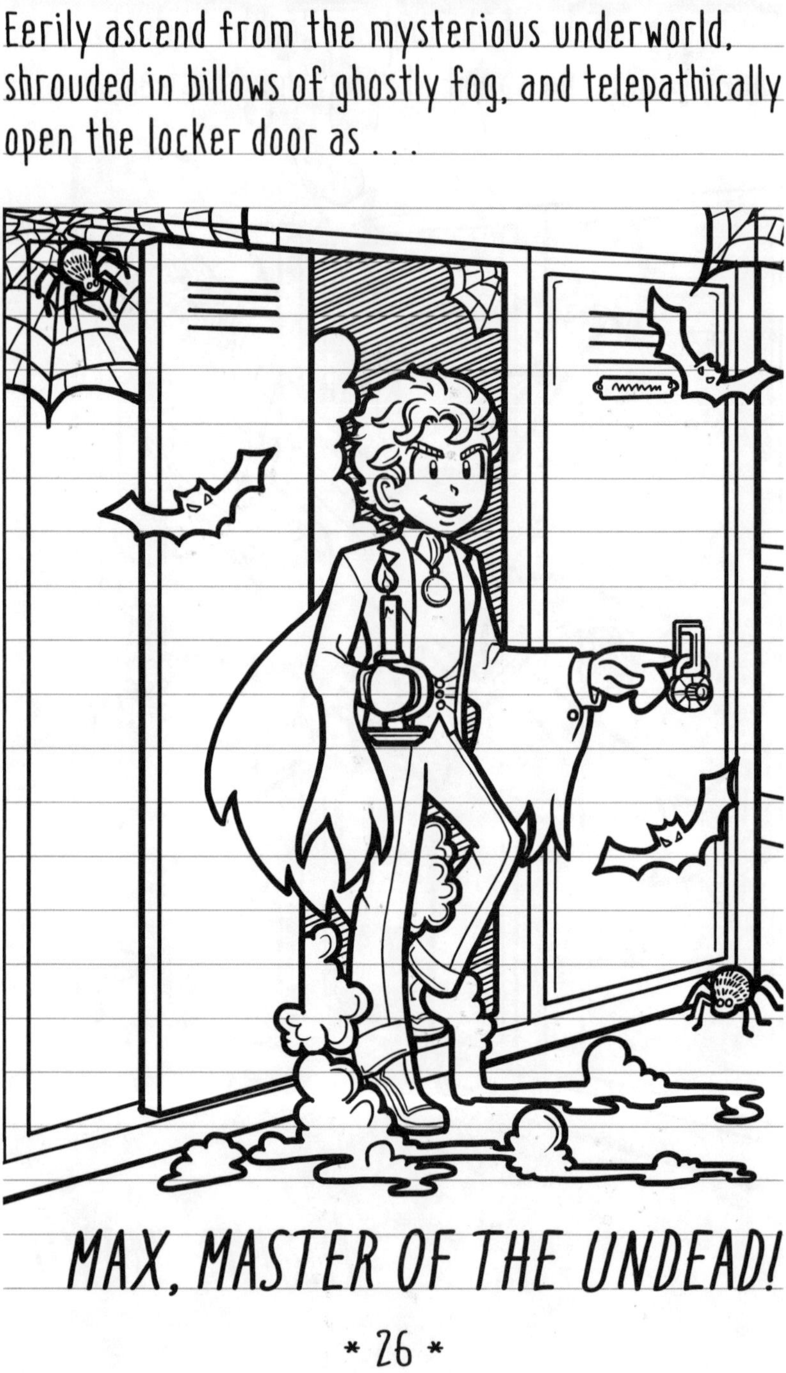

MAX, MASTER OF THE UNDEAD!

Violently smash my way out of my locker in a seething and uncontrollable fit of rage as . . .

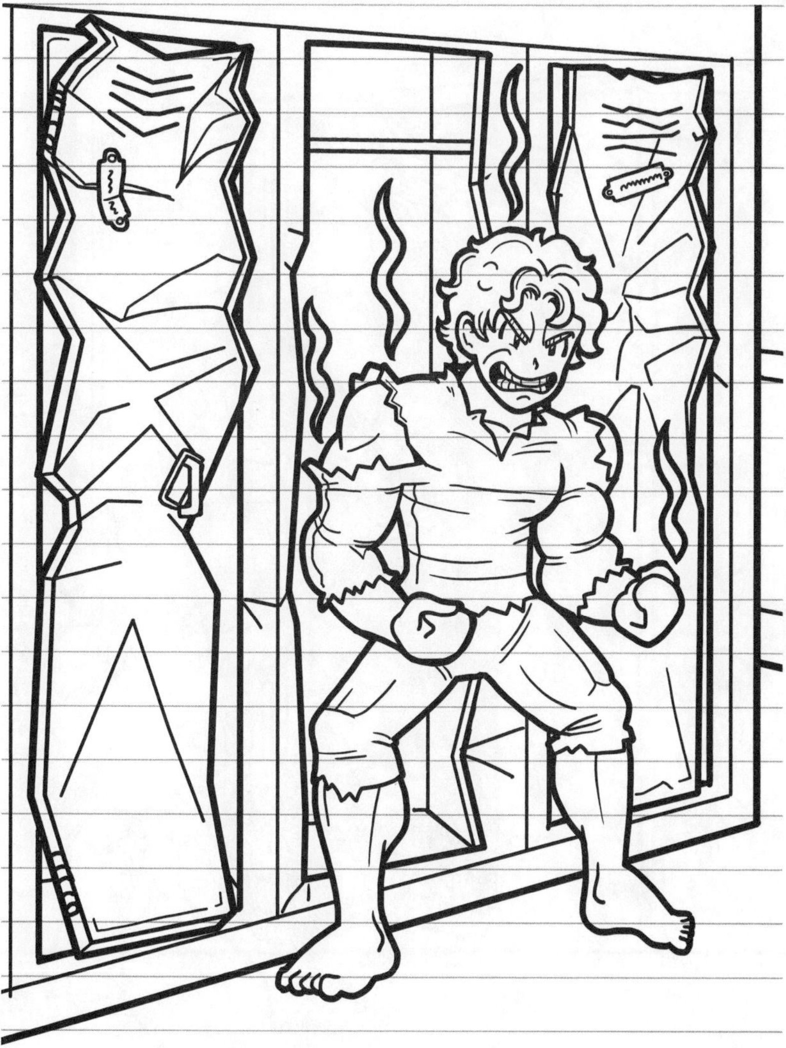

MAD MAX THE DESTROYER!

Pulverize my locker with earsplitting sonic blasts from my wicked guitar solo performed for a group of crazed and hysterical fans as . . .

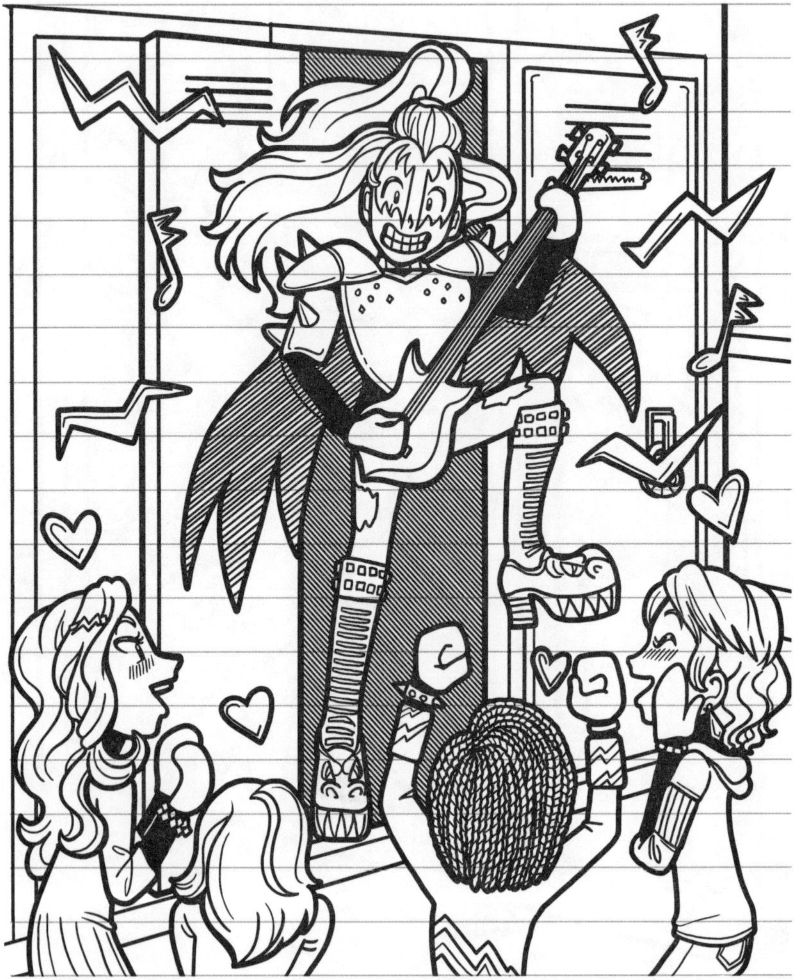

MAX MUSIX, HEAVY METAL ROCKER!

Completely annihilate my locker after transforming into a colossal, technologically advanced half-robot beast as . . .

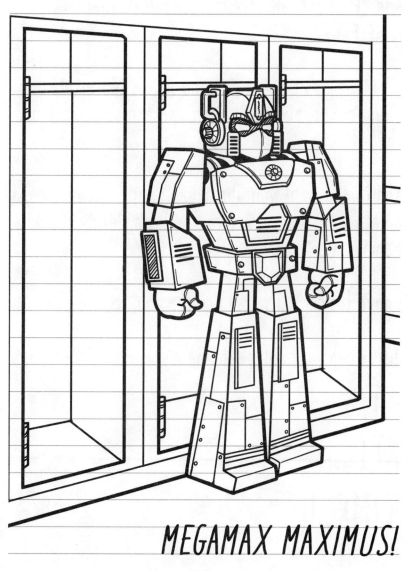

MEGAMAX MAXIMUS!

All these superheroes and their powers are pretty SICK, right?!

And YES! I actually created and drew them all MYSELF.

Now, the next time YOU end up locked inside your locker, please don't make the same mistake that I did.

And for those of you who haven't quite yet developed an AWESOME superpower that will completely DESTROY a locker, don't worry.

I have LIFESAVING advice for you, too.

Just keep your cell phone handy.

AT.

ALL.

TIMES!!

Then simply call or text a friend to come and RESCUE your embarrassed behind!

Works like a charm.

NO JOKE!!

4. WOULD YOU LIKE FRIES WITH THAT?

I know this is probably going to sound like your guidance counselor at school, but carefully selecting a career is really important, especially for a superhero.

RULE #2: A SUPERHERO SHOULD ALWAYS MAINTAIN A PART-TIME JOB.

WHY? So you can hide out and pretend to be a normal person ~~(on the days VILLAINS aren't trying to SLAY you)~~ while earning extra cash to pay your cell phone bill and other stuff. Don't believe me? How about some facts:

Spider-Man is a newspaper photographer, Superman is an investigative reporter, Thor is a doctor, the Hulk is a scientist, Iron Man is an inventor, and Wonder Woman is a nurse.

A job is ALSO needed because making the difficult transition from a normal person to a superhero takes a longer time for some than others, ~~and you could STARVE to DEATH during the process. . . .~~

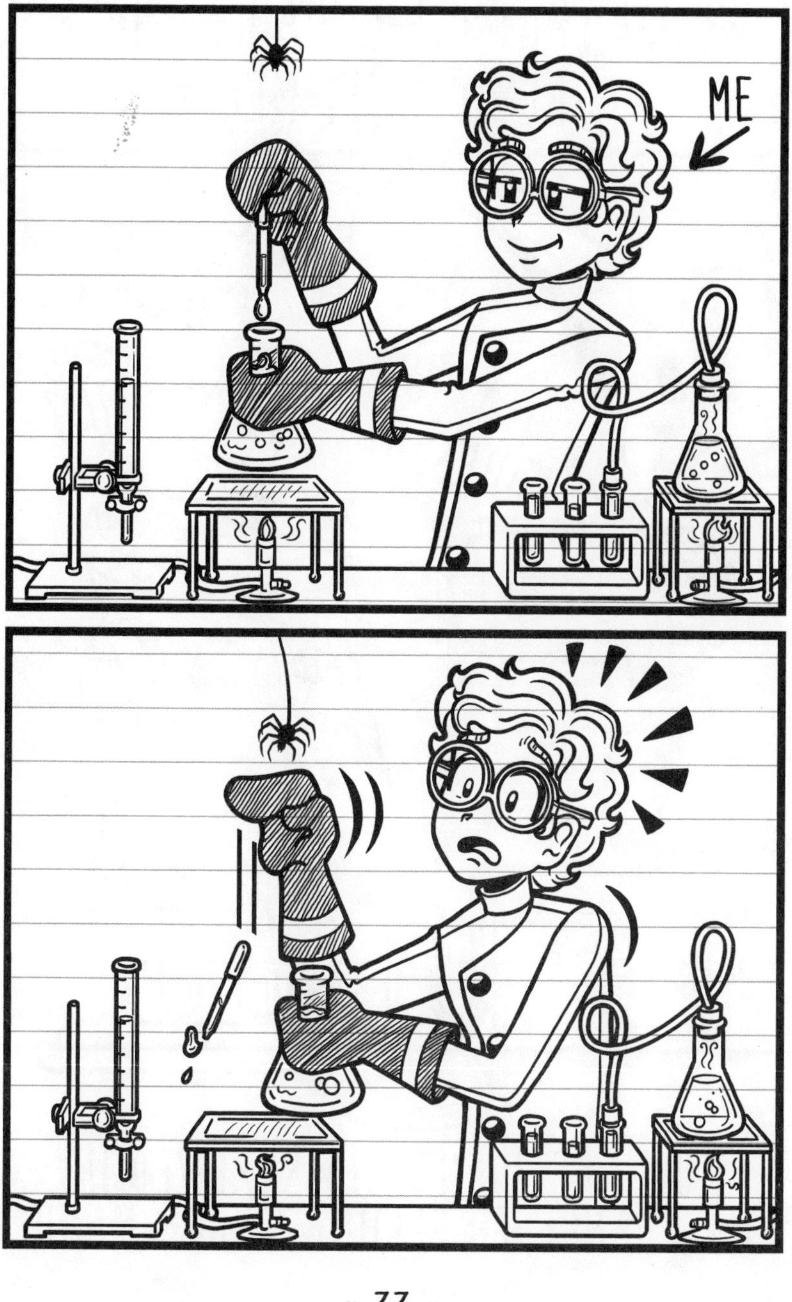
ME

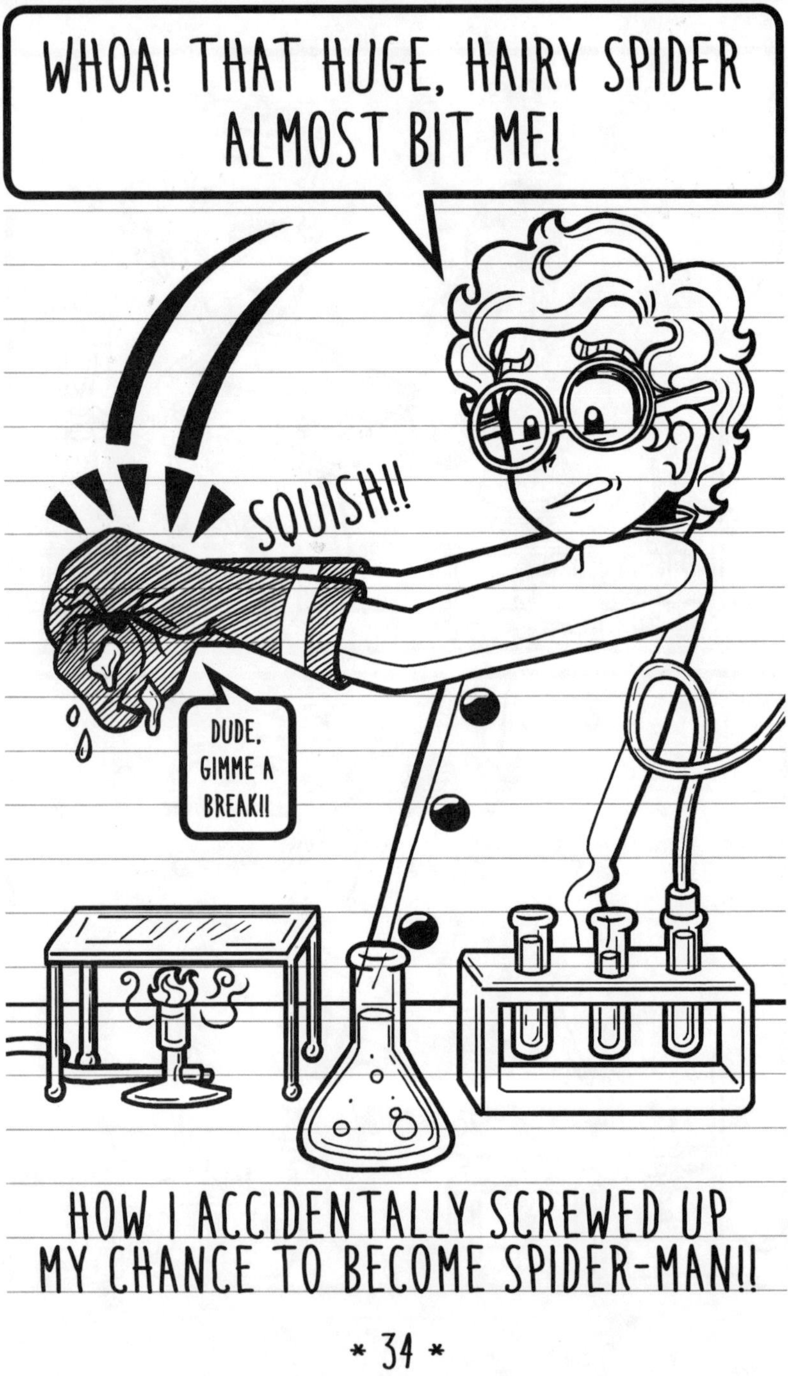
WHOA! THAT HUGE, HAIRY SPIDER ALMOST BIT ME!
SQUISH!!
DUDE, GIMME A BREAK!!

HOW I ACCIDENTALLY SCREWED UP MY CHANCE TO BECOME SPIDER-MAN!!

And once you FINALLY land your new job, there are two very important WORKPLACE TIPS that will be vital to your success:

1. WORKPLACE HYGIENE: After a long night of battling evil villains in an assortment of smelly places, like sewage tanks, fish markets, city dumps, and pig farms, you are probably going to work up a serious sweat. Always remember that superhuman BODY ODOR is so pungent that it can MELT the BOOGERS of any breathing man, woman, or child within one hundred feet. So PLEASE shower regularly!

2. WORKPLACE LUNCH ETIQUETTE: Even though you have the superhuman strength to open a can of pork-'n'-beans with your teeth, gulp it down in a single swallow, and then fart enough GAS to fuel a rocket launch to the planet Jupiter and back, PLEASE be considerate of others at your table during lunchtime!

Anyway, I plan to make millions of dollars as a rap artist, race car driver, or pro video gamer. But if none of these very lucrative careers works out, I plan to just get a job nearby . . .

...FLIPPING BURGERS!

I'm SERIOUS! My superpowers would totally rock in a job like this. . . .

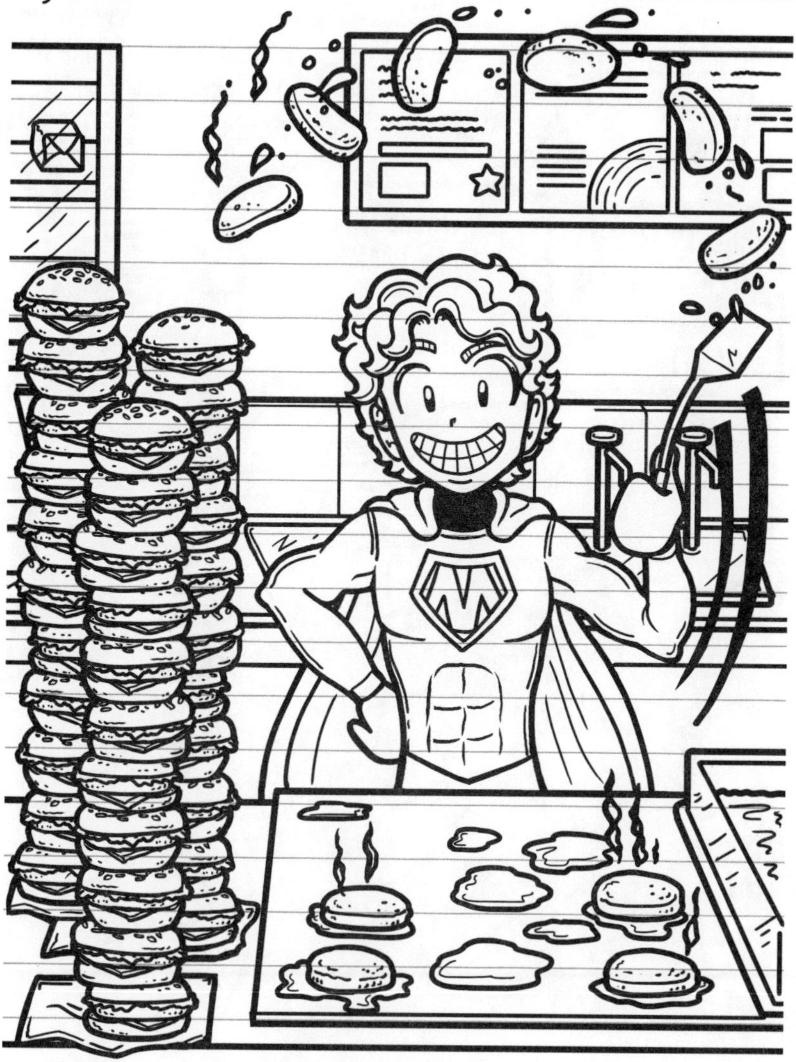

MIGHTY MAX,
SUPERPOWERED BURGER FLIPPER!!

Although, I have to admit, things could get a little AWKWARD, with me being a superhero and all. . .

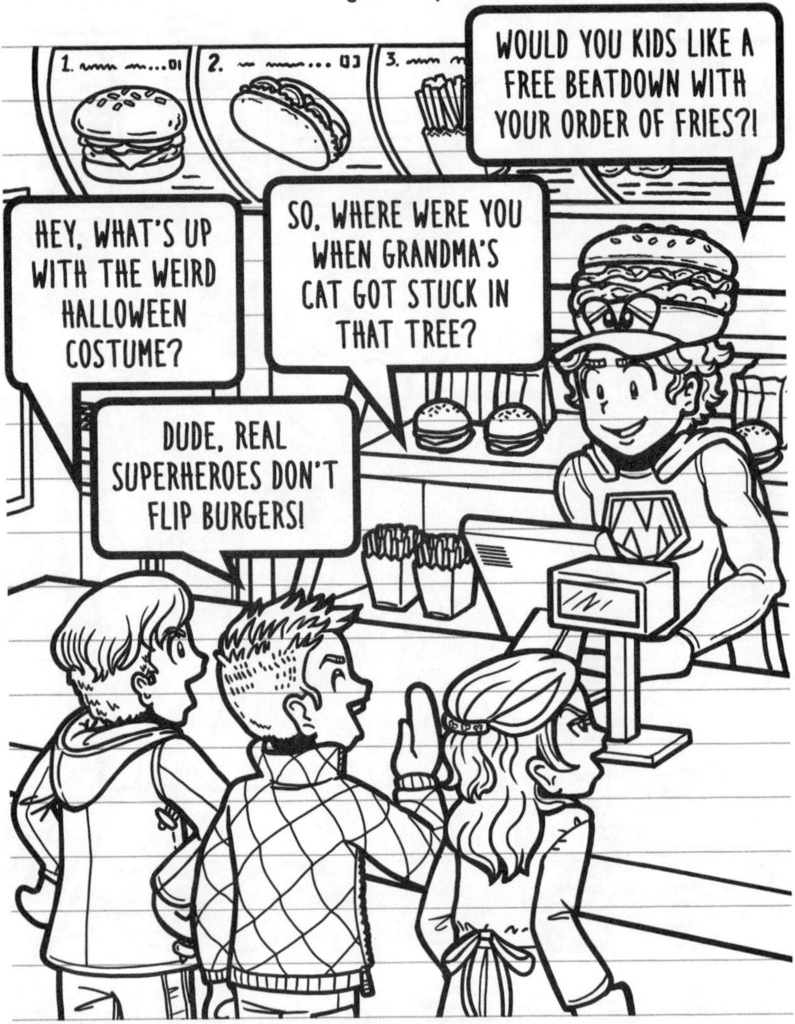
WOULD YOU KIDS LIKE A FREE BEATDOWN WITH YOUR ORDER OF FRIES?!
HEY, WHAT'S UP WITH THE WEIRD HALLOWEEN COSTUME?
SO, WHERE WERE YOU WHEN GRANDMA'S CAT GOT STUCK IN THAT TREE?
DUDE, REAL SUPERHEROES DON'T FLIP BURGERS!

ME, TRYING REALLY HARD **NOT** TO PUNCH ANNOYING CUSTOMERS!

However, the scariest part about working at a burger place when you're a superhero is that you can lose your temper and actually KILL someone!

If/when this happens, your BOSS will probably take one or more of the following actions:

1. Take you off the drive-through window ~~(which will be DEVASTATING because it means you will no longer be able to practice your raps OR do your Justin Bieber impersonation using that professional-looking microphone)~~.

2. Demote you ~~from the position of HEAD FRYER to ASSISTANT BATHROOM MOPPER~~.

3. Make you serve all the really old people ~~who keep ordering things like denture cream, adult diapers, and a refill of their high blood pressure medicine because for some reason they think they're at their neighborhood PHARMACY, not a fast-food restaurant~~.

4. Make you clean up after all the "Happy Me!" kiddie birthday parties, ~~which always include gallons~~

* 39 *

~~of fluorescent-orange-colored PUKE from kids who~~
~~binge drink the nasty "Happy Me!" fruit punch and~~
~~ride the "Happy Me!" merry-go-round nonstop,~~
~~then PROJECTILE VOMIT all over each other!~~

5. Call the police, press charges for murder, and
demand the DEATH penalty.

The only DOWNSIDE about my new job is that once
word gets around, ~~Thug~~ evil VILLAINS might show up
and start HARASSING me.

You know, like BURPING really loud into the drive-
through speaker after I say, "Welcome to Crazy
Burger, may I take your order, please?!"

Or trying to FREAK me out by tossing BOOGERS or
WORMS at me when I open the drive-through window.

And the worms could actually crawl into the fries!

Then WHAT am I supposed to do?!! Just shrug and
ask the customer . . .

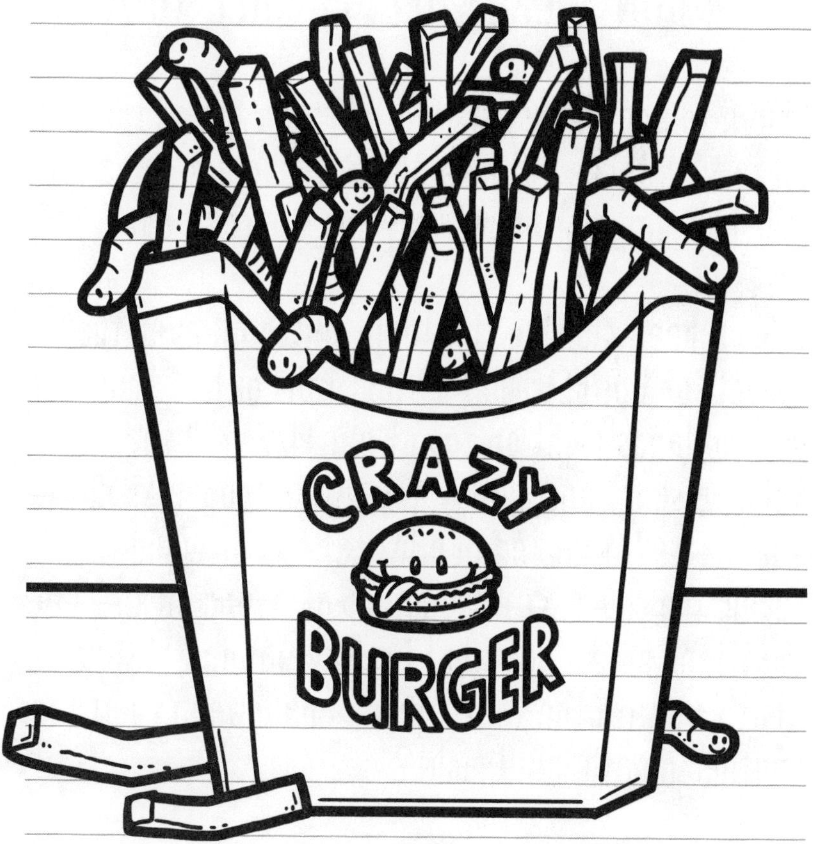
CRAZY
BURGER

"WOULD YOU LIKE SOME **WORMS** WITH THOSE FRIES?"

Sorry, but THAT would just be WRONG on so many levels!

5. DON'T CALL ME! I'LL CALL YOU!

I have to admit, just sitting there on top of that
pizza with three ruthless thugs eyeballing me all
evil-like was NOT helping my superhero image!

"We've been chasing this little snitch all over the
school for HOURS! Then he just falls out of thin
air and lands right on top of our PIZZA?!!" snarled
Ralph, a short and dumpy guy with a toupee so dirty
and matted it looked like his cat had dragged it
behind the couch, crawled on top of it, and given birth
to kittens on it. "But what I really wanna know is
what's up with the fancy getup? Halloween's not for
another month, am I right?"

Moose, a big, muscular guy with spiked hair and a
jean jacket, stared wide-eyed at my silver cape and
looked really worried. "I don't know, boss. He don't
look like a normal kid. Maybe he's a . . . SPACE ALIEN!
I saw a TV show where this space alien made a high-
pitched sound that would make human HEADS explode.
He would go, *SCREEEEEEEEEEEECH!!* And then, *KA-BOOM!*
You're dead! I'm not lying. That was so SCARY, I had

to sleep with a night-light for an entire week!"

"Sorry, bro! But you're NUTTIER than a Snickers bar, and you watch WAY too much TV!" sneered Tucker, a tall, skinny guy wearing a bandanna. "Maybe he's the tooth fairy. Or a wannabe superhero, like, I don't know . . . SUPER PIZZA BOY! I bet he's here to save innocent PIZZAS from being viciously EATEN by people around the world!"

Then the three men doubled over in laughter. I couldn't help but feel like a big, fat . . . JOKE wearing Erin's ~~ice princess costume~~ superhero outfit that I was forced to change into after my regular clothes were ruined in an unfortunate accident.

Finally Ralph leaned in so close to my face I could see his nose hairs. "You were Mr. Tough Guy when you were hiding up in those vents. But now it looks like you want your mommy! What happened . . . PIZZA BOY?!" he snarled.

I balled my fists and just glared at him. I wanted to yell at them and even throw a few punches. But I had a really bad feeling those criminals were probably NOT going to be very intimidated by a guy sitting on a pizza in a silver cape.

"We gotta get these computers loaded up! Which means we don't have time to be babysitting some silly kid who thinks he's a Saturday-morning cartoon. So, gentlemen, how are we gonna take care of this little problem?" Ralph said menacingly.

"Just finish him off!" Moose said angrily as he peeled a slice of pizza off his forehead.

"Why? To keep him from squealing to the police?" asked Tucker.

"NO! As punishment for TOTALLY RUINING a perfectly good PIZZA! Guys, I'm still STARVING! You know I get really GRUMPY when I'm hungry, right?" Moose whined. "It's hard to concentrate, and I just keep thinking about FOOD. Like burgers, pancakes, chocolate milk, macaroni and cheese—"

Moose was SO upset about me ruining his pizza, he looked like he was about to CRY. I suddenly had a flashback from my childhood. . . .

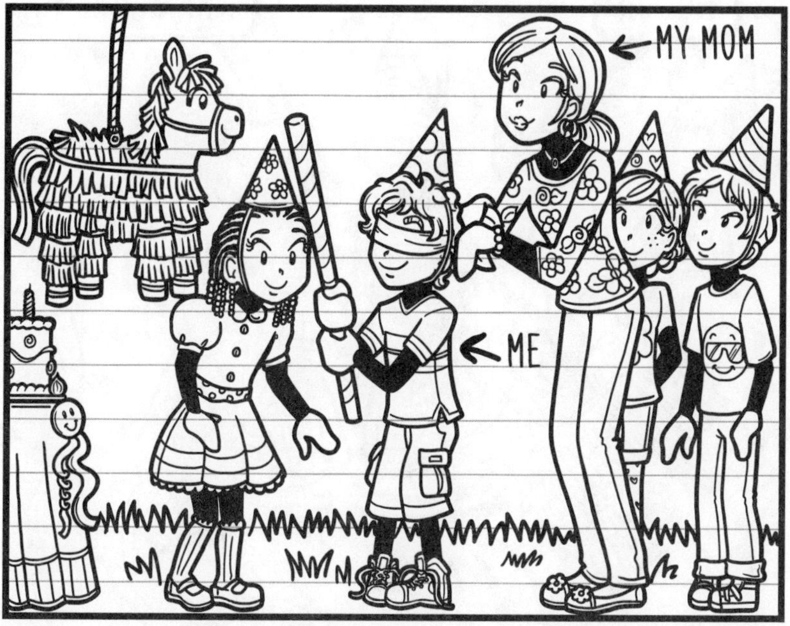
MY MOM
ME

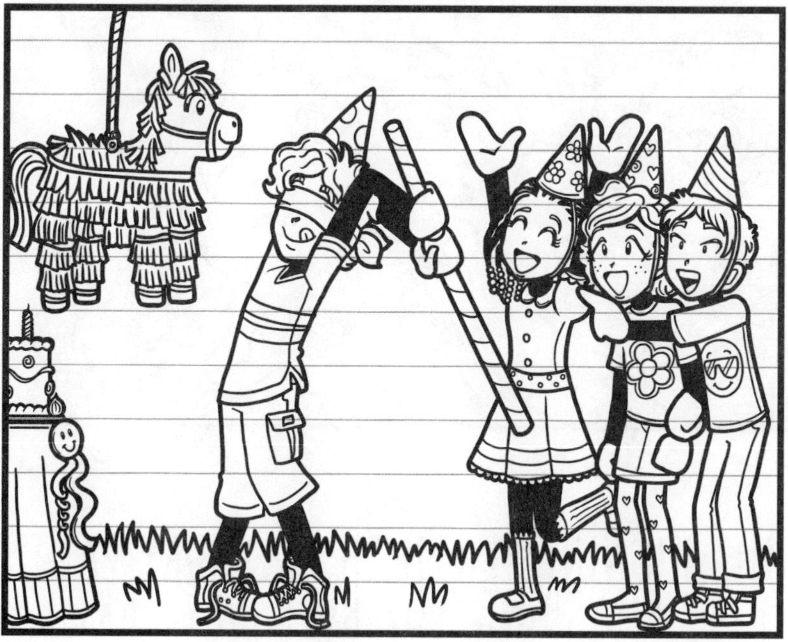

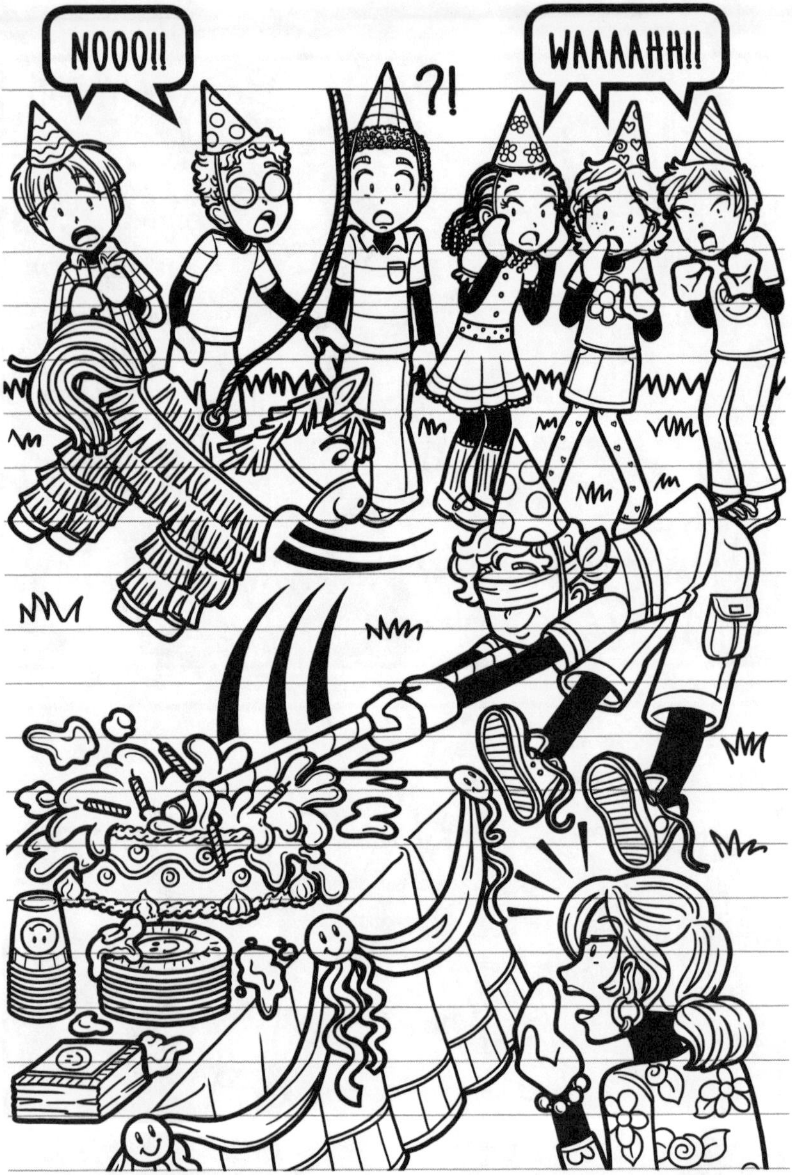
NOOO!!
?!
WAAAAHH!!

ME, RUINING MY FIFTH BIRTHDAY PARTY BY SMASHING THE BIRTHDAY CAKE!!

That was a pretty traumatic experience!

"Grow up, Moose!" Tucker grumbled. "And stop sniveling about food! You're making ME hungry!"

"You want me to STOP?! Then make me!" Moose shot back. "I'm WAY hungrier than you'll ever be!"

"No, you're not!"

"Yes, I am!"

"No, you're NOT!"

"JUST SHUT UP!" Ralph yelled. "You both are HUNGRY?! Then I'll give you a snack! How about I rip out your SPLEENS and shove 'em down your throats?! Then you won't be hungry anymore, you MORONS! Do you understand me?!"

"Yeah, boss," Moose and Tucker muttered as they shot each other dirty looks. JUST GREAT! That picture with all its GORY detail is forever SEARED into my BRAIN. . . .

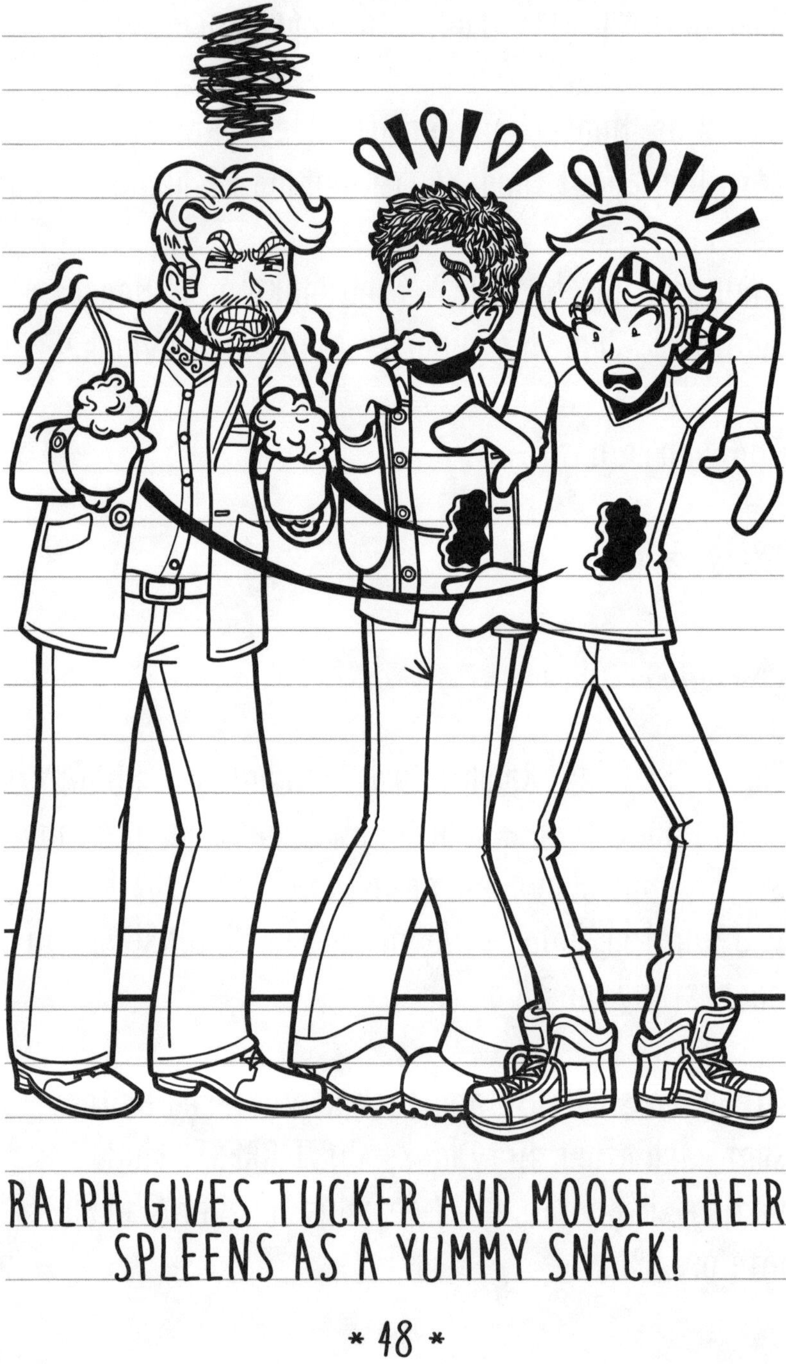

RALPH GIVES TUCKER AND MOOSE THEIR SPLEENS AS A YUMMY SNACK!

Just before I had accidentally crashed through the vent, I'd sent Erin the computer password for the school building's automated systems. This gave her remote access and control of the PA system, security cameras, lights, etc., which meant she could possibly see and hear everything.

After receiving her text that she'd call me in two minutes, I'd switched my cell phone from vibrate to ring so I wouldn't miss her call. But that seemed like ages ago.

I wasn't sure if Erin was aware of all the DRAMA going down in the computer lab. But the LAST thing I needed right then was for her to call me while those burglars were all up in my face like a bad case of acne!

"I'll keep an eye on the kid while you two dummies go find some rope so we can tie him up!" Ralph said, glaring at me. "Then we'll get rid of him!"

I broke into a cold sweat! Were they actually going to KILL me? WHY? And HOW? But my frantic thoughts were rudely interrupted when . . .

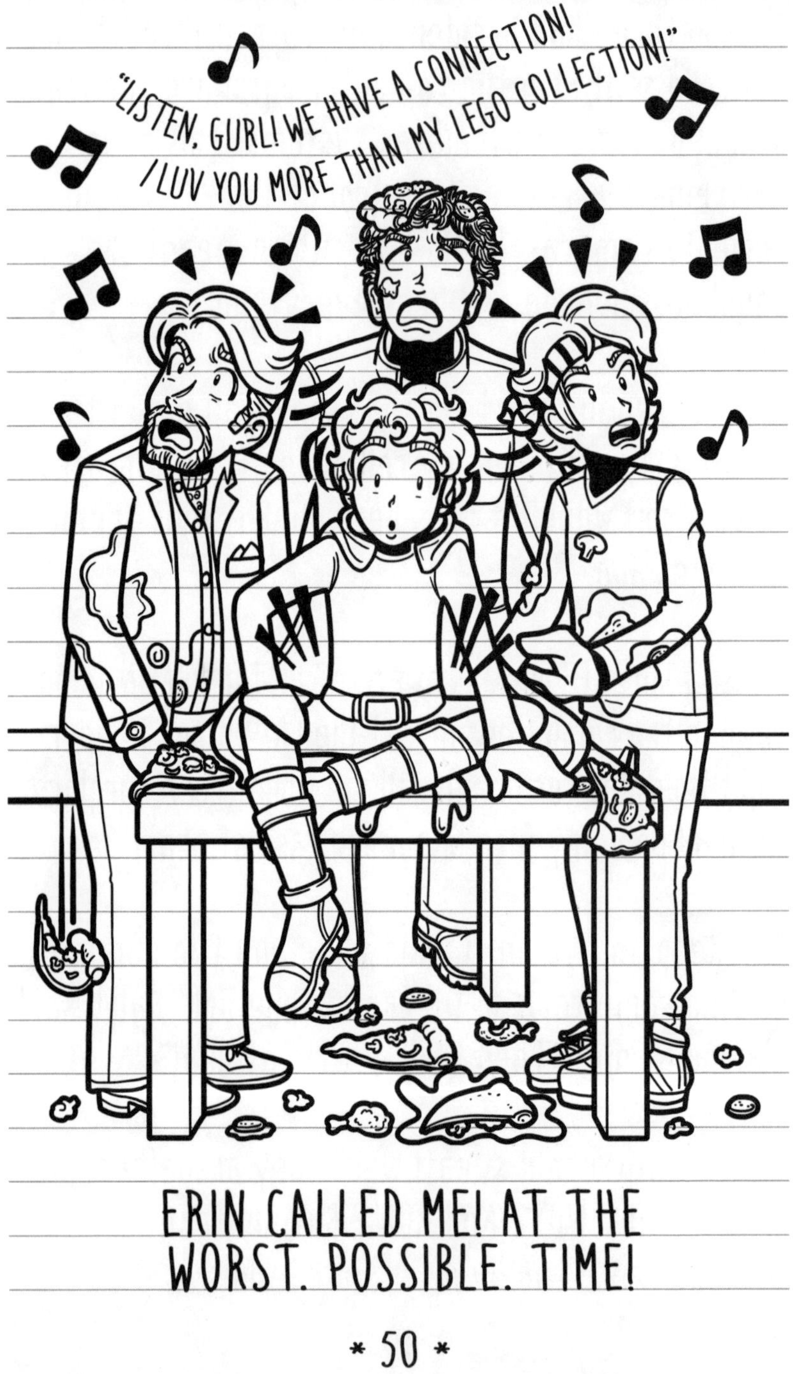
"LISTEN, GURL! WE HAVE A CONNECTION!
I LUV YOU MORE THAN MY LEGO COLLECTION!"

ERIN CALLED ME! AT THE WORST. POSSIBLE. TIME!

Okay, I ASSUMED it was Erin calling me.

I cringed and froze as the chorus to an annoying boy band ringtone blasted from my back pocket....

"LISTEN, GURL! WE HAVE A CONNECTION! I LUV U MORE THAN MY LEGO COLLECTION!"

Startled, Ralph, Tucker, and Moose immediately panicked and stared suspiciously around the room.

They were acting like they'd just heard a police siren and NOT the most annoying song EVER!

"There's that song again!" Tucker sputtered. "The same one I heard in the locker room!"

"But where in the HECK is it coming from?!" Ralph said as he spun 180 degrees, trying to locate the source of the music.

"How about a GHOST! I t-told you guys this p-place was haunted!" Moose stuttered in fear.

I was dying to reach down and turn off the ringer.

But I couldn't risk those criminals discovering I had a cell phone in my back pocket, which meant the police and a twenty-year prison sentence were merely a 911 call away.

Forget the rope! They'd probably KILL ME on the spot because of the phone. Just the thought of it made me so nervous I could barely breathe.

At all.

Way to go, Barf! This is the PERFECT time to have a PANIC ATTACK and stop breathing!

And it didn't help matters that my inhaler was in my pocket right next to the ringing phone.

JUST GREAT!!

"Wait a dang-gone minute!" Ralph said, cupping his hand over his ear and narrowing his eyes. "It sounds to me like the music is coming from . . . from . . ."

The three of them lunged at me as they yelled . . .

"THE KID!"

I gasped and gulped like a fish out of water, but I STILL couldn't breathe.

I felt REALLY dizzy.

I tried to grab my inhaler, but the room started to spin.

And then, suddenly, everything went completely . . .

DARK!

6. A VERY DARK AND TWISTED TALE

No, REALLY! I'm not lying! The room ACTUALLY went completely DARK. . . .

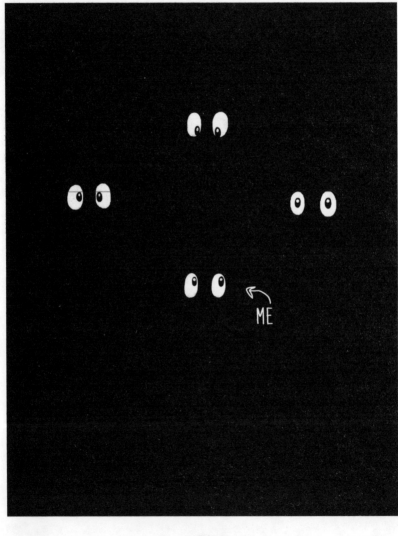

ME

At first I thought I had DIED!

And since my phone had finally stopped ringing, everything was really quiet. Like, DEAD quiet!

Weirdly, I didn't feel any pain. Not from my panic attack or from possibly being strangled by those burglars once they'd figured out I had a phone.

Thank goodness I finally noticed I wasn't breathing! Because THAT would've definitely KILLED me. Assuming, of course, I wasn't ALREADY dead.

I reached into my pocket and grabbed my inhaler. Then I took two deep breaths.

Sorry, but Max Crumbly was NOT going down like this!

I climbed off the ~~pizza~~ table and groped through the dark to the nearest wall.

All I remember is grabbing my flashlight from my boot and shining its light on that vent as a surge of pure adrenaline started to pump through my veins. . . .

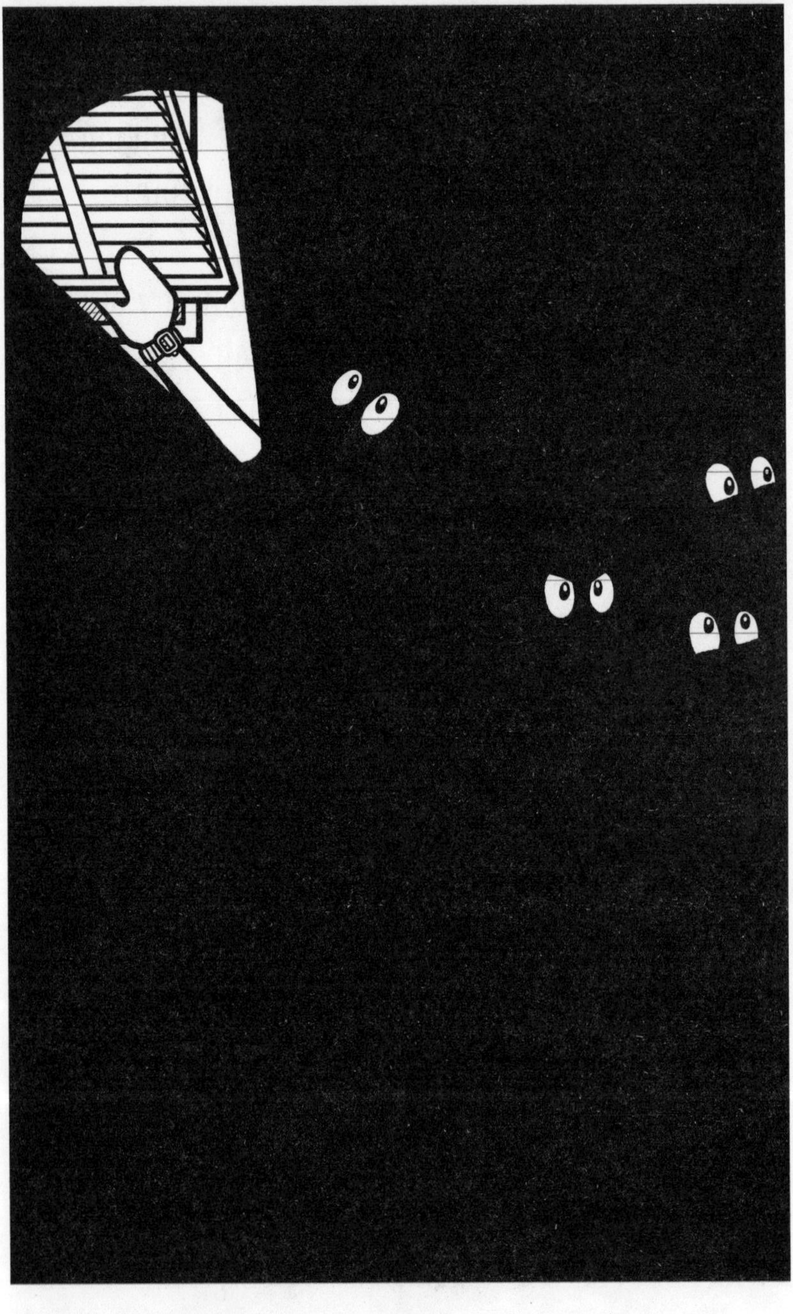

I don't have the slightest idea how I made it up into that vent. But I did. No joke!

And just in the nick of time. As soon as the burglars got over the initial shock of the lights being off, they completely FLIPPED OUT!

"Hey, who turned out the lights?" Tucker shrieked.

"A G-G-GHOST!" Moose screeched again.

"JUST GRAB THE KID, YOU KNUCKLEHEADS!!" Ralph screamed. "Don't let him get away!"

"I think I have him!" Tucker yelled. "OUCH!"

"GOTCHA!" Moose hollered. "OW!"

"Hold still, you little RAT!" Ralph snarled. "UGH!"

When the lights finally came back on, I couldn't believe my eyes! I don't think Ralph, Tucker, and Moose could believe their eyes EITHER. . . .

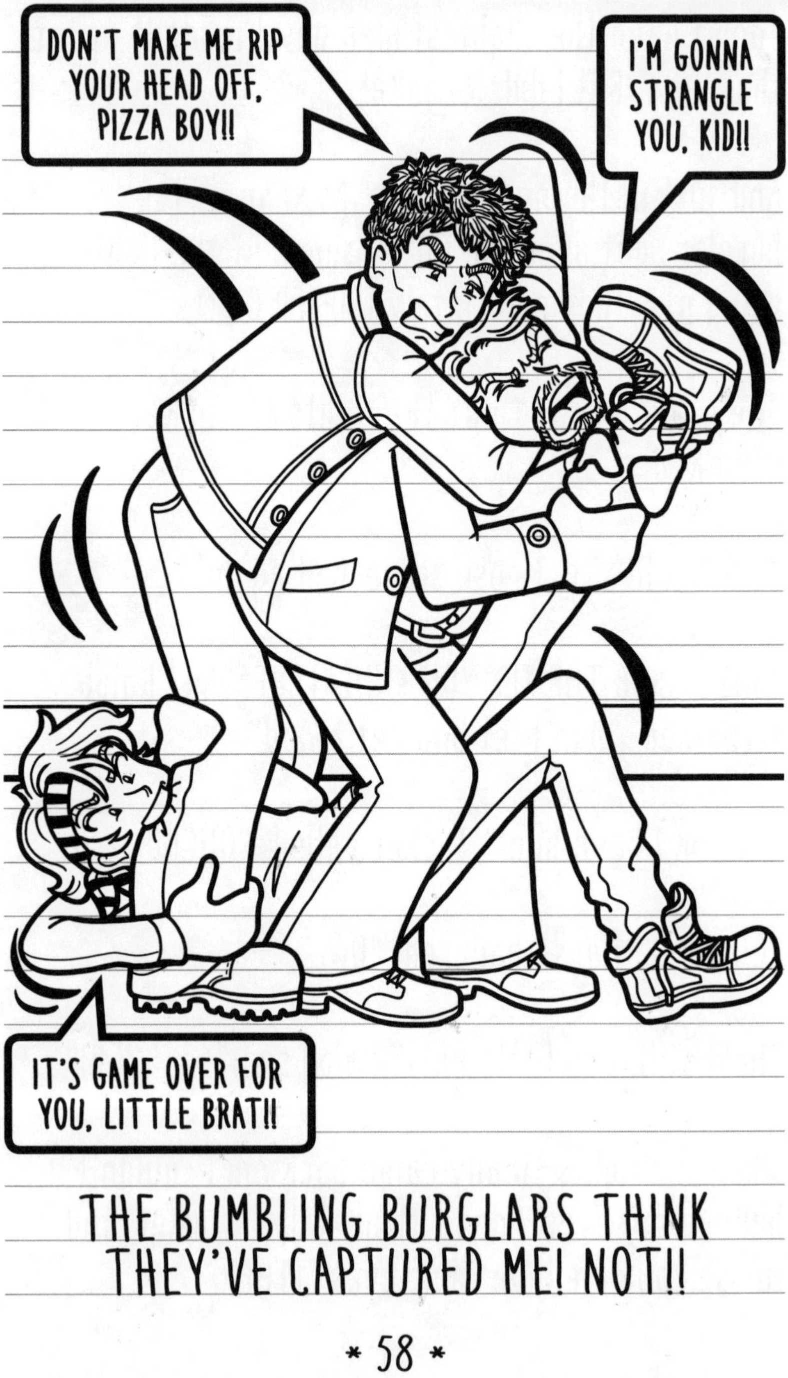
DON'T MAKE ME RIP YOUR HEAD OFF, PIZZA BOY!!
I'M GONNA STRANGLE YOU, KID!!
IT'S GAME OVER FOR YOU, LITTLE BRAT!!

THE BUMBLING BURGLARS THINK THEY'VE CAPTURED ME! NOT!!

They looked like something straight out of one of those fake WRESTLEMANIA matches on TV!!

Only these guys were totally NOT faking! They thought they were attacking ME.

But, in reality, they were giving EACH OTHER a BEATDOWN.

FOR REAL!! I couldn't make this stuff up.

It took a while for them to untangle themselves from their massive BRAWL.

And when they finally noticed me up in the vent laughing my behind off, they were FURIOUS!

The burglars started yelling and screaming stuff at me that would get your mouth washed out with soap.

I just smiled at those idiots, waved, and said, "What's up, dudes! I hope you enjoyed that fight. Sorry I couldn't make it!!" . . .

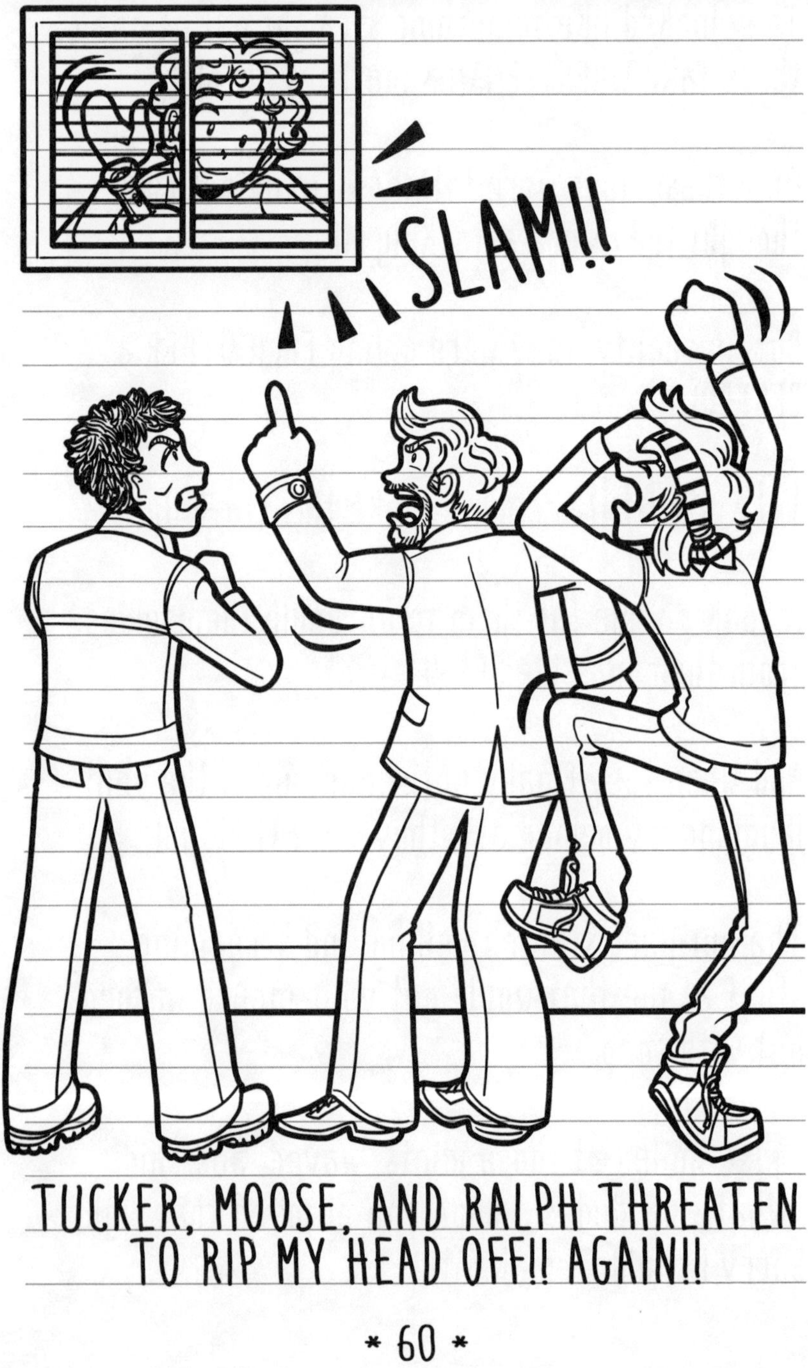
SLAM!!

TUCKER, MOOSE, AND RALPH THREATEN TO RIP MY HEAD OFF!! AGAIN!!

With all the lights going on and off, it seemed like Erin was FINALLY in control of things.

And not a minute too soon. For a while there, I thought I was TOAST!

Erin's a LIFESAVER!

But we STILL needed to talk on the phone to come up with a brilliant plan to stop the burglars from stealing the school's computers AND get my dad's comic book back. You know, the collectible comic I accidentally left in the computer lab when I was playing video games after school.

I decided to send Erin a quick text to let her know I was on my way to the boiler room (AGAIN!) and that I would call her in about ten minutes.

But first I needed to do a little surveillance to try to locate that book.

I crawled a safe distance away from all the drama and then made myself comfortable.

7. RALPH VENTS HIS FRUSTRATIONS

"THAT was the last straw!" Ralph bellowed. "I've had it with that kid! I'm going up into that vent to hunt him down MYSELF! And I am not coming out without him!"

"Listen, boss! I know you're mad, but going up into those vents is a really BAD idea!" Moose argued.

"I agree! Especially since you're a little on the, um . . . CHUNKY side!" Tucker explained nervously.

"When I want the opinion of two MEATBALLS, I'll go ask a plate of spaghetti! So just keep your worthless opinions to yourself!" Ralph shot back.

"I don't know, boss! I've got a really bad feeling about this. Deep down in my gut!" Moose said.

"That's just INDIGESTION from the baloney, mustard, and pickle sandwich you ate for breakfast! So get over here and help me up into this vent! NOW!" Ralph said.

That's when Tucker glared angrily at Moose. . . .

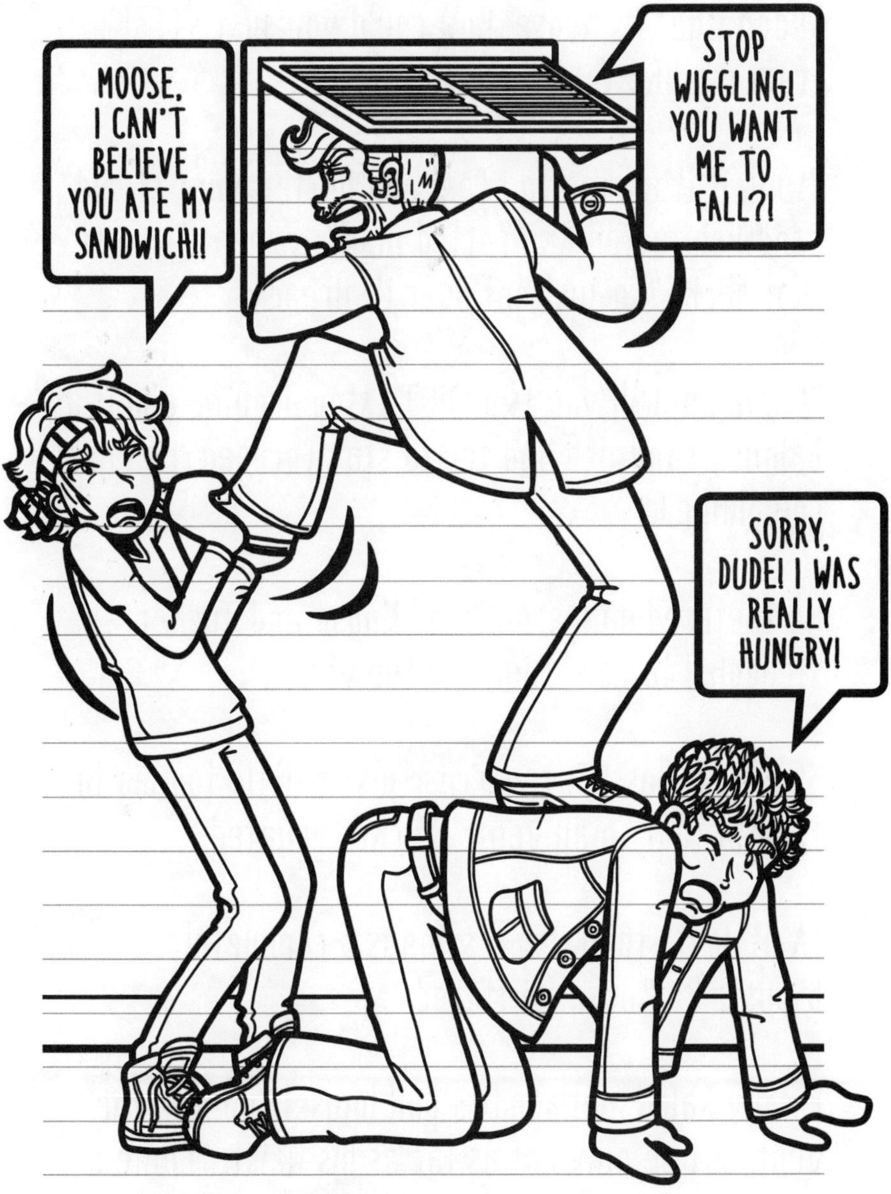
MOOSE, I CAN'T BELIEVE YOU ATE MY SANDWICH!!
STOP WIGGLING! YOU WANT ME TO FALL?!
SORRY, DUDE! I WAS REALLY HUNGRY!

RALPH CLIMBS INTO THE VENT!

"I don't get it, Moose. How could you just STEAL from me like that?" Tucker asked.

"Well, if it makes you feel any better, your stupid sandwich tasted like rotted monkey meat!" Moose shot back. "So just get over it already!"

"Come on! Will you two IDIOTS stop arguing about a baloney sandwich and try to stay focused?!" Ralph complained.

He teetered dangerously as Moose and Tucker struggled to hoist him into the vent.

"Sorry, b-boss! But you're j-just a little too big to fit into that small vent!" Tucker grunted.

"A little?! I think my s-spine is c-completely b-busted!" Moose muttered.

Finally Ralph managed to pull himself up into the vent. But he only got as far as his waist. "Come on, guys! Push! I'm almost inside! Just keep PUSHING!" Ralph yelled. "What's the problem?!" . . .

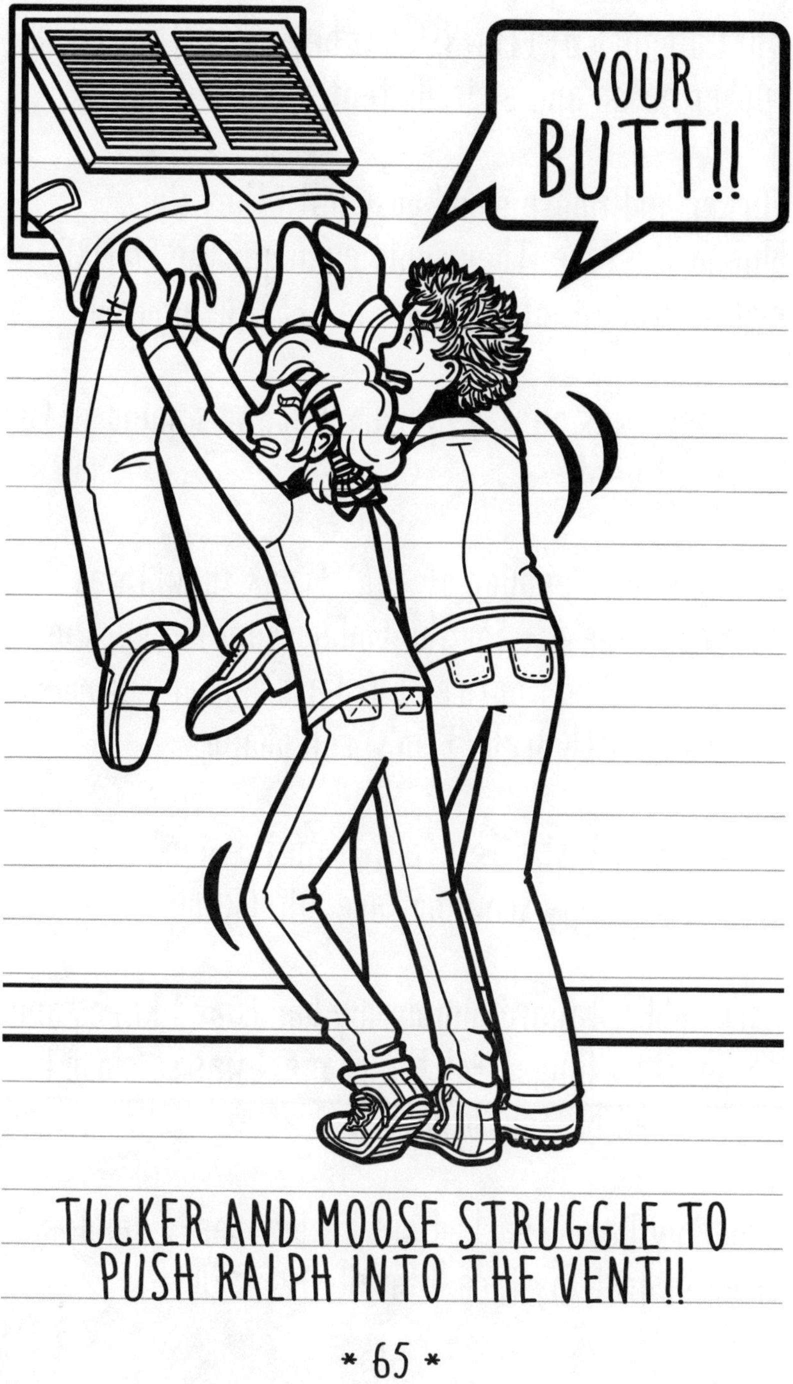
YOUR BUTT!!

TUCKER AND MOOSE STRUGGLE TO PUSH RALPH INTO THE VENT!!

What a bunch of CLOWNS!! All they needed were red rubber noses and a circus tent!

Tucker and Moose could push until they were blue in the face. They could even get the ENTIRE eighth-grade football team to HELP them push!

But there was no way in HECK Ralph was going to fit into that vent.

I'd seen quite enough of THAT freak show! I was about to take off for the boiler room to check in with Erin, when I noticed I had accidentally dropped my (okay, technically Erin's) cell phone.

It was lying just a few feet from the vent entrance and Ralph's ~~ugly~~ scowling face. OH, CRUD!!

I scrambled toward him on my hands and knees and desperately lunged for the phone. I was so close I could smell his foul breath.

Suddenly Ralph reached out his big, beefy hand and tried to grab my face. I totally FREAKED!! . . .

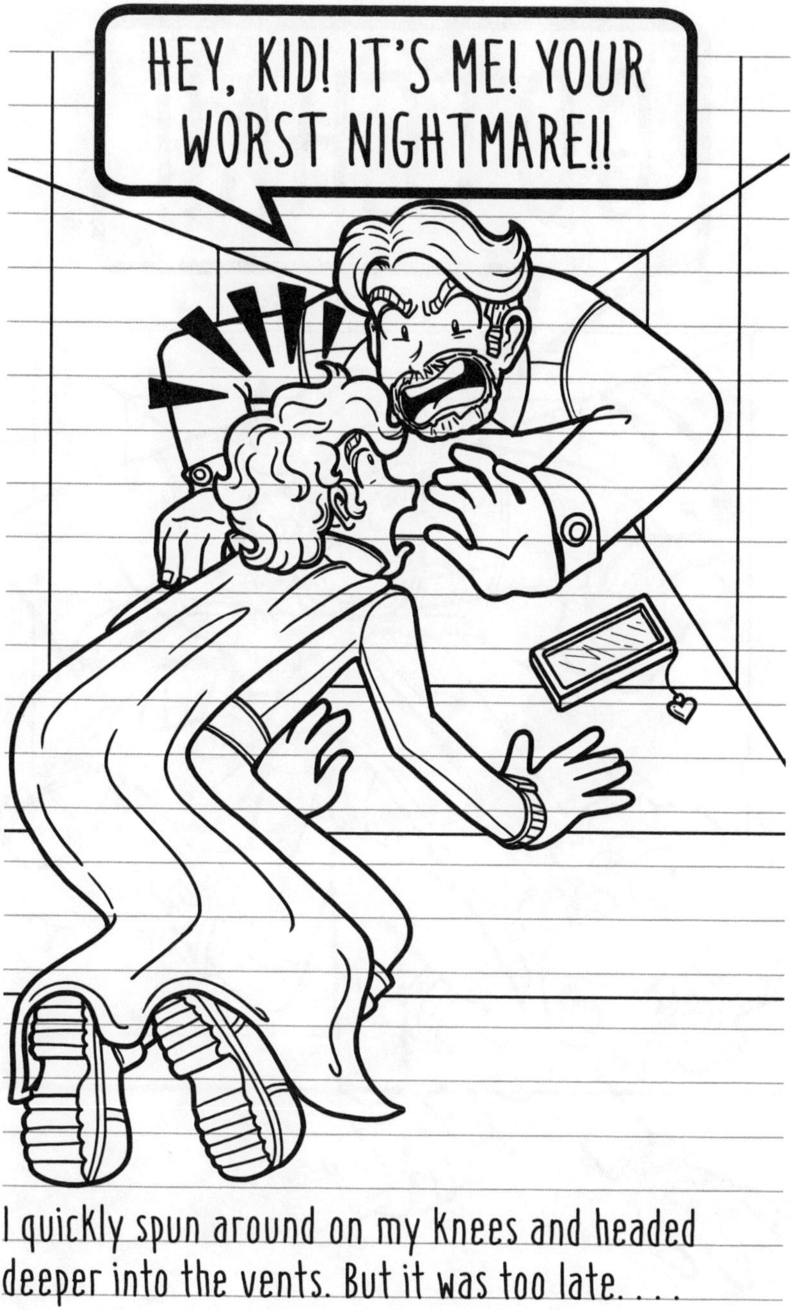
HEY, KID! IT'S ME! YOUR WORST NIGHTMARE!!

I quickly spun around on my knees and headed deeper into the vents. But it was too late. . . .

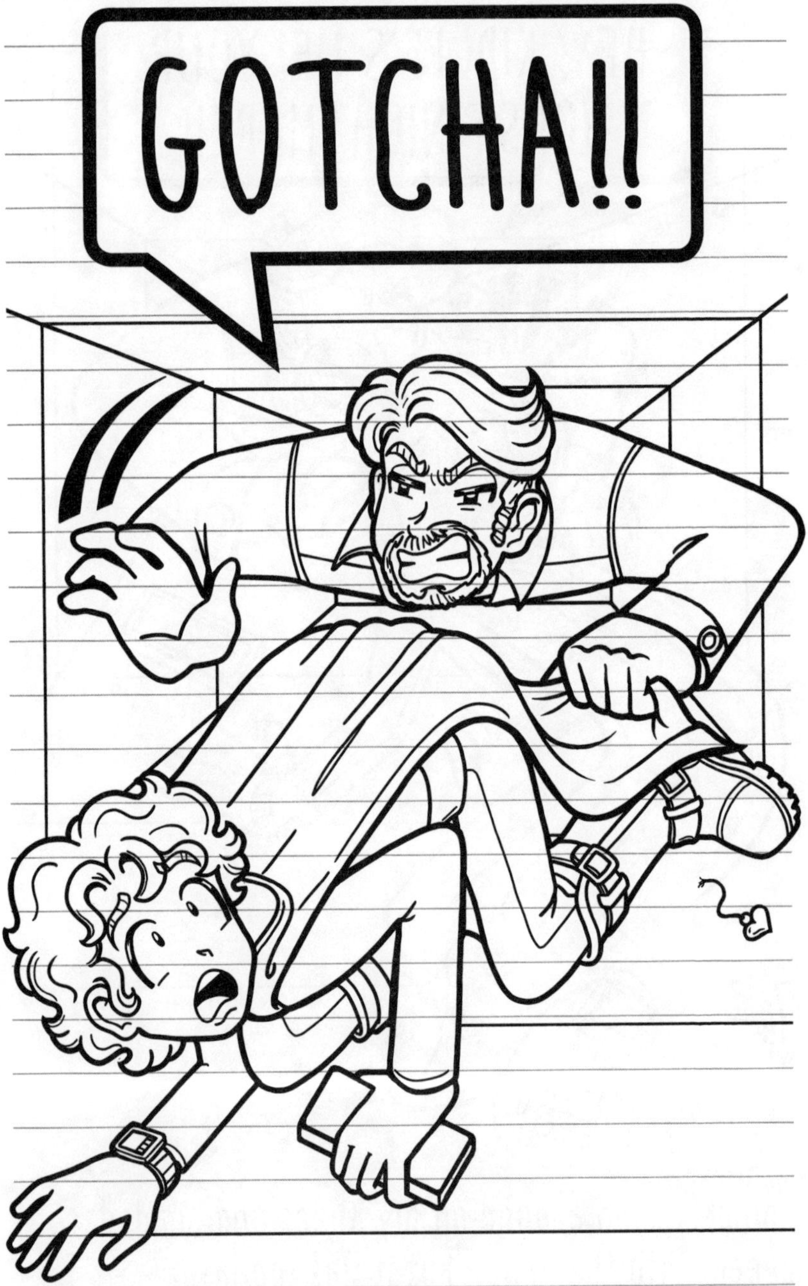
GOTCHA!!

Ralph grabbed my cape!

Then he started pulling me toward him.

"Let GO of me!"

I yelled as I struggled in vain to pull my cape out of his vise-like grip.

I glanced at the phone and wondered if, somehow, Erin could help me.

But short of me asking Ralph for a quick time-out to call and update her on my very dire situation, there was no way she would know what was going on inside the vents.

Erin had saved my behind back in the computer lab by strategically shutting off the lights.

But now I was on my own!

8. WHY OLD DUDES SHOULD NEVER, EVER WEAR SAGGY PANTS!

Note to self: Seriously think about losing the cape.

I was no match for Ralph! No matter how hard I struggled, he dragged me backward toward the vent opening.

"It's the end of the line for you, kid!" Ralph growled. "Just FACE IT!"

Ironically, his threat gave me a really good idea.

I rolled over onto my back, brought both of my knees to my chest, and then kicked with all my might. The chunky soles of my lost-and-found motorcycle boots landed squarely on Ralph's very sweaty and very surprised FACE!!

BAM!!

"OOOOOOOW!!" Ralph howled in pain.

"HELP! THAT LITTLE BRAT JUST VICIOUSLY KICKED ME IN MY FACE!"

"Boss! Are you okay?!!" Tucker exclaimed.

"What's going on up there?!" Moose asked.

"GET ME OUT OF HERE!! NOW!! I MEAN IT!"

"Just jump down. We're right here to catch you!" Moose said. "Jump, boss! JUMP!"

"I CAN'T DO IT! I JUST . . . CAN'T!!"

Tucker and Moose looked at each other and rolled their eyes. Ralph was acting like a big baby.

"You can't jump?!" Tucker asked. "But WHY?!"

That's when Ralph yelled so loudly his voice actually reverberated through the vents. . . .

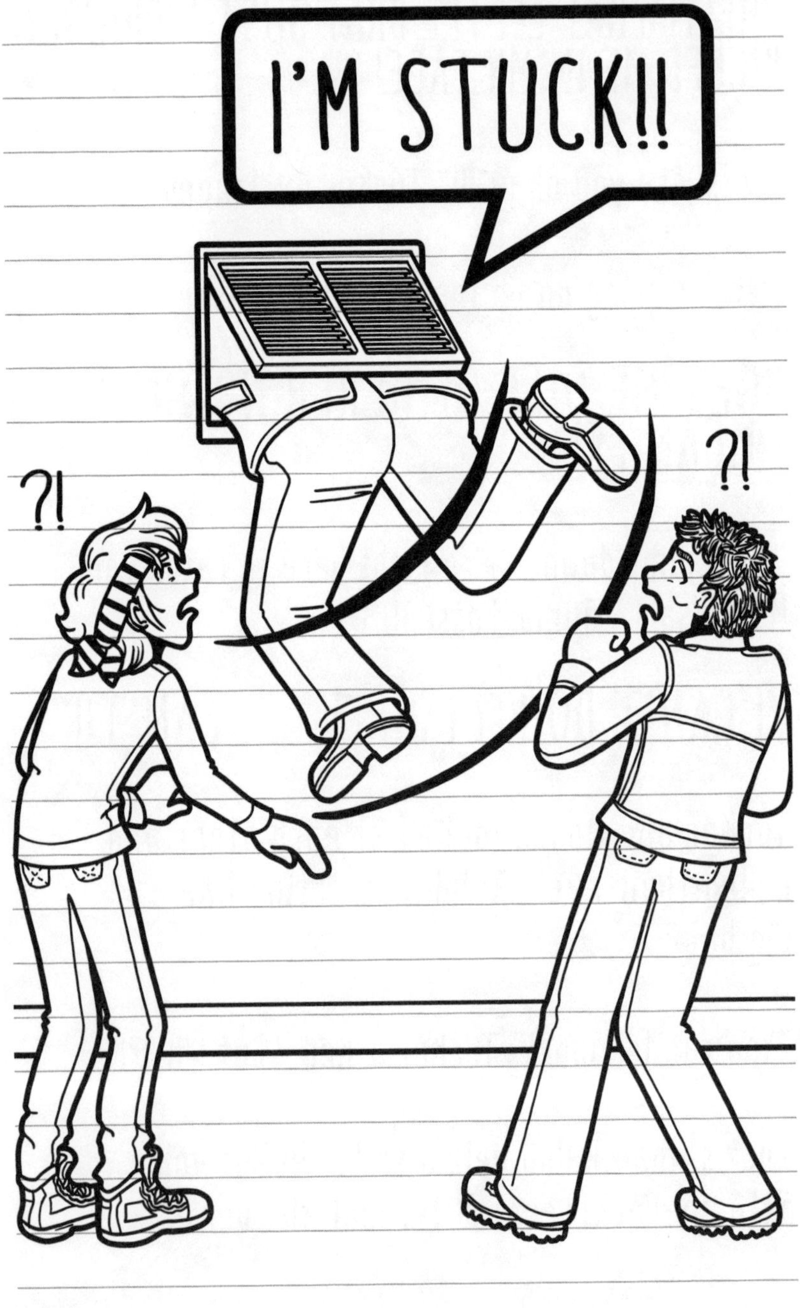
I'M STUCK!!
?!
?!

Tucker and Moose just stared in disbelief. Ralph yelled a bunch of not-so-nice words as he kicked his legs back and forth like he was swimming a fifty-meter race.

"GET. ME. OUTTA HERE!!"

"But, boss, what do you want us to do?" Tucker asked.

"DO SOMETHING! ANYTHING!!"

"Hey, I saw a situation just like this on TV last week!" Moose exclaimed excitedly. "A man got his head stuck in a sewer pipe, and every time someone flushed the toilet, he almost drowned! Let's dial 911 and ask them to bring over the Jaws of Life! They'll cut Ralph out!"

"YOU FOOLS!! DID IT EVER OCCUR TO YOU THAT WE'RE BURGLARIZING A SCHOOL?! IF YOU CALL THE COPS, WE'RE GOING STRAIGHT TO JAIL! SO JUST PULL ME OUT!! RIGHT NOW!! DO YOU HEAR ME?! PULL!" . . .

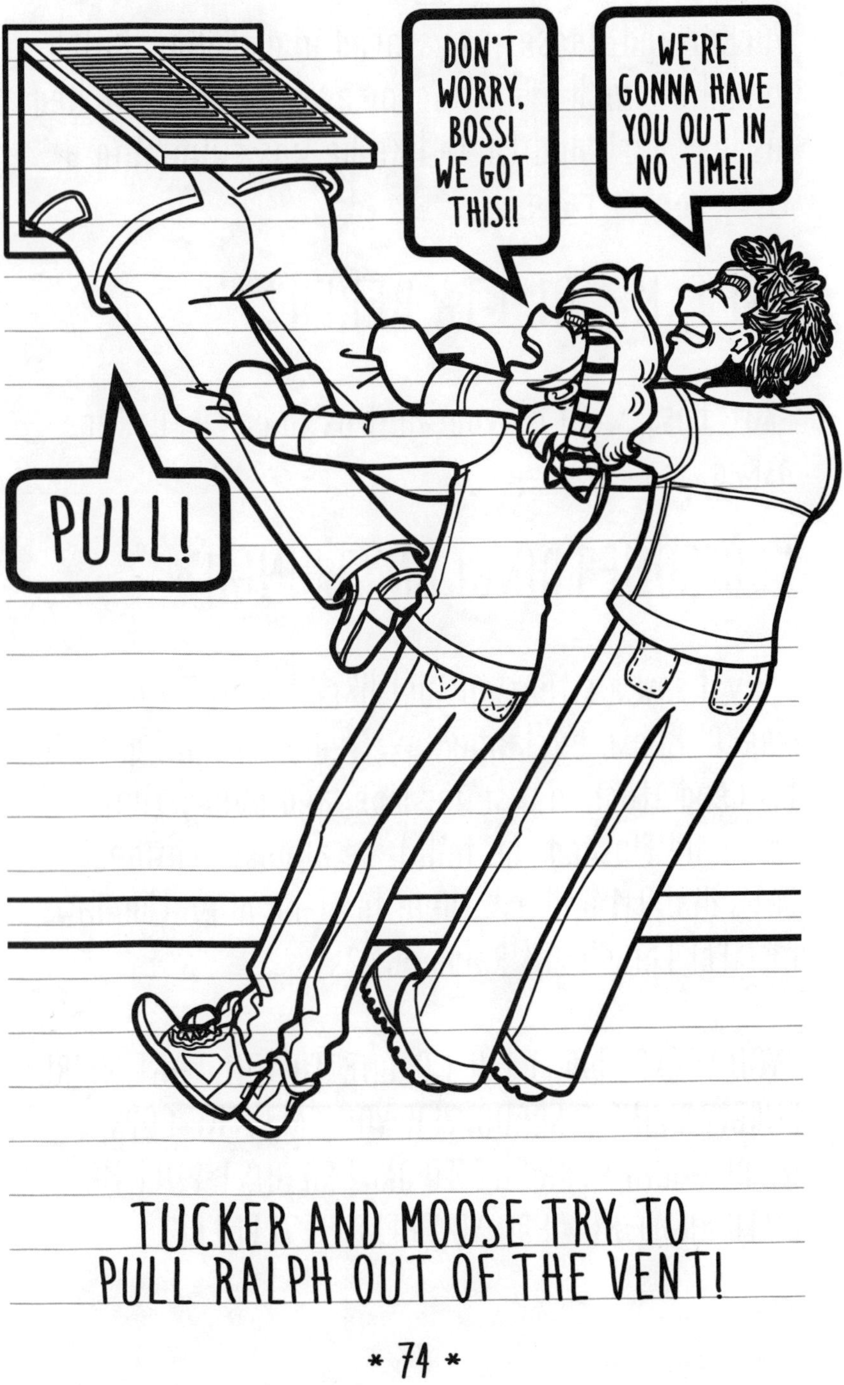
PULL!
DON'T WORRY, BOSS! WE GOT THIS!!
WE'RE GONNA HAVE YOU OUT IN NO TIME!!

TUCKER AND MOOSE TRY TO PULL RALPH OUT OF THE VENT!

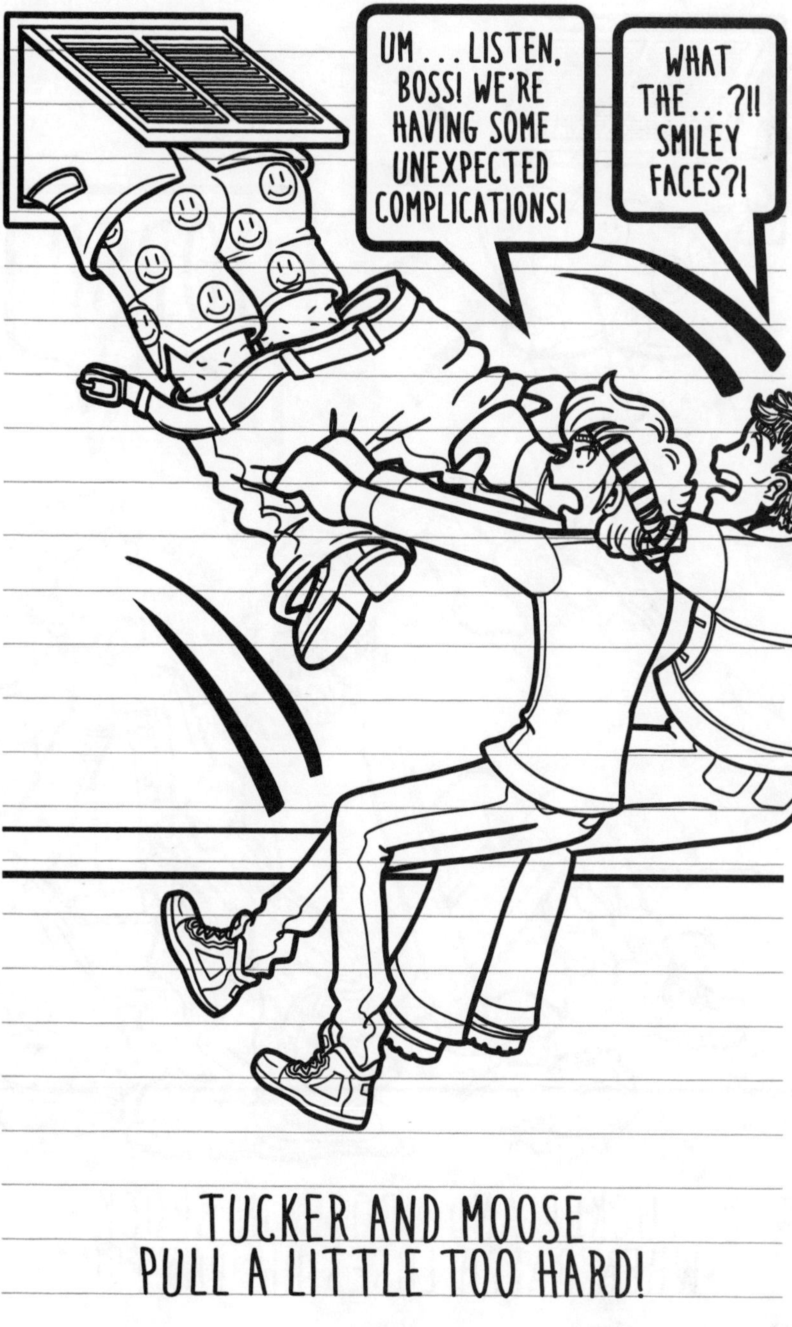
UM . . . LISTEN, BOSS! WE'RE HAVING SOME UNEXPECTED COMPLICATIONS!
WHAT THE . . . ?!! SMILEY FACES?!

TUCKER AND MOOSE PULL A LITTLE TOO HARD!

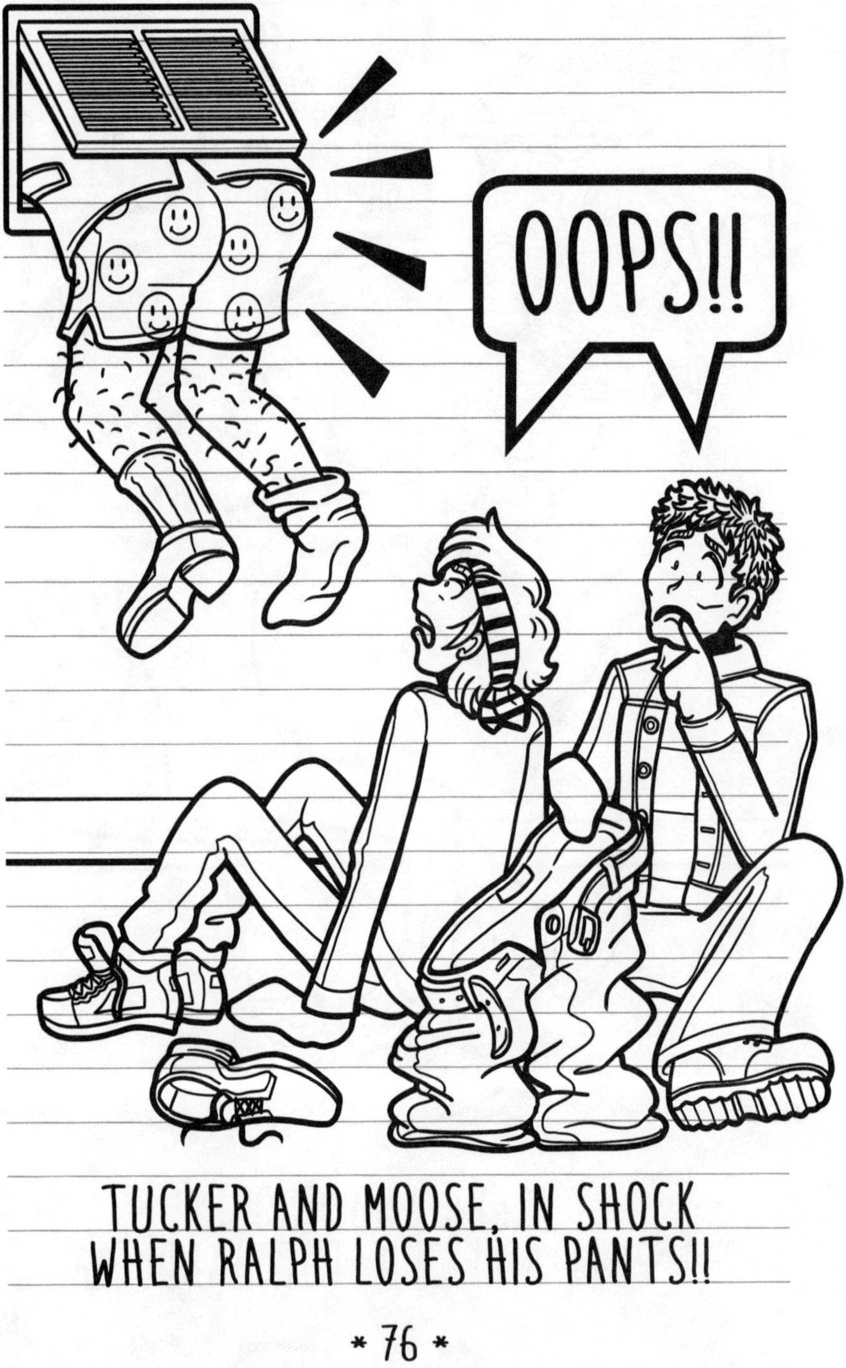
OOPS!!

TUCKER AND MOOSE, IN SHOCK WHEN RALPH LOSES HIS PANTS!!

"TUCKER! MOOSE! WHAT IN THE HECK IS GOING ON OUT THERE?! I FEEL COLD AIR ON MY . . . BACKSIDE!"

"Don't worry! We just opened a window to get a little fresh air, that's all!" Tucker lied.

"Listen, Tucker!" Moose exclaimed. "This is hopeless! Maybe we should take the computers and get out of here. Ralph can just catch up with us later, and we'll give him his cut of the loot!"

"I don't know, Moose! When Ralph finally gets down from there and figures out we left him, he's going to be REALLY mad! Then he might actually fire us—or worse!" Tucker argued.

Finally the two men came up with a plan. Tucker climbed up on Moose's shoulders. Then they forcefully tugged on the vent door until the frame came loose from the wall.

Ralph was kicking and hollering at the top of his lungs until they FINALLY pulled him out. . . .

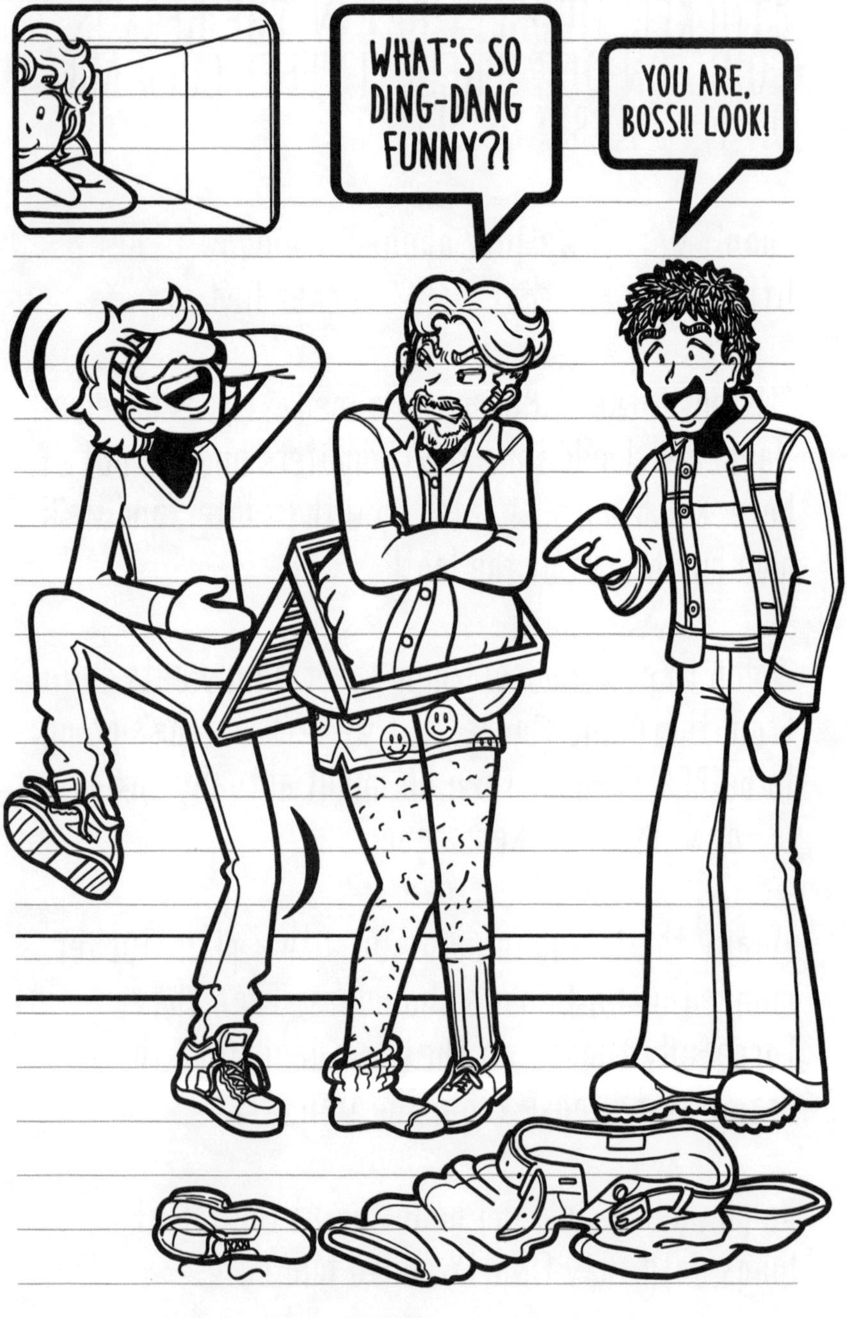
WHAT'S SO DING-DANG FUNNY?!
YOU ARE, BOSS!! LOOK!

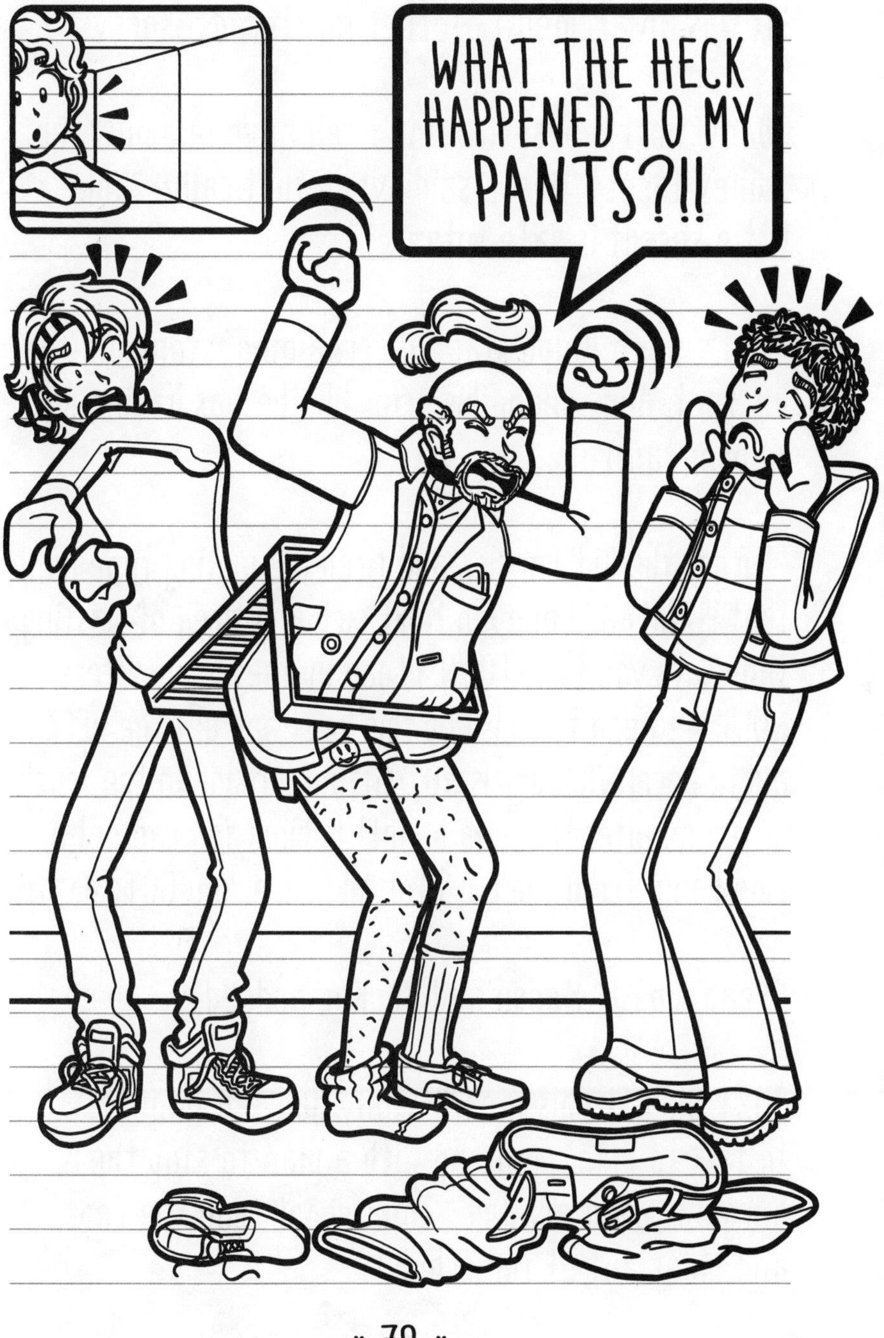
WHAT THE HECK HAPPENED TO MY PANTS?!!

"It was an accident!" Tucker muttered. "Sorry!"

"Don't worry, boss. We won't tell anyone about the smiley faces," Moose said sympathetically. "Your little secret is safe with us."

That's when Ralph started screaming, stomping his feet, and waving his arms like he was having a temper tantrum.

"Forget the kid! I'm sick and tired of wasting time on that PUNK! And I'm even MORE sick and tired of wasting time with you two CLOWNS! Load up these computers NOW!! We need to finish up this heist and get the HECK outta here! Whoever is NOT sitting outside in the truck in ten minutes is gonna be left behind! You can get a ride home from the COPS for all I care. You GOT that?!"

"Yeah, boss!" Moose and Tucker nodded.

JUST GREAT! This meant I only had ten minutes to talk to Erin, come up with a plan to stop the burglars, find my dad's comic book, call the cops, and clear out of the school!

I needed to get moving, and FAST! I was trying to figure out where I'd left the janitor's cart when I remembered it was STILL in the computer lab, completely covered with pizza.

GIVE ME A BREAK!! It was going to take MORE than ten minutes just to crawl through the vents to get back to the boiler room.

My situation was HOPELESS! My body was starting to ache all over from crashing through that vent, and my head was pounding.

I was totally EXHAUSTED, and my battle with the burglars was just getting started. I pulled out my inhaler, checked the dose counter, and gasped. It was at ZERO?!

JUST GREAT! My medicine had run out! If the burglars didn't KILL me, THAT surely could!

Maybe it was finally time to give up and go home. A loser named BARF, like me, was obviously no match for these RUTHLESS criminals!

9. HANGING OUT IN MY ~~MAN~~ MAX CAVE

As I crawled toward the boiler room, I couldn't help but feel depressed. . . .

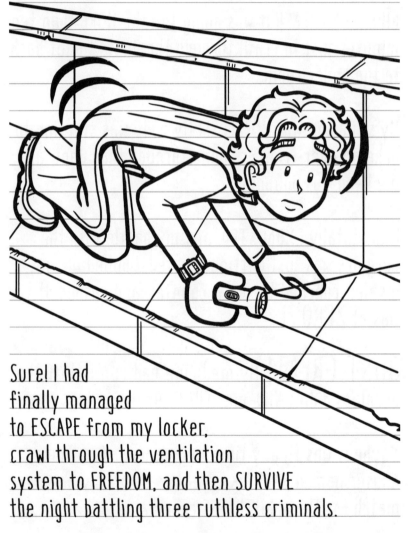

Sure! I had
finally managed
to ESCAPE from my locker,
crawl through the ventilation
system to FREEDOM, and then SURVIVE
the night battling three ruthless criminals.

But sadly, none of my accomplishments really mattered anymore. As soon as I got home, my parents were going to be so ANGRY with me that they'd insist on my grandma homeschooling me again.

I didn't have a choice but to break the bad news to Erin. I was a complete FAILURE and couldn't stop the burglars from stealing the school's computers.

By now those burglars had already loaded their truck and were probably on their way to Queasy Cheesy to pick up a new pizza to replace the one I had completely destroyed. I hoped Erin wouldn't hate me for letting her down.

I was just starting to worry that I'd taken a wrong turn (AGAIN!), when I finally spotted a weird glow coming from a large vent at the end of a corridor.

I scrambled toward it and popped the vent open.

Then I carefully climbed down a metal ladder into a damp, musty, dimly lit area . . . the BOILER ROOM!

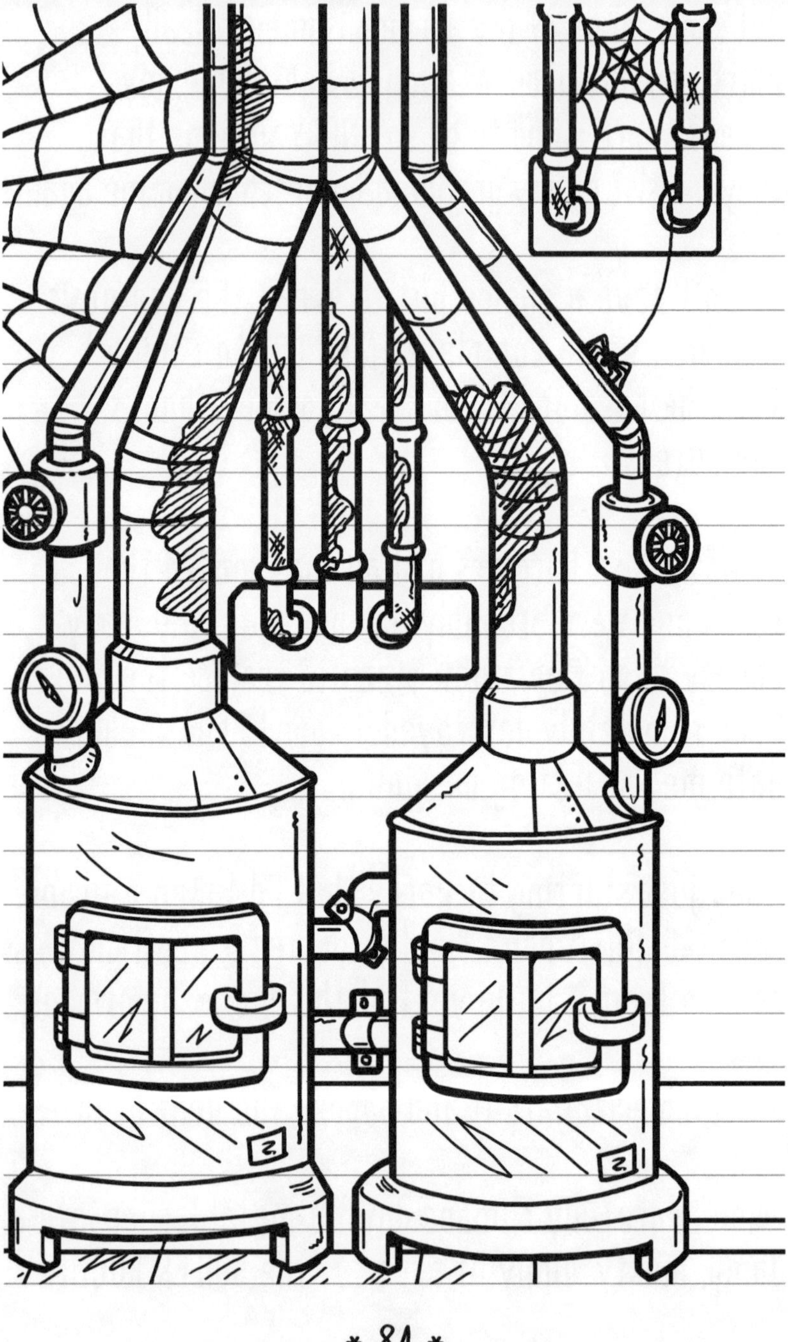

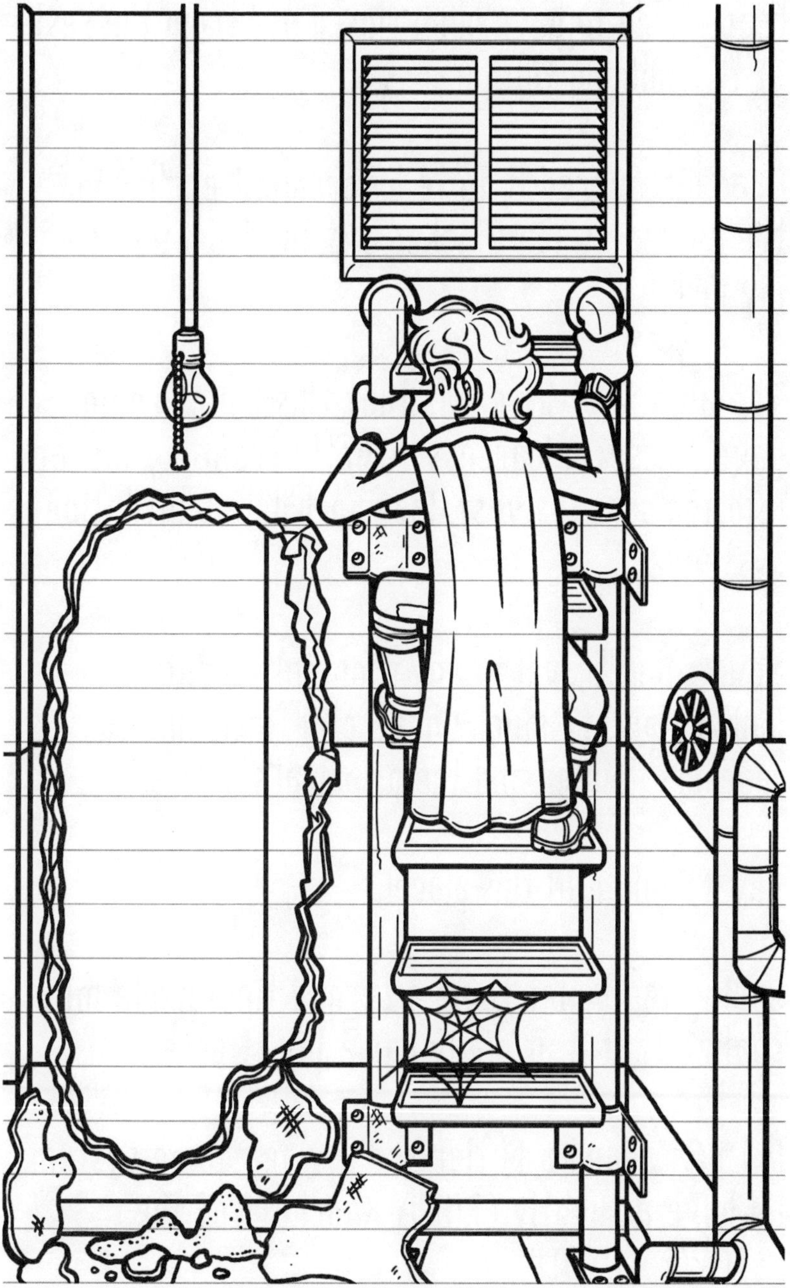

It appeared to have been closed off from the rest of the building for decades.

I had discovered it quite by accident earlier in the evening when I kicked out the back wall of my locker.

The amazing thing was that this boiler room gave me secret access directly from my locker into the school's vast, labyrinth-like ventilation system.

Now I could travel to any room in the entire building pretty much undetected, including the teachers' lounge and the principal's office.

Hey, I could RUN this place!

Seeing the boiler room a second time made me realize that it actually had a lot of potential.

If I just added a butler and a video game system, I'd have a slightly CRUDDY knockoff of the BATCAVE. SWEET!! . . .

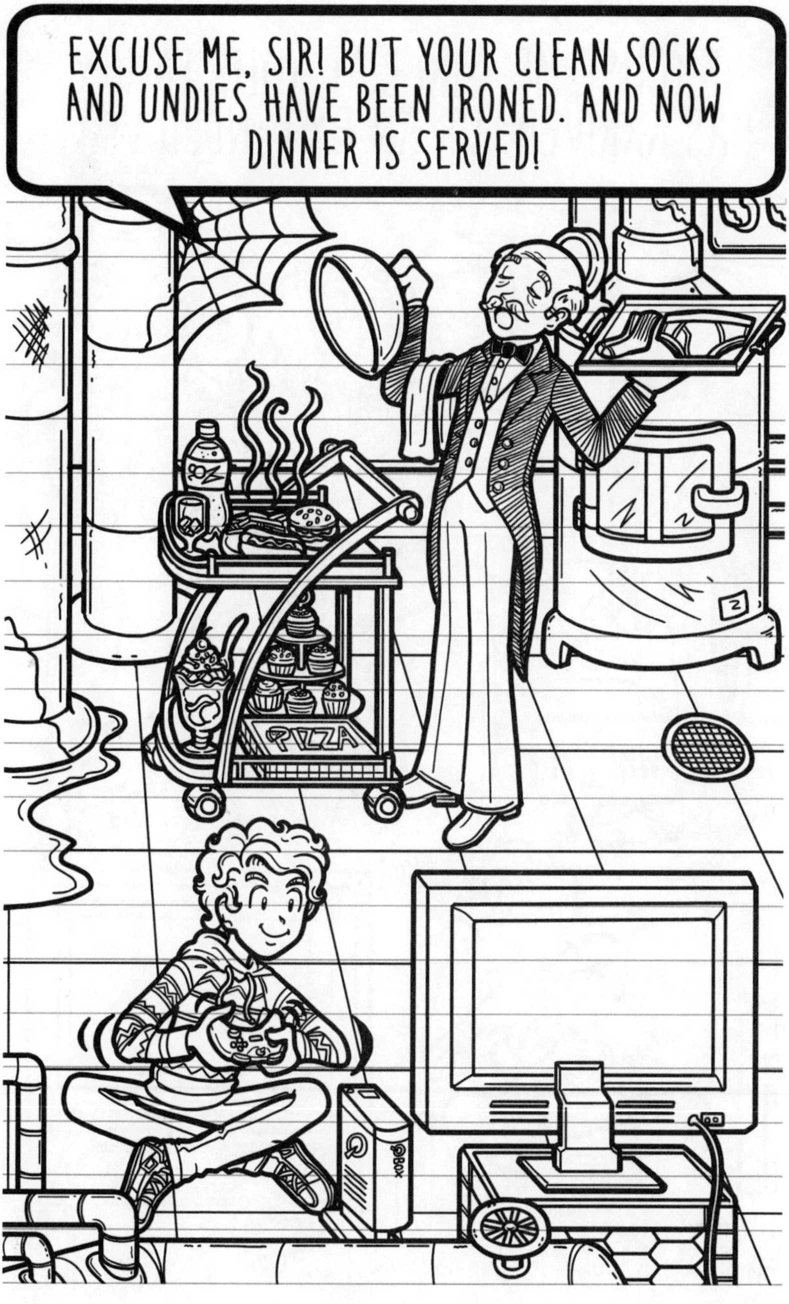
EXCUSE ME, SIR! BUT YOUR CLEAN SOCKS AND UNDIES HAVE BEEN IRONED. AND NOW DINNER IS SERVED!
PIZZA

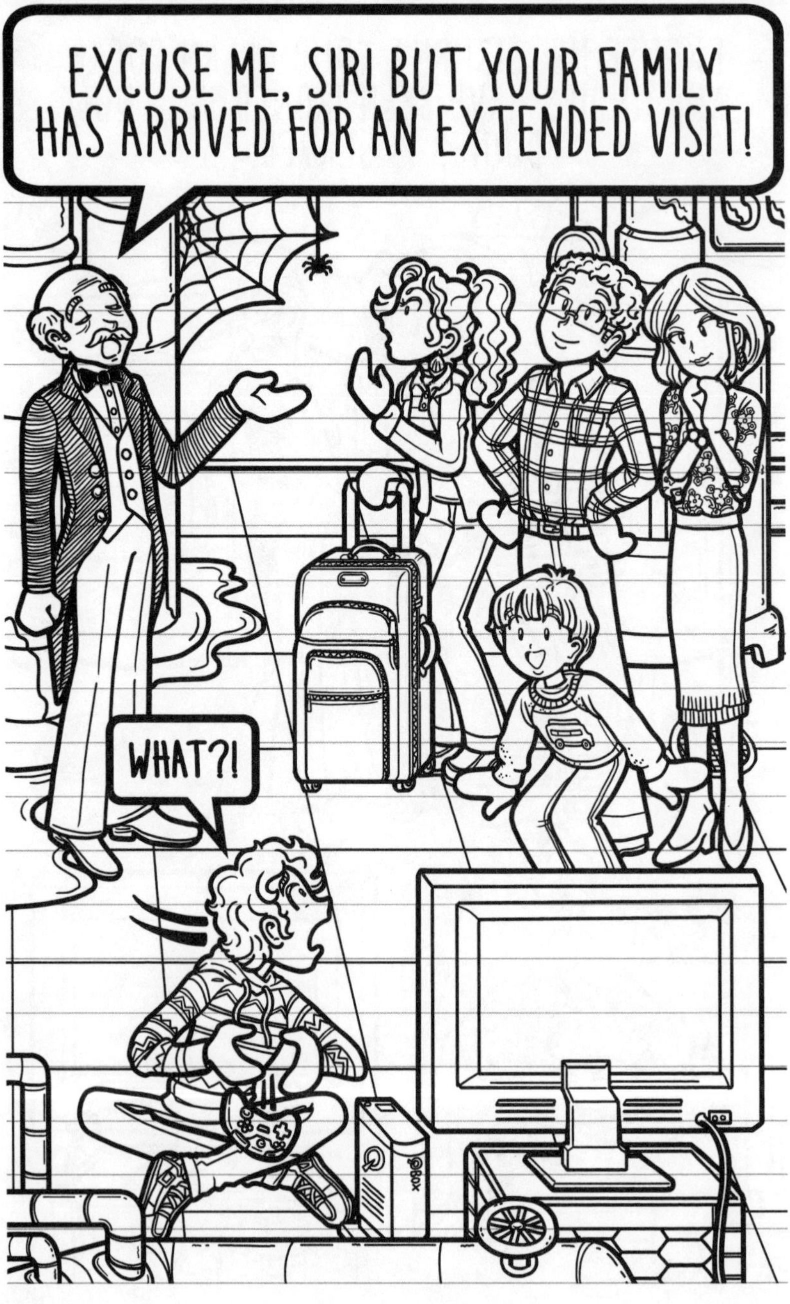
EXCUSE ME, SIR! BUT YOUR FAMILY HAS ARRIVED FOR AN EXTENDED VISIT!
WHAT?!

Hey! I love my family as much as the next kid!

But sometimes they can be super annoying!

Anyway, I needed to call Erin, but I was kind of worried.

She was a good friend at my school, and I didn't want to mess things up.

Correction!...

She was my ONLY friend at my school, and I didn't want to mess things up.

Finally I took my cell phone out of my pocket and nervously dialed Erin's cell phone number.

10. PHONE-Y FRIENDS FOREVER?

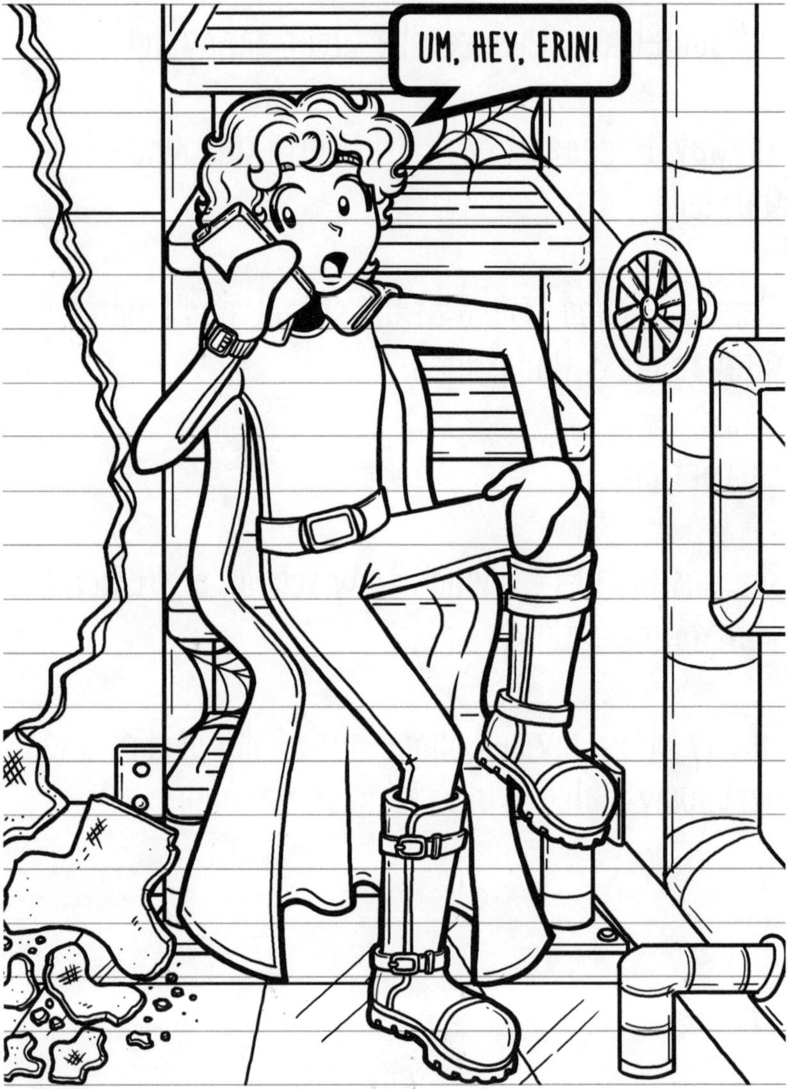
UM, HEY, ERIN!

"OMG! Max, where ARE you?!" Erin said frantically.

"I completely lost track of you. I could hear the men talking, but not YOU. I was about to call the police when I got your text!"

"Sorry!" I muttered. "I've mostly been hiding out in the vents. And right now I'm in the boiler room."

"I even tried CALLING you, but you didn't answer the cell phone. What happened?!" Erin asked.

"I heard it ringing and I REALLY wanted to pick up. But I was worried those crooks were going to get upset," I explained.

"But why would they get upset about the phone?!"

"Who knows?! Maybe it was that annoying RINGTONE?! I know 'Lego Luv' is your favorite song, but it's so SICKENING, it should come with a free BARF BAG!"

"Listen up, dude!" she shot back. "Thanks to that SICKENING song, I was finally able to figure out you were in the computer lab. And it sounded to me like you were in BIG trouble with those burglars."

"Yeah, but I was only in trouble because you called me. I was just about to, um . . . give them a beatdown when the phone rang," I said lied.

"Sure, Max! Whatever you say. I'm really sorry I interrupted that beatdown you'd planned. But I turned off the lights to give YOU time to escape."

"Really?! I wondered what was up with the lights. That was a smart move, Erin. Thanks! For real!"

"You're welcome. I didn't mean to give you a hard time or come off as a drama queen. I was just worried because I really like you a lot."

"Um . . . you DO?!" I stammered. "Well . . . same here."

"Actually, what I meant by 'like' was not . . . you know! We're, um . . . friends."

"Yeah, I understand . . . friends. Same here." There was a long silence, and I could feel my cheeks burning. Erin actually liked me! SWEET! But NOT liked me, liked me. Which was totally cool.

After that, things got a little AWKWARD . . .

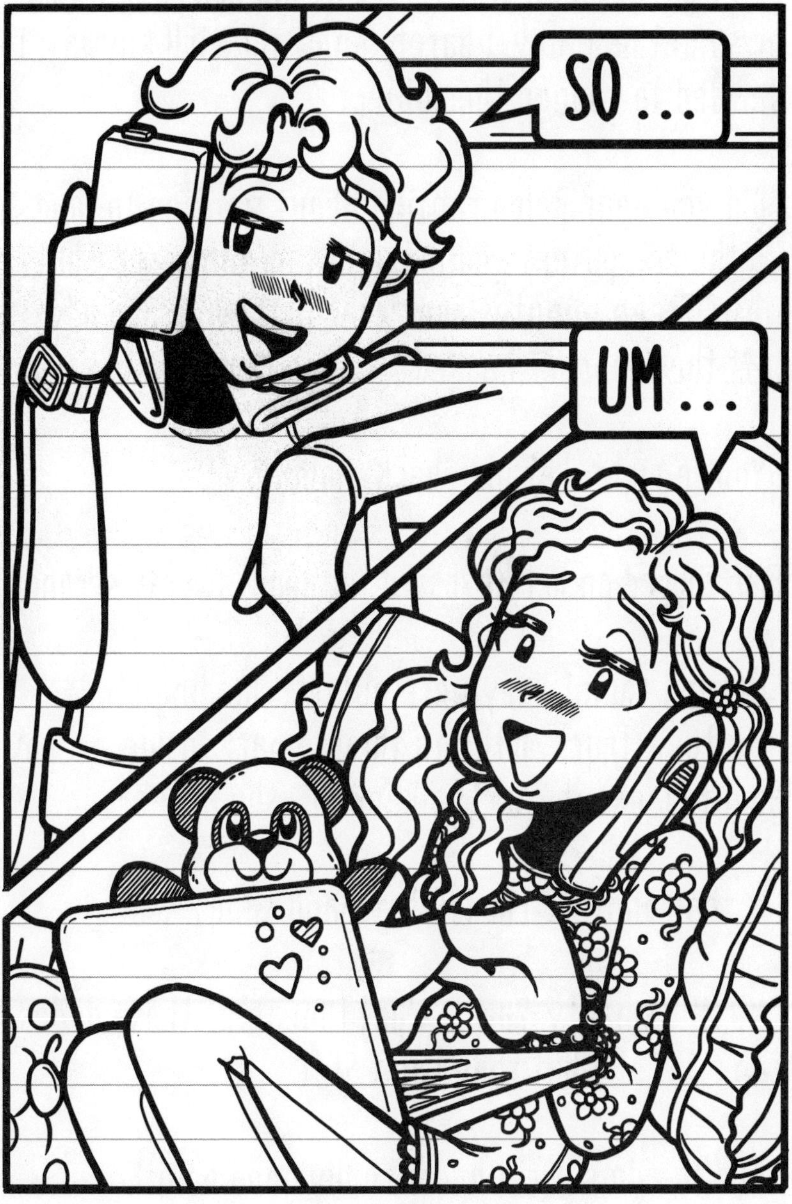
SO . . .
UM . . .

It was nice to know Erin was worried about me. But don't get it twisted! It's not like I'm crushing on her or something. Hey, I barely know the girl! Anyway, I decided to change the subject.

"Did you hear Ralph ranting about wanting to load up the computers and leave in ten minutes? That was fifteen minutes ago. What if they've already left the school?" I asked.

"You're right. Let me check. Hold on. . . ."

Erin tapped on her keyboard for about twenty seconds.

"I found them! They were outside, loading stuff into their truck, but now they're back inside. So how about Blackout 2.0: The Remix?" she asked.

"Is that another cruddy boy band song?"

"NO, Mr. Smarty-Pants. What I mean is, those dudes can't STEAL what they can't SEE!"

I had to admit, Erin had a really good point! . . .

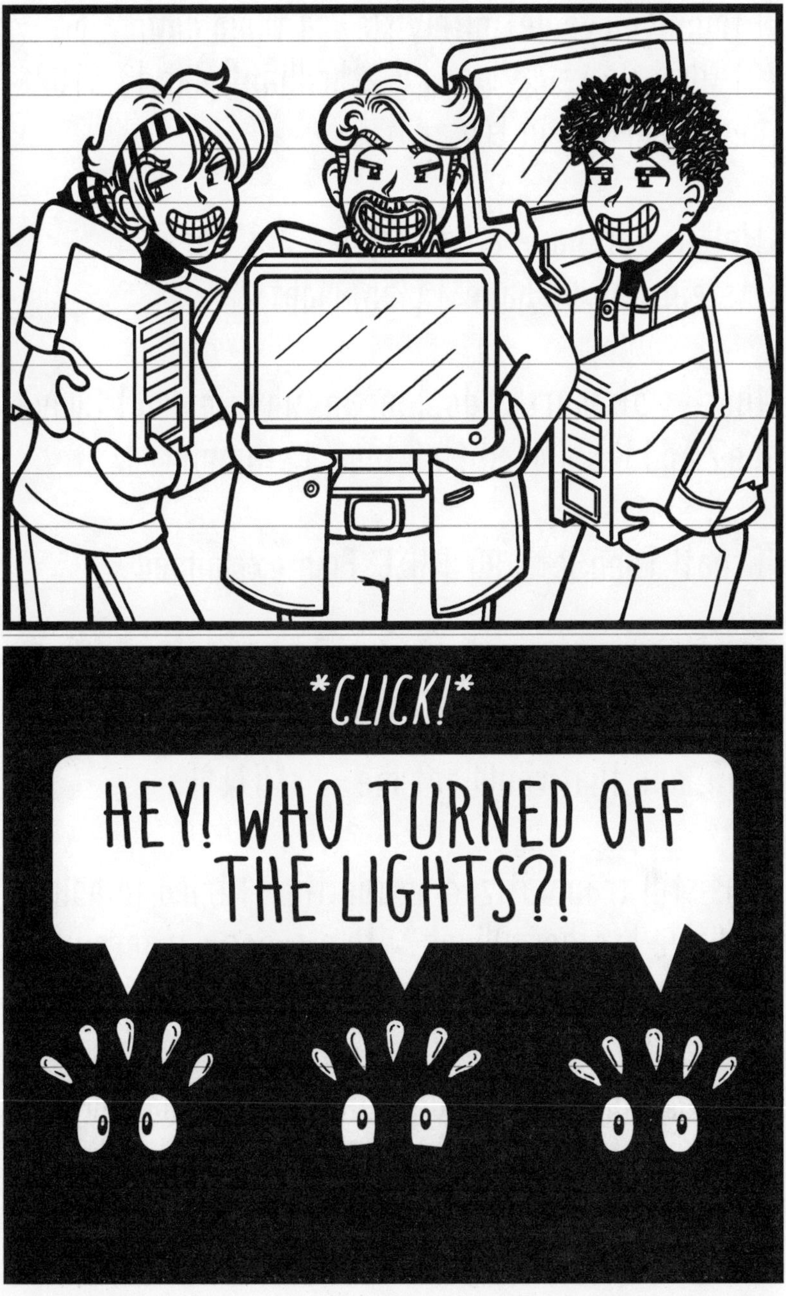
CLICK!
HEY! WHO TURNED OFF THE LIGHTS?!

"I think you've definitely slowed them down a bit. But what we really need is a brilliant plan to STOP them!" I sighed in frustration.

"Well, if YOU have a better idea, let's hear it, Einstein. You DO have a plan, right, Max?!"

"Um . . . of course I do. I mean, why wouldn't I have one? And it's a good plan too!" I stammered.

"Great! Then let's DO THIS!" Erin exclaimed.

Okay. I'm not gonna lie. I was really nervous about tackling a huge project like this with Erin. You know, one that could get me . . . KILLED!

I was still traumatized by the time I tried to help my little brother, Oliver, with a super-dangerous task. So, WHAT was it, you ask?

I helped him build a SNOWMAN. Hey, don't laugh! Sounds simple enough, right?

WRONG!! I almost DIED!! . . .

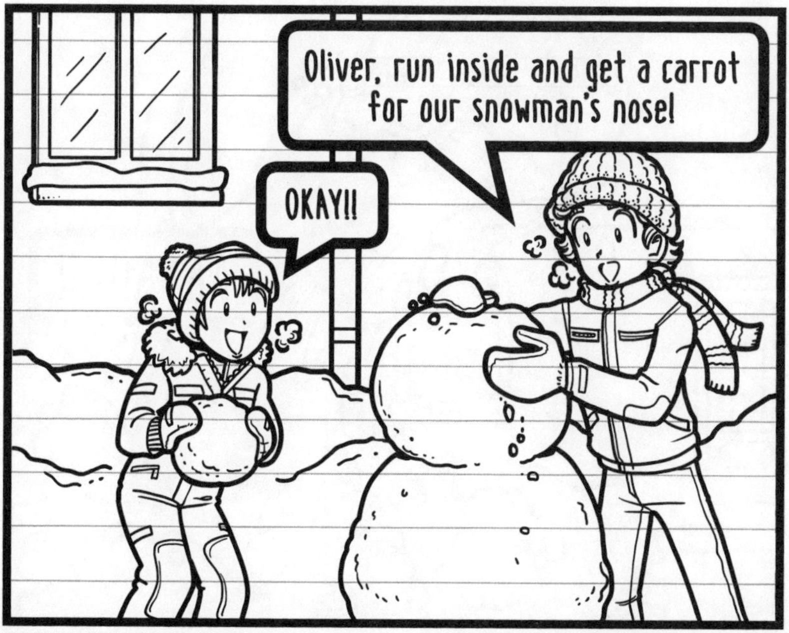
Oliver, run inside and get a carrot for our snowman's nose!
OKAY!!

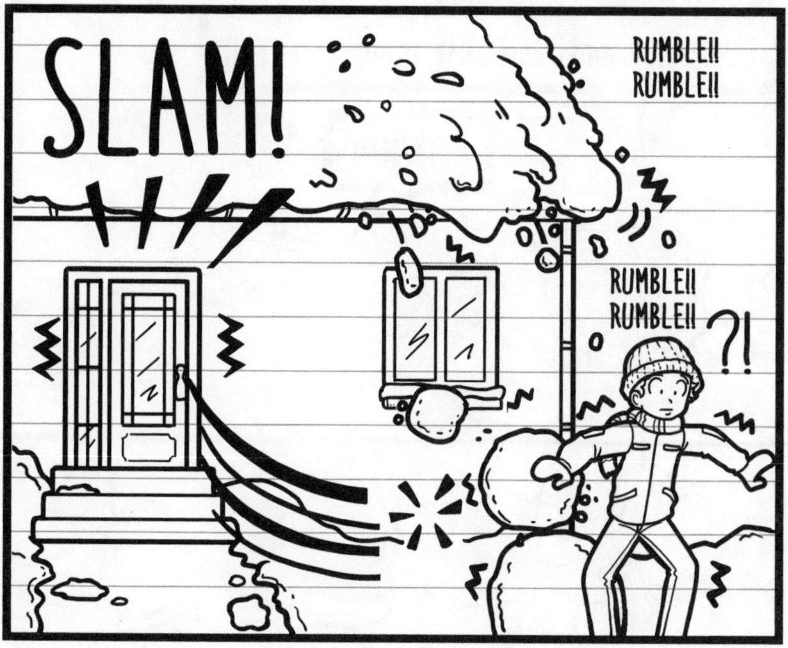
SLAM!
RUMBLE!! RUMBLE!!
RUMBLE!! RUMBLE!!
?!

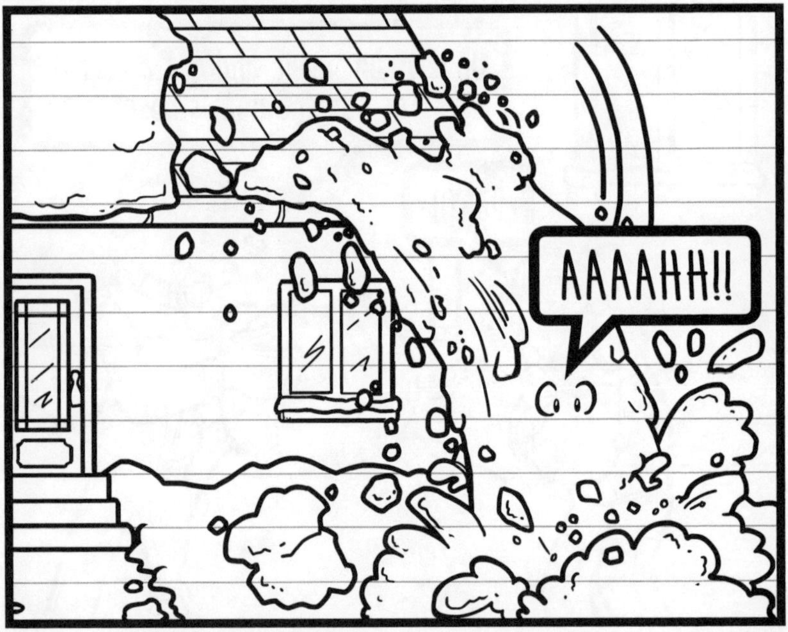
AAAAHH!!

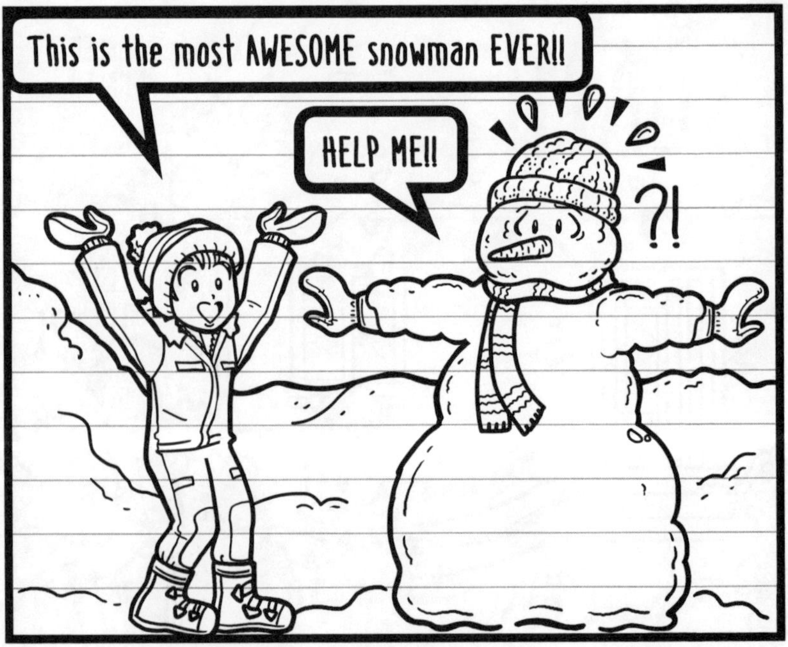
This is the most AWESOME snowman EVER!!
HELP ME!!
?!

It took an entire HOUR for me to finally convince Oliver that I was his brother and NOT his cool new magical snow buddy, Frosty the Snowman!

And by then my butt cheeks had frozen into two big chunks of ice. I thought for sure I was going to DIE from a terminal case of ~~frostbutt~~ frostbite. Since I obviously couldn't defrost my behind in the microwave, I didn't have a choice but to use my sister's hair dryer ~~without her permission!~~

I know Oliver is just a little kid, but sometimes I think he has the IQ of belly button lint.

Anyway, I was really hoping things would go better with Erin than they did with that stupid snowman.

"Okay, Erin, here's the plan. For starters, we'll need to keep a close eye on those three goofballs. So what exactly are you able to see and hear?"

"Let me pull up that information," Erin said. It sounded like her fingers were tap-dancing on her laptop keyboard.

"The school PA system is in every room and hallway, so I can hear just about everything," she explained. "But the only security cameras that are showing up on my computer are for the front and south doors. For some reason I can't access the other nine cameras. And since we're on the subject, I just got an idea. Hang up and call me back so we can video chat. Okay, Max?"

Before I could protest, I heard a *CLICK!* and Erin was gone.

That's when I suddenly broke into a cold sweat. The last thing I wanted was for Erin to actually SEE me!!

I had completely FORGOTTEN! I was wearing her ICE PRINCESS COSTUME!! JUST GREAT ☹!

I was relieved that Erin only had a very limited view through two cameras. I planned to avoid them like the plague.

I called Erin back on video chat. But I held the cell phone really close to my face so she couldn't see what I was wearing. . . .

Yes, I know! I was weirdly distorted and Erin could probably count the number of boogers in my nose.

But that was WAY better than her totally FREAKING OUT after seeing ME in her STOLEN princess costume, looking like her UGLY twin sister with a starter MUSTACHE.

~~I'm serious! It's just peach fuzz today, but I'll probably need to start shaving in the next month or two.~~

Anyway, after an intense brainstorming session, Erin and I came up with a pretty decent plan.

My job was to scope out three locations, set up booby traps, lure the burglars, and then capture them one by one.

Erin's job was to closely monitor the burglars' whereabouts (for MY safety), keep them busy and/or distracted using the building's automated systems, prevent them from leaving the school property with stolen goods, locate my dad's missing comic book, call the police to report the burglary once everything was finished, and, most important, make sure I actually SURVIVED this fiasco.

And, if you ask me, I had the EASY part!

NO JOKE!!

11. TALES FROM A MIDDLE SCHOOL NINJA

I was happy and relieved when Erin agreed to help me try to take out those burglars.

But I have to admit, all of her pointless WORRYING was starting to get a little annoying.

She was worried when she lost contact with me, she was worried when I didn't call her back, and she was worried when I didn't answer the phone.

But get this! NOW she was INSISTING that we stay on the phone with each other, just so she could call the police if I had an "emergency situation"! The girl was TRIPPIN'!

"Sorry, Erin! No way am I going to agree to that! I probably only have about forty-five minutes of battery life left on this phone, and I need to conserve as much of it as I can. I'm NOT going to stay on the phone with you every second like you're my BABYSITTER!"

"Actually, Max, you have only FORTY minutes to make this plan work. Because that's when I'm calling the police. You can use your LAST five minutes of battery life to call your PARENTS and explain why the police need them to come pick YOU up from school in the middle of the night. I NEED to be on the phone with you every second if we're going to do this!"

"Erin, I GOT this! Come on! WHY are you making such a big deal out of everything?!"

"WHY? Because it IS a big deal! And if you don't agree to MY terms, I'll call the police AND your parents RIGHT NOW! I'll never forgive myself if something bad happens to you, Max. And I REFUSE to get expelled from this school and ruin my chance to go to a major university, all because I helped YOU break thirty-nine school rules in one night due to YOUR unresolved issues with THUG! So it's your choice, dude!"

Right then Erin and I were so exasperated with each other that we'd have UNFRIENDED each other on Facebook (IF we'd ACTUALLY ever been friends on Facebook)....

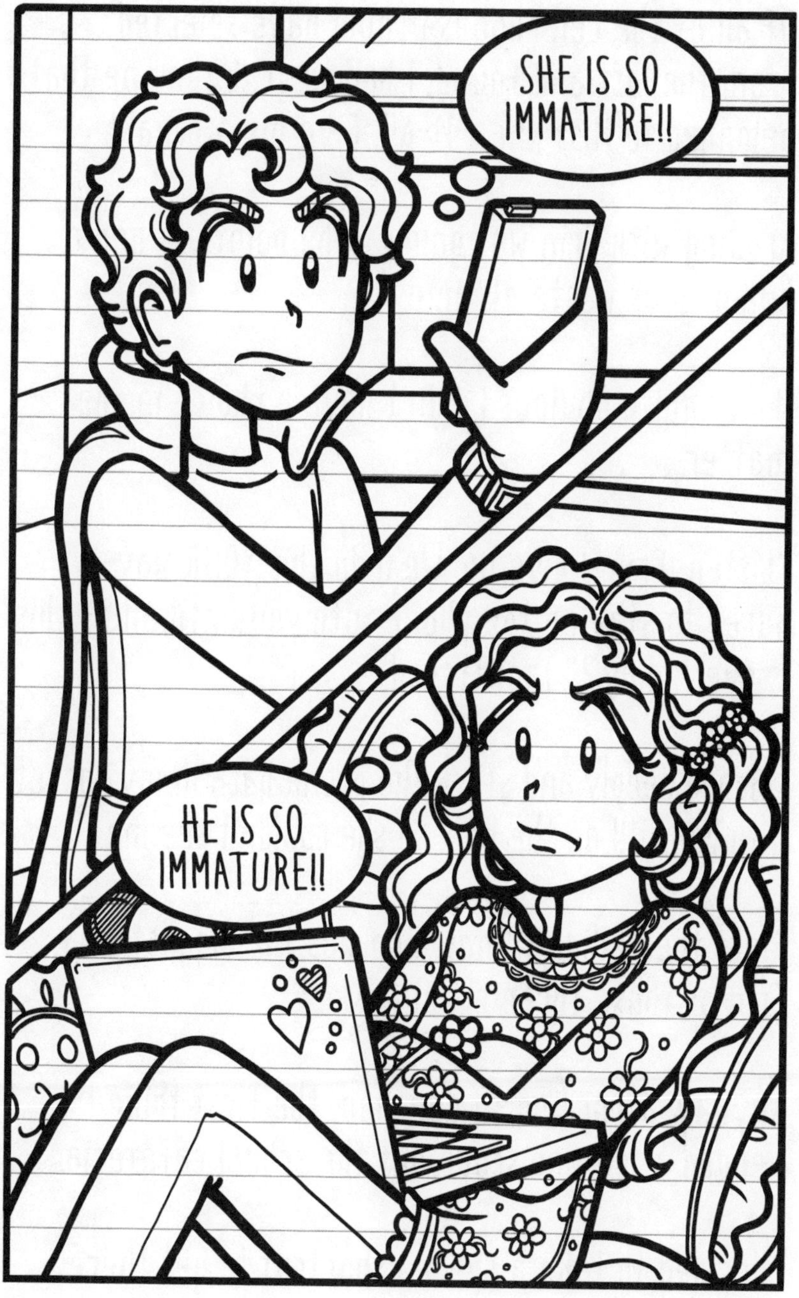
SHE IS SO IMMATURE!!
HE IS SO IMMATURE!!

Of all of the cell phones I could have selected from the lost and found, I had to grab the one that belonged to Miss Know-It-All. Give me a break!

Arguing with Erin was going to be pointless and a humongous waste of time.

It was quite obvious I didn't have a choice in the matter.

"Listen, Erin, I give up. We'll do this YOUR way. I agree to stay on the phone with you until all of this is over, okay?" I muttered.

I sighed deeply and stuck the phone back in my pocket with her still on the line, so she couldn't see me.

Right then I didn't know who was the biggest PAIN, Erin or those three criminals.

Anyway, according to our plan, the first thing I needed to do was scope out the school cafeteria.

I decided to take a special shortcut to get there.

So I went through that big hole in the boiler room wall . . .

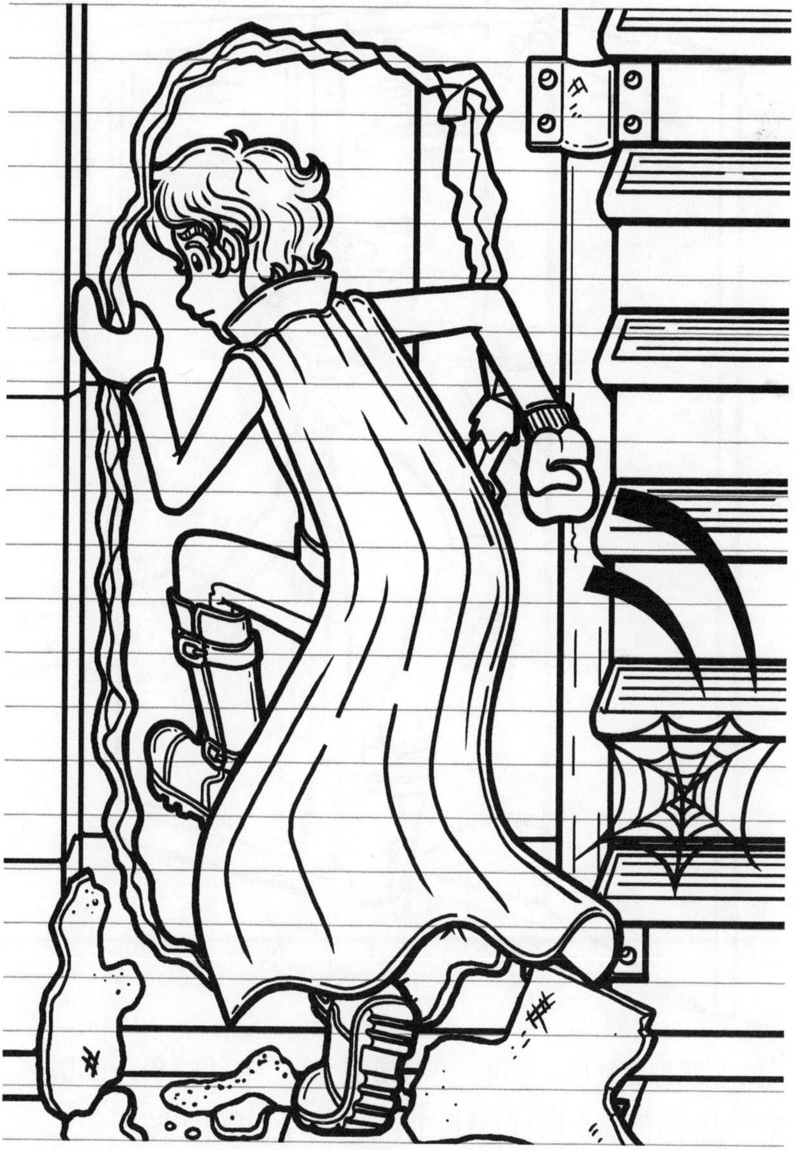

. . . that led directly into my locker and out into the main hall. . . .

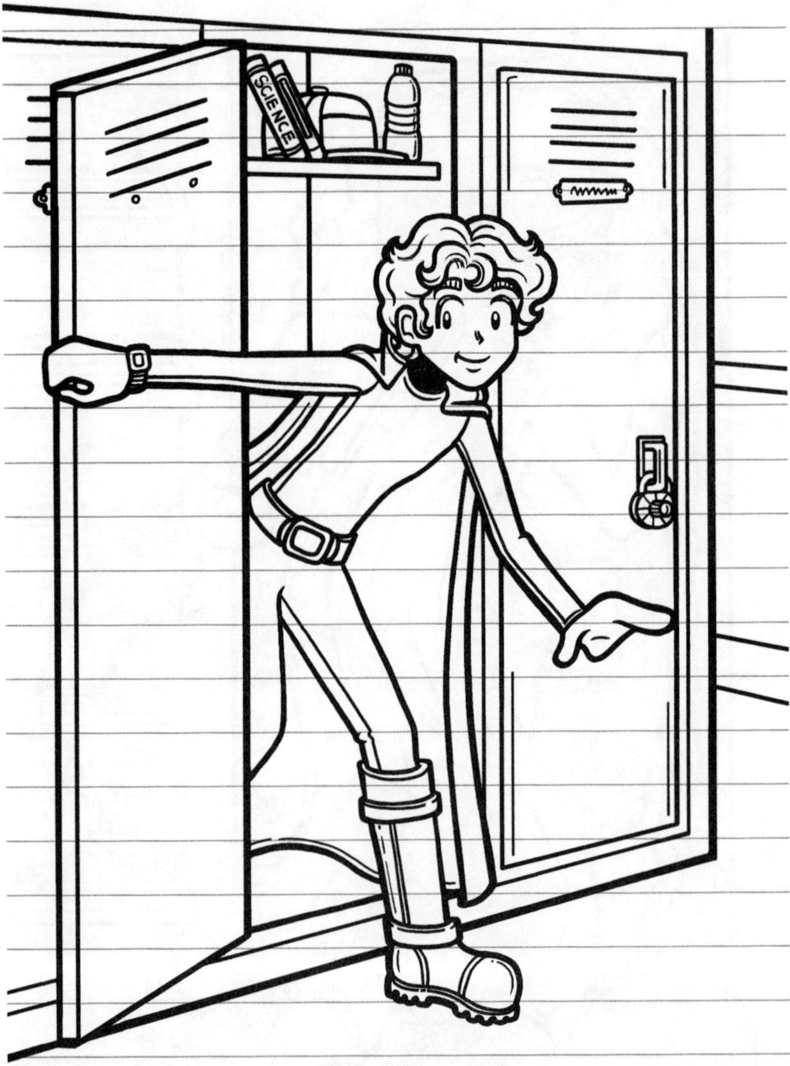
SCIENCE

However, before I made it out of my locker, Erin decided it was VITAL that I get my first update.

"Listen, Max, it sounds like Ralph is on his cell phone getting yelled at by his wife, Tina; Tucker is in the boys' bathroom; and Moose is at a drinking fountain, guzzling water because he's starving. So it's all clear from your locker to the cafeteria."

I can't believe I'm actually saying this, but maybe Erin is right. Staying in close communication with her might be a game changer.

Instead of crawling through the vents on my hands and knees, now I could roam the halls without having to worry about accidentally running into any of those crooks ~~and getting my head ripped off~~.

But the best news was that not a single computer had been stolen since Erin turned off the lights.

I feel like I'm part of a high-tech ninja operation. Just call me NINJA MAX, STEALTH WARRIOR! When I was younger, I was totally obsessed with the *Teenage Mutant Ninja Turtles* TV show. While most kids were begging their parents for a dog or cat, all I wanted was a regular ol' turtle. Kind of. . . .

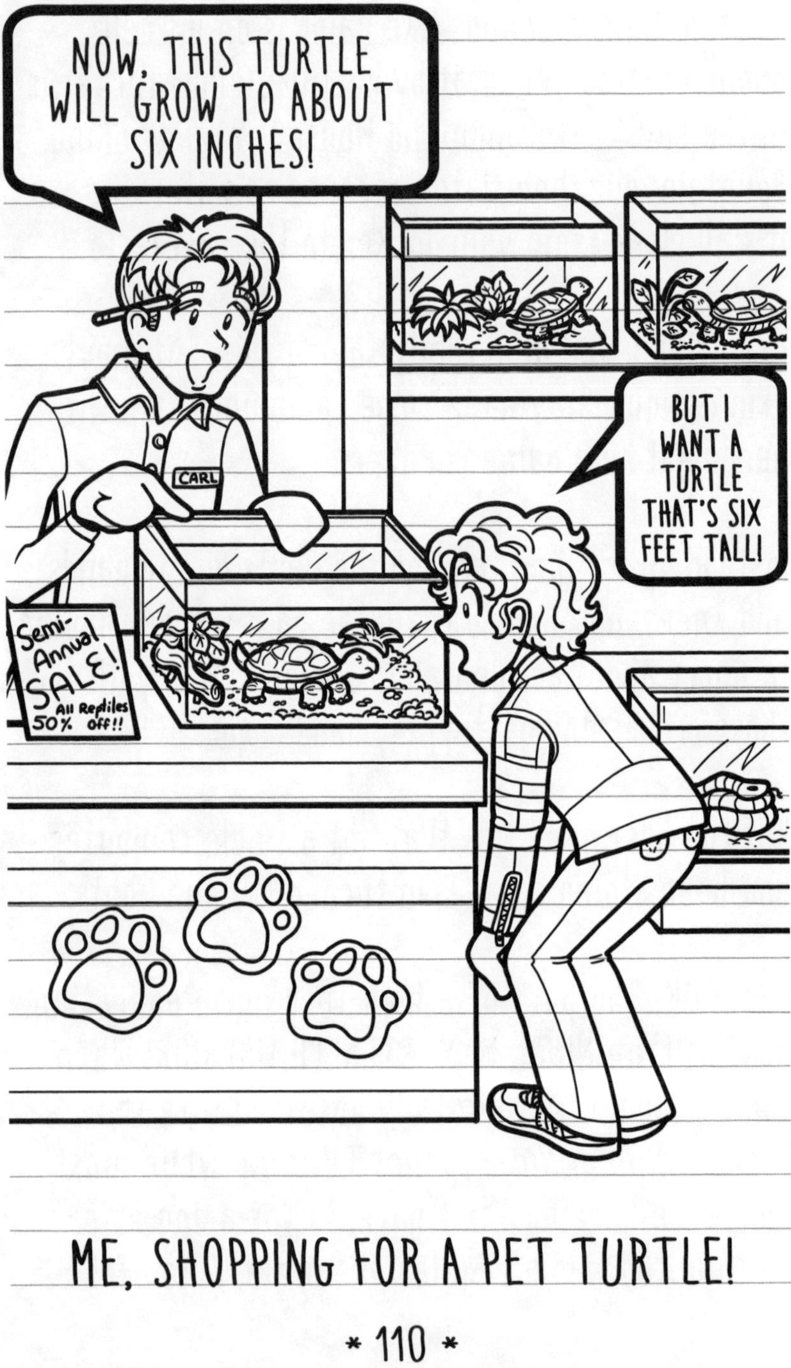
NOW, THIS TURTLE WILL GROW TO ABOUT SIX INCHES!
CARL
BUT I WANT A TURTLE THAT'S SIX FEET TALL!
Semi-Annual SALE! All Reptiles 50% off!!

ME, SHOPPING FOR A PET TURTLE!

I definitely wasn't the kind of kid you would call a spoiled brat, and I wasn't super demanding. I just had my little heart set on getting a turtle that would grow to be six feet TALL....

And eat pizza, live in a sewer, act like a teenager, and do martial arts. And wear cool clothes, like khakis, bandannas, boots, and gold chains.

Come on! Was THAT too much to ASK?!

Since my family and friends knew I had turtle fever, I ended up getting FOUR of them for my birthday, along with $50 cash! I was THRILLED!

Even though my turtles were little, I decided I'd feed them a lot so they would get really big. So all I needed were some cool clothes for them to wear.

I was really happy when my older sister, Megan, offered to sell me her old doll clothes for ONLY $50, which was ALL of my birthday money.

But that deal turned out to be a total RIP-OFF!...

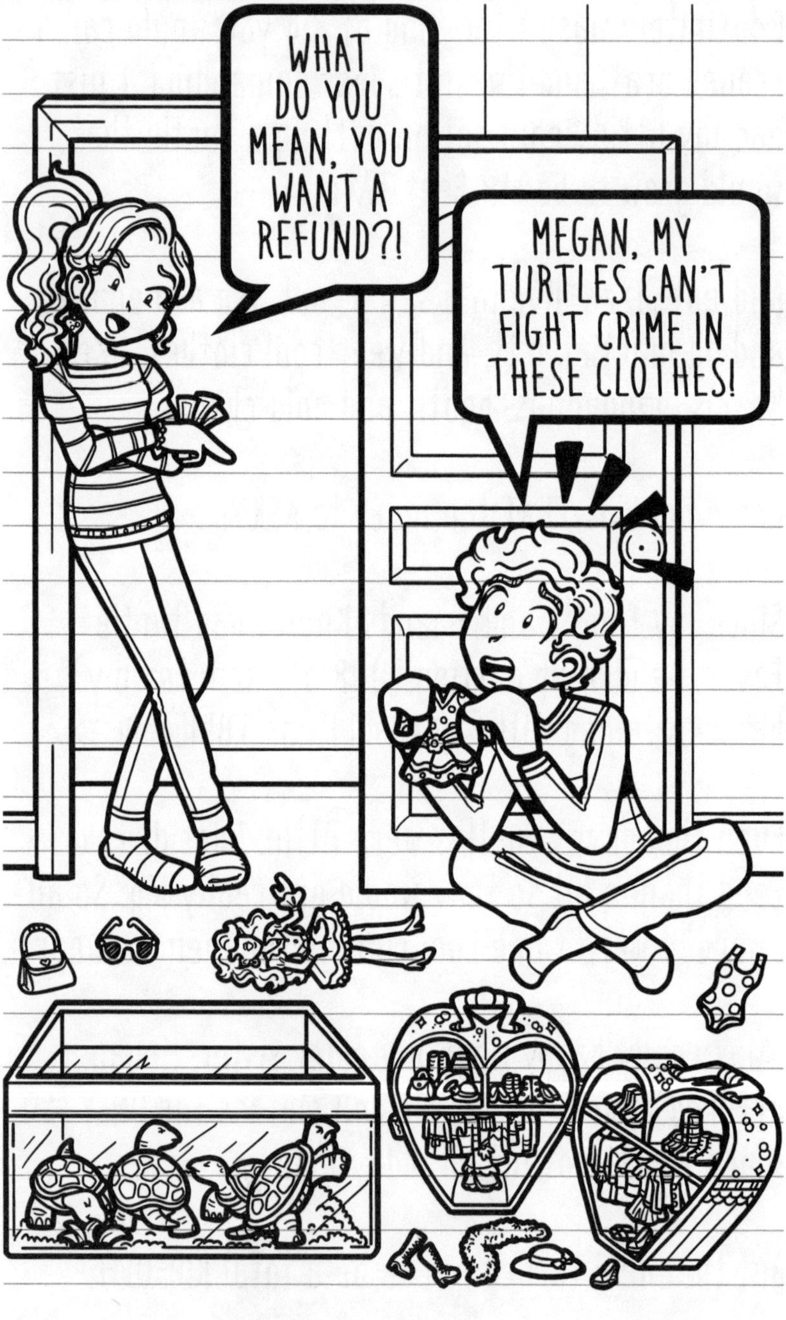
WHAT DO YOU MEAN, YOU WANT A REFUND?!
MEGAN, MY TURTLES CAN'T FIGHT CRIME IN THESE CLOTHES!

Anyway, when I finally outgrew my Ninja Turtles phase, I took my four turtles to the pond in the park and let them go.

They seemed really happy to be free and actually swam off together to find a new home.

I think all of this probably meant that I was no longer a naive child and was finally blossoming into a mature young adult.

Since my turtles were best friends, I believe they STILL hang out together. By now they're probably HUGE from eating a fresh pond diet. Like maybe six feet tall! And they probably do martial arts, fight crime, eat pizza, and wear really cool clothes. Which is why, to this day, I totally REGRET that I set my turtles FREE!

That was the STUPIDEST thing I've ever done in my life!!

Okay! I won't LIE to you. It was just ONE of the MANY stupid things I've done in my life!! For real!

12. BEWARE OF FUZZY GREEN BUNS!

As I headed to the cafeteria, my stomach suddenly started making garbage disposal sounds. I was praying that Erin didn't hear it, but she did.

"Max, WHAT is that strange noise?! Um . . . on second thought, maybe I DON'T want to know . . . !"

"It's NOT what you think! I haven't eaten in hours, and my stomach is growling. That's all," I explained.

I couldn't believe what Erin did next. She gave me her locker combo and told me to go grab a box of cookies.

And it was my favorite, chocolate chip! So I'd finally get to eat dinner tonight! SWEET!!

When I arrived at the cafeteria, I almost didn't recognize the place.

It seemed completely different without the huge crowds, grumpy cooks in hairnets, and foul smells. It's really DANGEROUS to eat the food in there! . . .

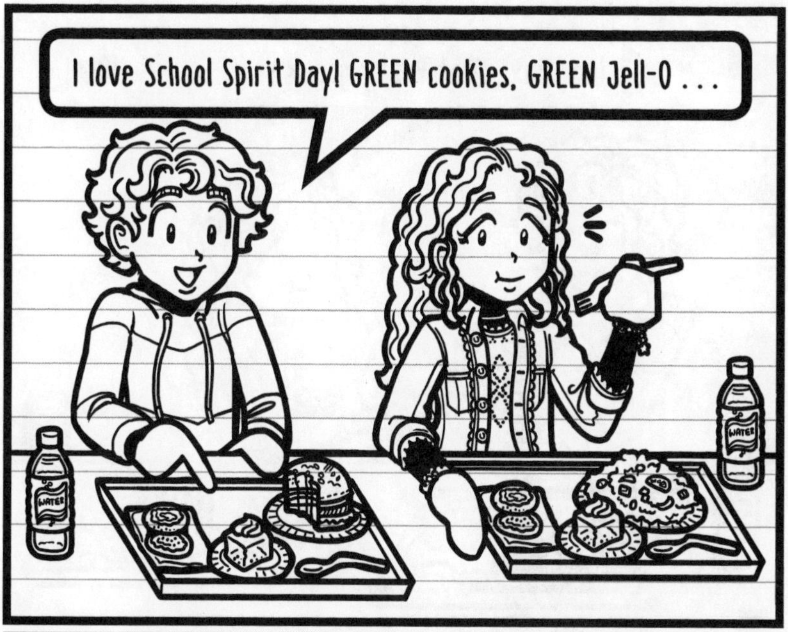
I love School Spirit Day! GREEN cookies, GREEN Jell-O . . .

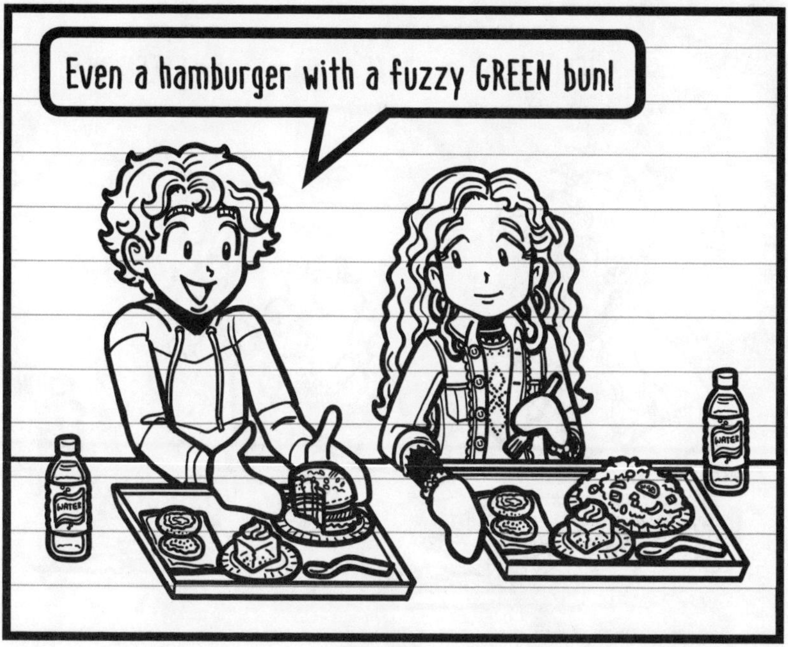
Even a hamburger with a fuzzy GREEN bun!

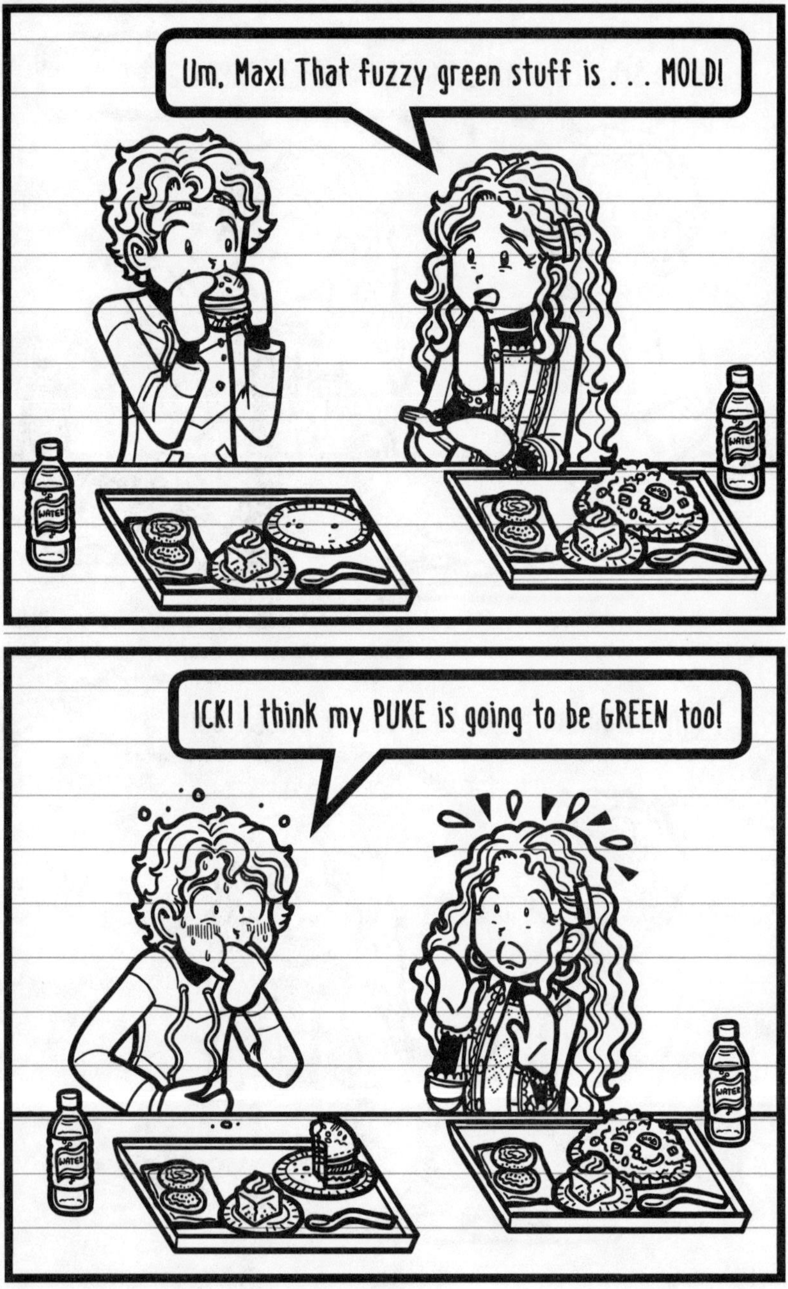
Um, Max! That fuzzy green stuff is . . . MOLD!
WATER
WATER
ICK! I think my PUKE is going to be GREEN too!
WATER
WATER

True story!! I almost threw up on Erin.

Luckily, I made it to the boys' bathroom.

But, unfortunately, all the stalls were filled up, and guys were washing their hands at all the sinks.

So, luckily, I managed to make it to the bathroom in the eighth-grade hall.

But, unfortunately, it was locked because they were painting it.

So I threw up down the front of my shirt.

And yes! It was GREEN!!

My vomit, not my shirt.

That was the LAST time I actually ate cafeteria food.

Anyway, when I tried the door to the school kitchen, it was unlocked. So I went inside to take a look around. . . .

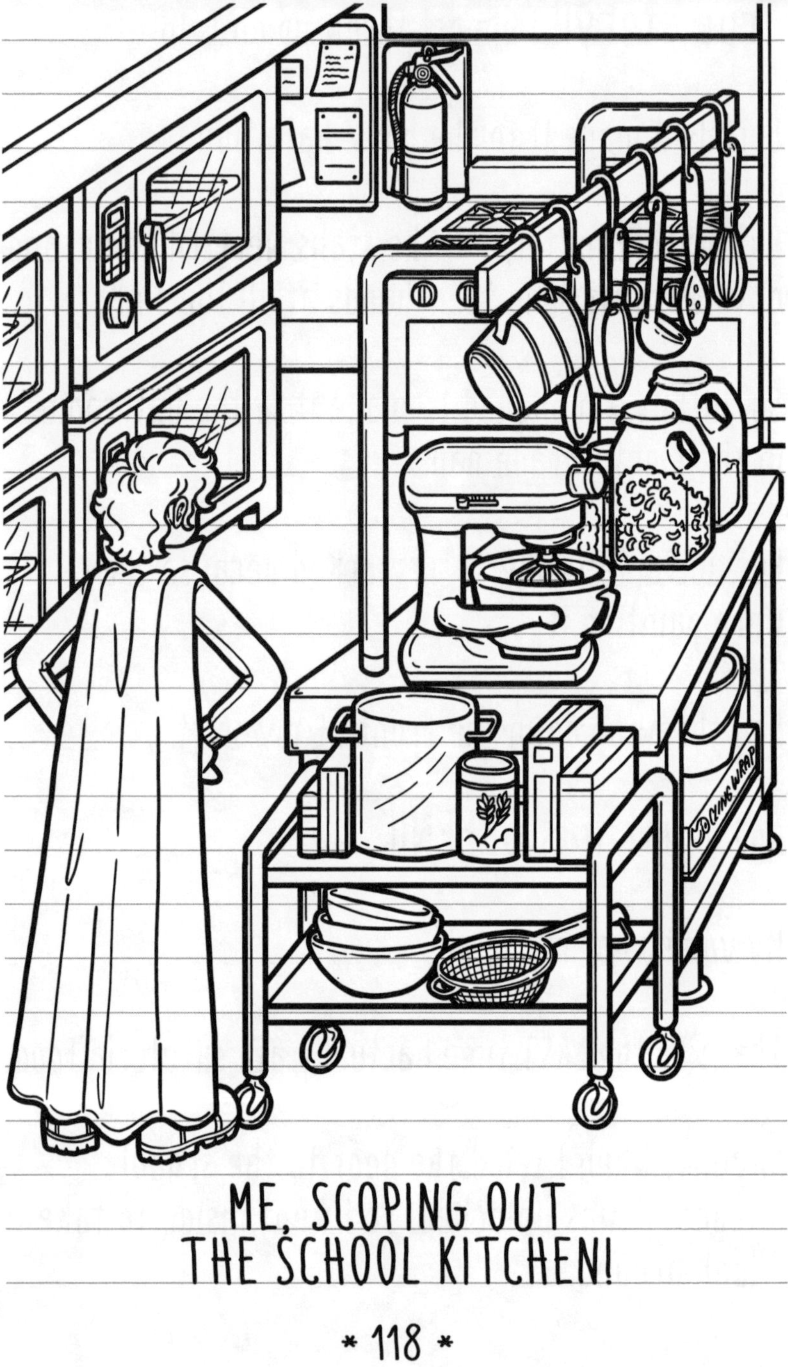
CLING WRAP

ME, SCOPING OUT
THE SCHOOL KITCHEN!

"Erin, I'm in the kitchen. There's a lot of stuff in here. But I don't see anything we could use to catch a criminal. Unless we want to drop a microwave on them."

"Come on, Max! Think outside the box!"

"Well, if I could get my hands on a few of those green fuzzy hamburger buns, I could serve up a severe case of FOOD POISONING, with a side dish of vomiting and diarrhea!" I snarked.

"Yeah! We could call it Operation Fuzzy Burger!" Erin laughed.

"That's a hilarious code name. Let's use it!" I chuckled.

"Hey, I know something else that's super gross. How about some of that SLIMY chicken soup?!" Erin suggested.

Suddenly an idea hit me like a bolt of lightning.

"THAT'S IT!" I shouted. "It'll be PERFECT!"

"What?! Force them to eat SLIMY chicken soup?!"

"NO! I'm going to COOK UP a booby trap that will stop 'em in their tracks! Can you help me out with a recipe?" I asked.

"Sure, Max! I just hope you can cook FAST! According to my calculations, your phone battery life is now down to thirty-nine minutes!"

"PLEASE! Don't remind me!" I muttered as I grabbed a huge mixing bowl and headed into the pantry to see what food items I had to work with.

I was about to prepare something so GROSS, just thinking about it made me throw up in my mouth a little.

ICK!

I just hoped I could COOK UP something that would completely incapacitate a ruthless burglar.

13. ATTACK OF THE COOKIE MUNCHER!

I had just finished mixing up my concoction in the kitchen when I got another update from Erin.

"Max, I have some bad news! Those guys have been searching the seventh-grade classrooms for flashlights. Although they didn't find any, they DID come across some candles in one of the science rooms. Can you believe they're actually planning to steal the rest of our computers by candlelight?! And they just might pull it off. I really think it's time to call the police!"

"Wait a minute! We can't do that. I haven't found my dad's comic book yet. There has to be something we can do to stop them!" I protested.

"Sorry! But unless you know kung fu or an ancient Jedi mind trick, it's game over!" Erin sighed.

I groaned and stared at the ceiling in frustration. That's when I noticed something that could possibly shut down those crooks. Instantly!

I told Erin my CRAZY idea, and she agreed it just might work. IF she could figure out how to turn on a system right at their exact spot. . . .

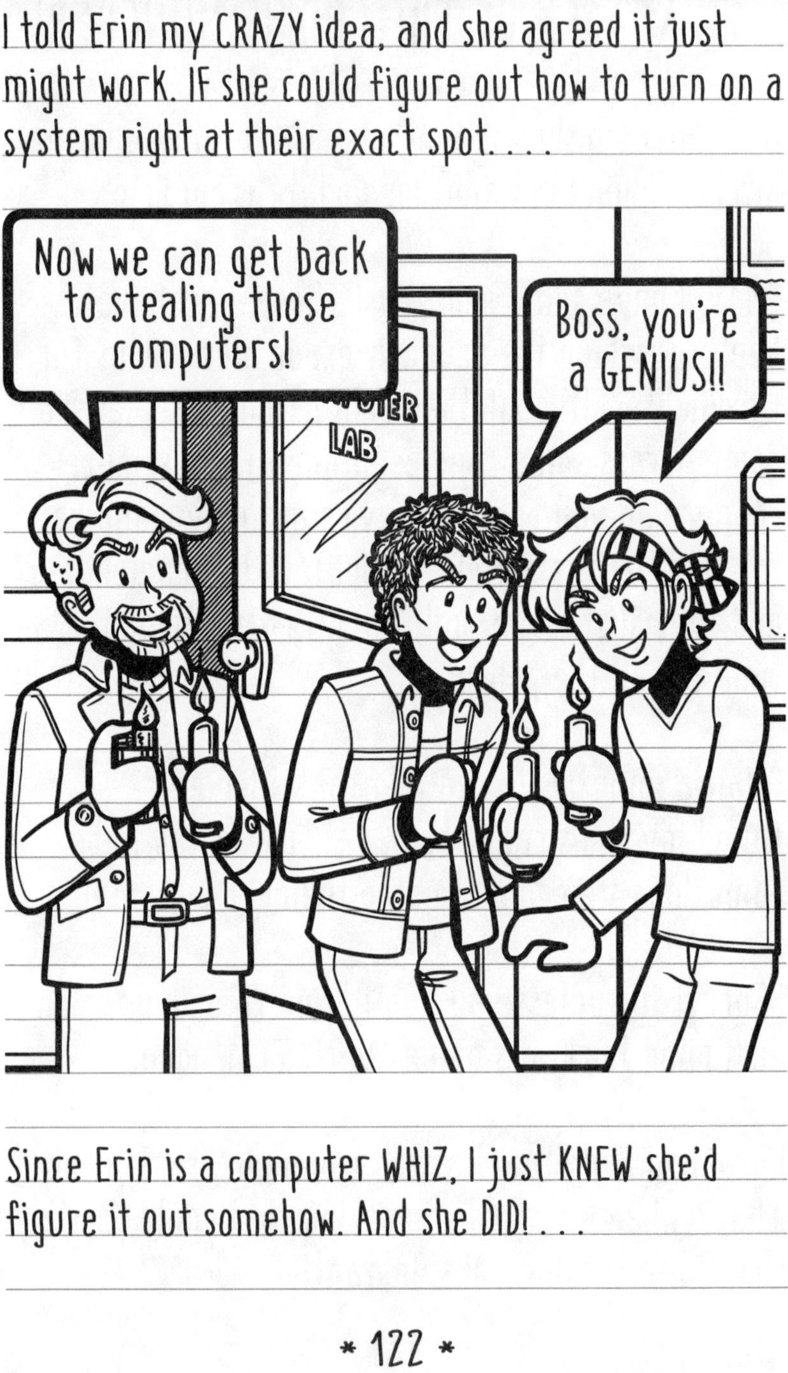
Now we can get back to stealing those computers!
Boss, you're a GENIUS!!
LAB

Since Erin is a computer WHIZ, I just KNEW she'd figure it out somehow. And she DID! . . .

It was PERFECT timing!

Boy, were those burglars ticked off. We could hear them yelling and screaming at each other while they stood in front of the hand dryers in the boys' bathroom.

Since we had successfully thwarted their attempts to steal from the computer lab, Ralph sent Moose to grab equipment from the main office.

After that pizza fiasco, I was pretty sure Moose was still STARVING. So I decided to use his personal issues to our advantage.

I stood right outside the glass wall of the office and munched greedily on my cookies. Then I happily did a little cookie dance, like they were the BEST in the entire universe.

Finally I waved the box at Moose, as if to say, "You want some cookies? Then come and get 'em!"

I was so UTTERLY annoying, I wanted to SLAP myself so I'd stop getting on my OWN nerves!

Moose just glared at me. Then he smacked his lips and swallowed, like his mouth was watering. Unfortunately, he could take only so much of my silly antics. And soon he was FURIOUS!! . . .

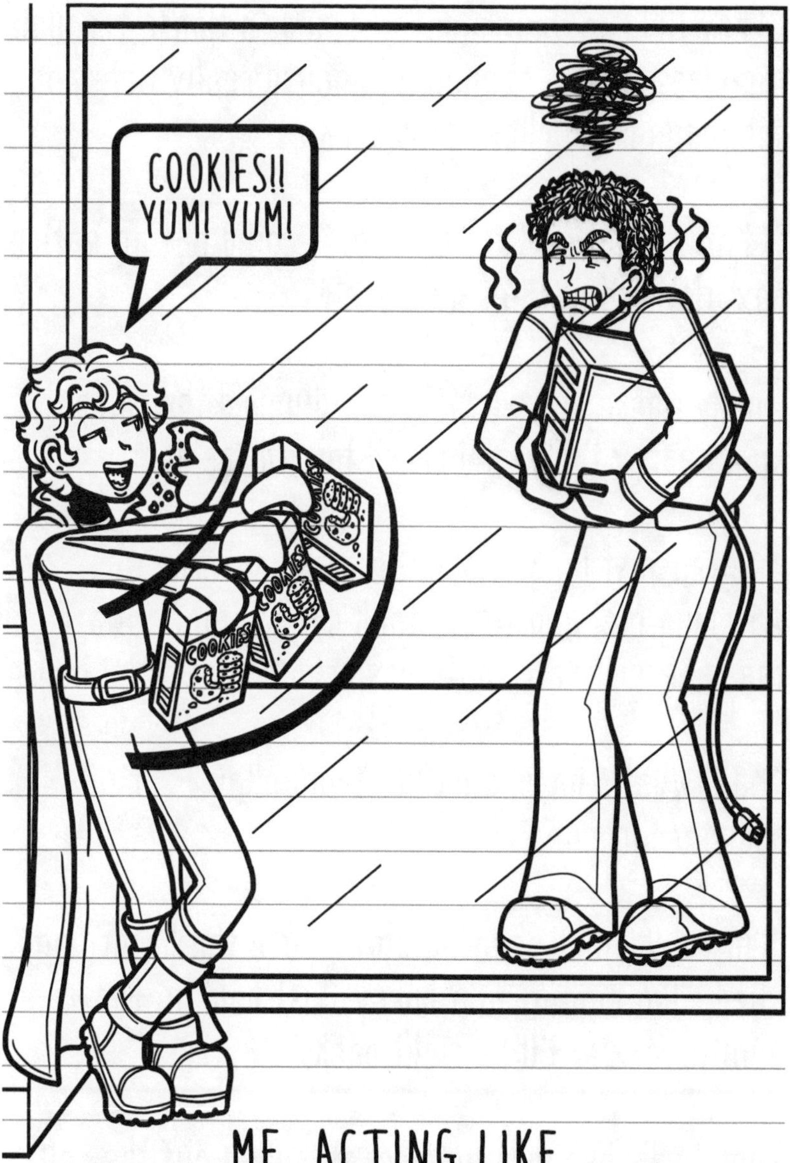
COOKIES!! YUM! YUM!

ME, ACTING LIKE
THE COOKIE ~~MONSTER~~ MUNCHER!

"They MELT in your mouth!" I said to Moose through the glass. Then I opened my mouth really wide and showed him my chewed-up cookies.

"I know, right?!" Erin agreed. "I could eat an entire box of those cookies by myself."

Finally Moose gritted his teeth, dumped the computer on a nearby table, and raced toward the door.

I waited just long enough to make sure he was watching me, and then I took off running toward the cafeteria, my footsteps echoing down the hall.

"Max! What's happening? Are you okay?" Erin asked, concerned.

"I'm fine! I just need to, um . . . use the bathroom," I lied. "I'm kind of in a hurry. Just hold on for a minute, okay? I'll be right back."

Then I reached into my pocket, pulled out the cell phone, and clicked the MUTE button. Some serious stuff was about to go down. **No joke!**

14. LIAR, LIAR, PANTS ON FIRE!

Things were going just as I had planned. Moose was chasing me into the kitchen and yelling not-so-nice things.

All I had to do was get into position behind the counter, wait for him to come running in . . .

And then . . . *BAM!!*

We'd have one less burglar on our hands!

But, unfortunately, something went wrong.

I must have accidentally spilled some of that stuff I was making, because I hit a slippery spot on the floor and completely WIPED OUT!

I slid across the kitchen on my belly and just barely missed crashing headfirst into the stove.

When Moose finally caught up with me, he reached down and snatched me up off the floor. Literally!! . . .

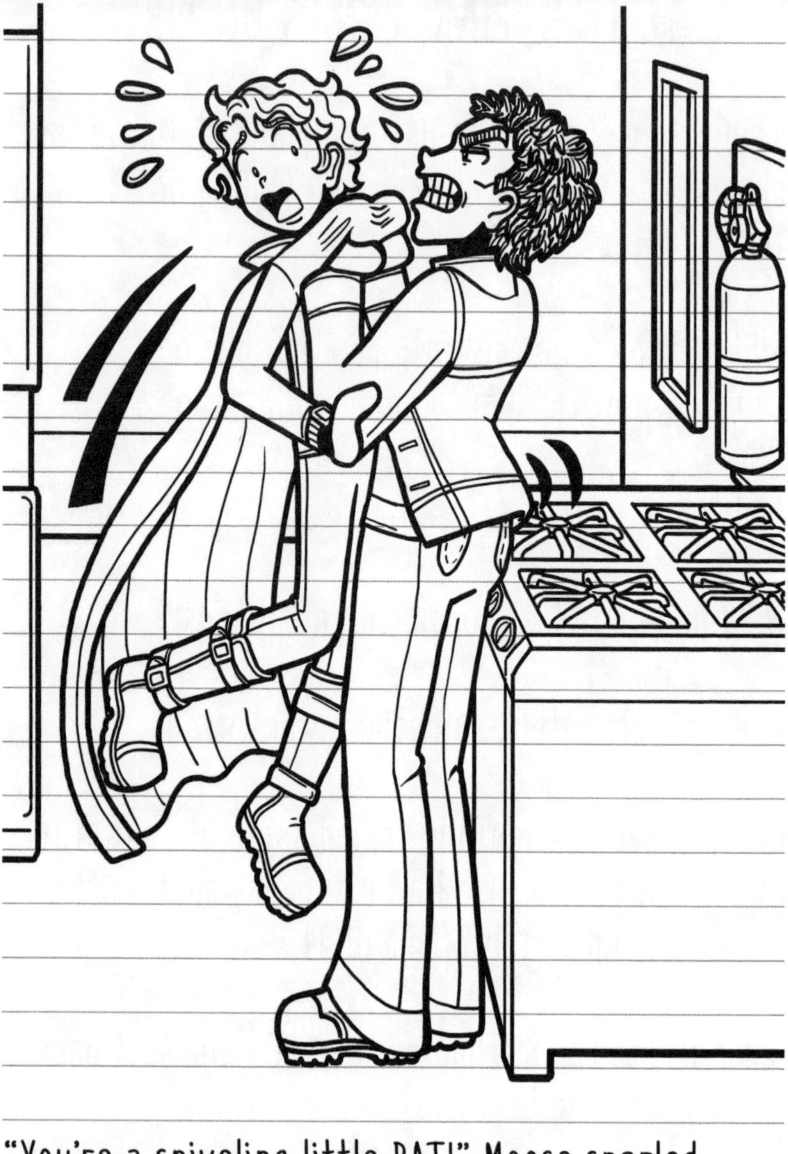

"You're a sniveling little RAT!" Moose snarled as he shook me. "What do you have to say NOW, TOUGH GUY?!"

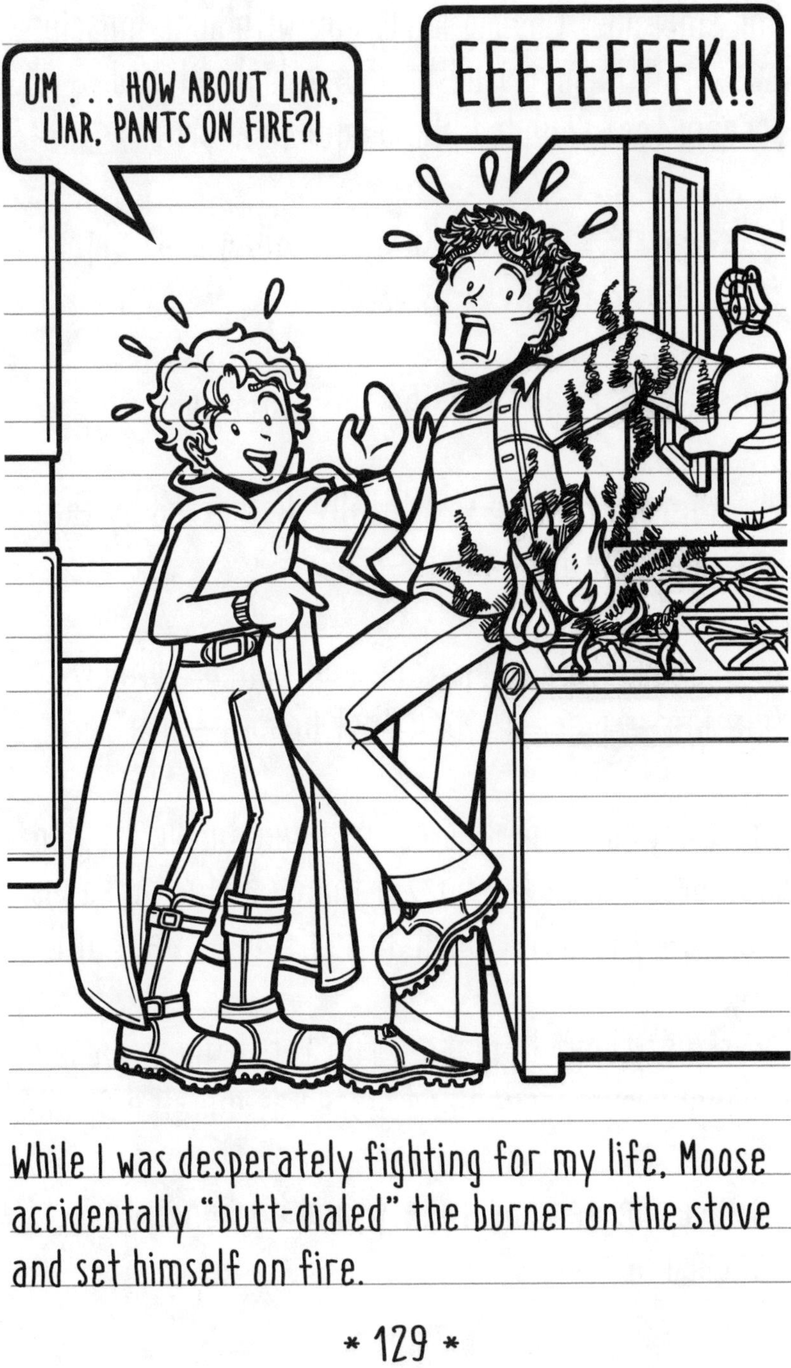
EEEEEEEEK!!
UM . . . HOW ABOUT LIAR, LIAR, PANTS ON FIRE?!

While I was desperately fighting for my life, Moose accidentally "butt-dialed" the burner on the stove and set himself on fire.

And since he's this big burly guy with huge muscles, I was a little surprised to hear a high-pitched scream that sounded like a squealing pig.

Actually, he sounded like a squealing BABY pig. You know, a PIGLET!

Honestly! I am NOT making this stuff up!

~~The fact that Moose was totally distracted by that fire made me feel a little braver.~~

~~So I got right up in his face and yelled, "DUDE! You want a piece of ME?! Just bring it, bro!"~~

Moose let go of me and rushed over to the kitchen sink. He grabbed the nozzle thingy and sprayed his backside with water until all the flames went out.

I was just about to make a run for it when Moose suddenly spun around and glared at me all evil-like.

His face was red and sweaty, and his hands were clenched into fists.

The back of his jacket and jeans were black and sooty and smelled like, um . . . burnt hot dogs.

I had a really BAD feeling about what was going to happen next. And it would probably be PAINFUL!

That's when I finally realized that NOW was probably a REALLY good time for Erin to call the POLICE. You know, since I was about to DIE!

Then I suddenly remembered that I had put that STUPID phone on MUTE. My BAD!

I was about to give up hope when the WEIRDEST thing happened. Moose stared right past me as his FURIOUS scowl slowly melted into a DERANGED smile.

He had spotted my chocolate chip cookies!

"Lucky for you, kid, I'm STARVING! So I'm gonna rip your face off AFTER I have a little SNACK!"

He rushed right over to my cookies! And just as he was about to grab the box . . .

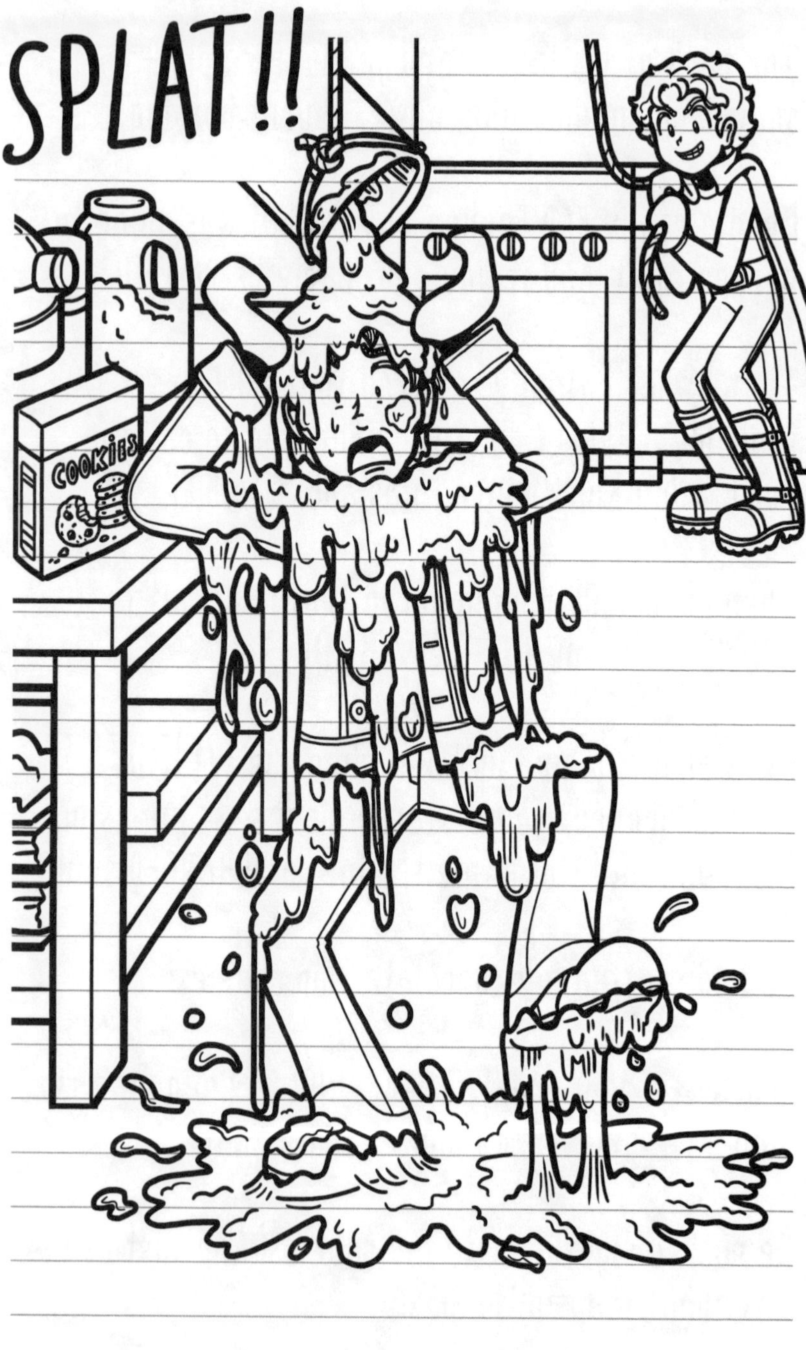
SPLAT!!
COOKIES

YES! I actually SLIMED Moose!

It was the perfect distraction I needed to take him down.

When the bucket landed on top of his head, he started yelling and screaming. . . .

"HELP! HELP! GET THIS BUCKET OFF OF MY HEAD! IT'S STUCK! I CAN'T SEE! GET IT OFF OF ME! HEEEELP!!"

I was definitely going to HELP Moose. Help END his career as a burglar.

HOW?! With a box of plastic cling wrap.

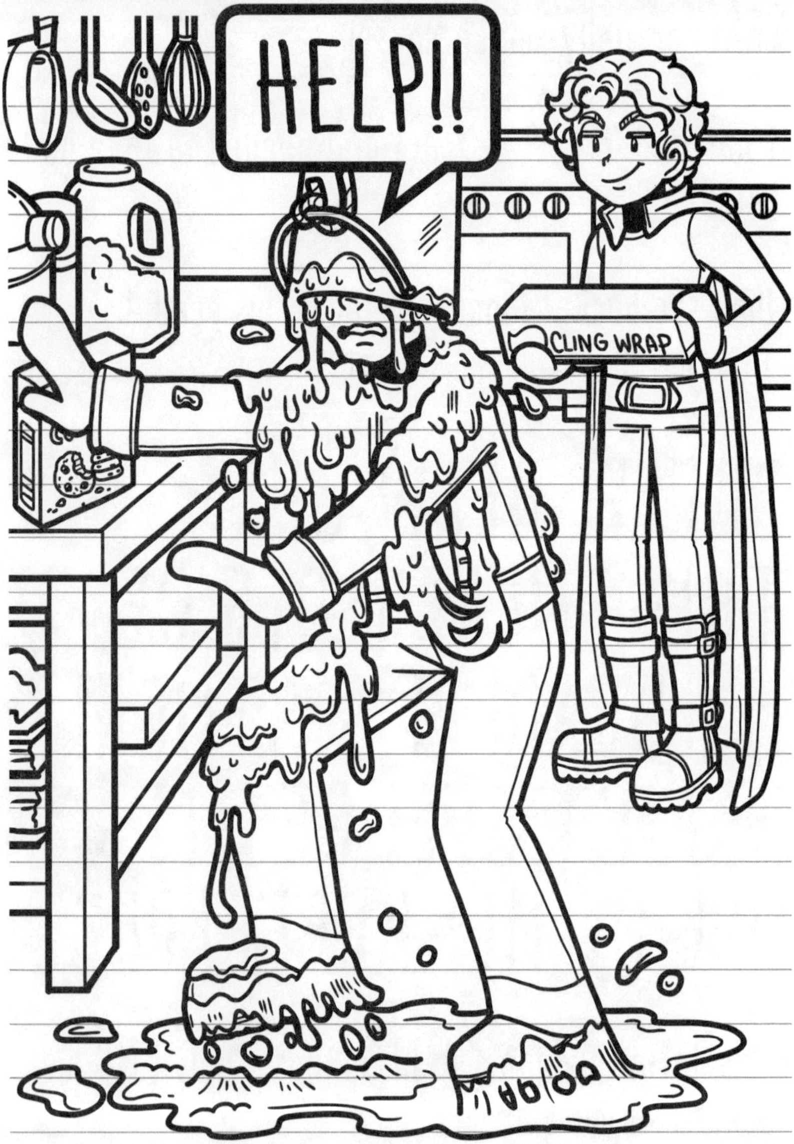
HELP!!
CLING WRAP

I wasn't planning to wrap up a baloney-'n'-mustard sandwich for Moose. Instead, I was going to . . .

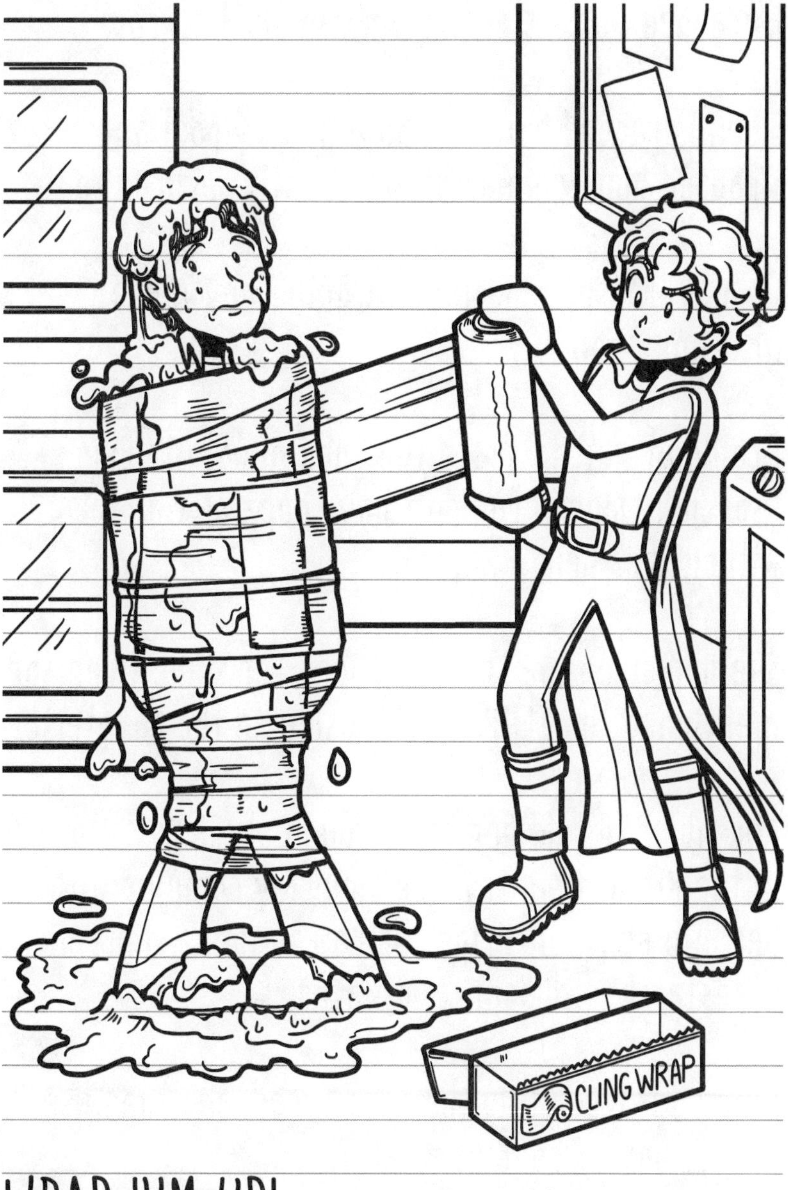
CLING WRAP

WRAP HIM UP! I guess you could say I was FINALLY starting to think outside the box!

I wrapped Moose's entire body in plastic wrap.

Then I dragged him over to a nearby post and wrapped him again so he was tightly secured to it.

I was VERY sure he was not going anywhere anytime soon.

I couldn't wait to share the good news with Erin. Especially since I couldn't have done ANY of this without her help!

She had given me the great idea for slime when she mentioned the SLIMY chicken soup in the cafeteria.

And when I'd told her the random stuff I'd seen in the kitchen pantry, she'd quickly come up with her own original recipe for how to make slime with cornstarch, dish soap, and water.

I mixed it up, set up the booby trap, and then used ~~her~~ MY box of cookies as BAIT.

And IT WORKED! LIKE. A. CHARM!!

I pulled out my phone and hit the mute button so she could hear me again.

"Hi, Erin! Are you still there?! I'm back!"

"Yeah, I'm here. I decided to take a bathroom break too. Listen, Max, you really need to stop wasting time. According to my calculations, you have about twenty-six minutes of battery life left. And we haven't even started looking for your comic book yet!"

"Thanks for the update, Erin. But at least we don't have to worry about Moose anymore. I guess you could say he's all tied up."

"WHAT?!! Are you kidding me?! I step away for one minute just to go to the bathroom and—"

"Hey! It's not my fault YOUR slime recipe took him out like that. You must be either a really GOOD cook or a really BAD one!" I teased.

"Okay, let me get this straight, Max! Our plan actually worked?! Moose is out of the picture?"

"No doubt! Hold on a second. I'll put him back IN the picture."

I held up my phone.

This is what Erin saw....

OUR MUG SHOT OF MOOSE

"OMG! I guess you could say we really WRAPPED UP that situation!" Erin giggled.

"Yeah, the plan we COOKED UP was brilliant!"
I laughed.

All joking aside, I was totally relieved that Moose was finally out of the way.

But things could have gone very badly.

NOTE TO SELF: Do **NOT** put cell phone on mute.
NEVER! EVER!!

Anyway, now we only had twenty-six minutes—no, make that twenty-five minutes—to take out Tucker and Ralph.

15. HOW NOT TO WRESTLE A THUG

I grabbed the box of cookies, hurried through the cafeteria, and cautiously peeked into the hall. "Erin, how about an update on Ralph and Tucker? I need to get to the gym."

"Sure, Max. They're both in the eighth-grade math classroom next to the computer lab, waiting on Moose to come back with the office computers. Ralph is still on his cell phone talking to his wife. And Tucker said he was going to draw a picture of his cat, Mr. Fuzzybottoms, on the board."

"Thanks! I'm on my way to the gym right now."

"Just stay clear of the room they're hanging out in and you should be fine. I'll turn the lights on in the gym for you," Erin said. "But hurry! We don't want them to get impatient and go looking for Moose."

I jogged toward the gym, hoping that the doors weren't locked. About thirty seconds later I held my breath, pressed the gym door handle, pulled, and . . .

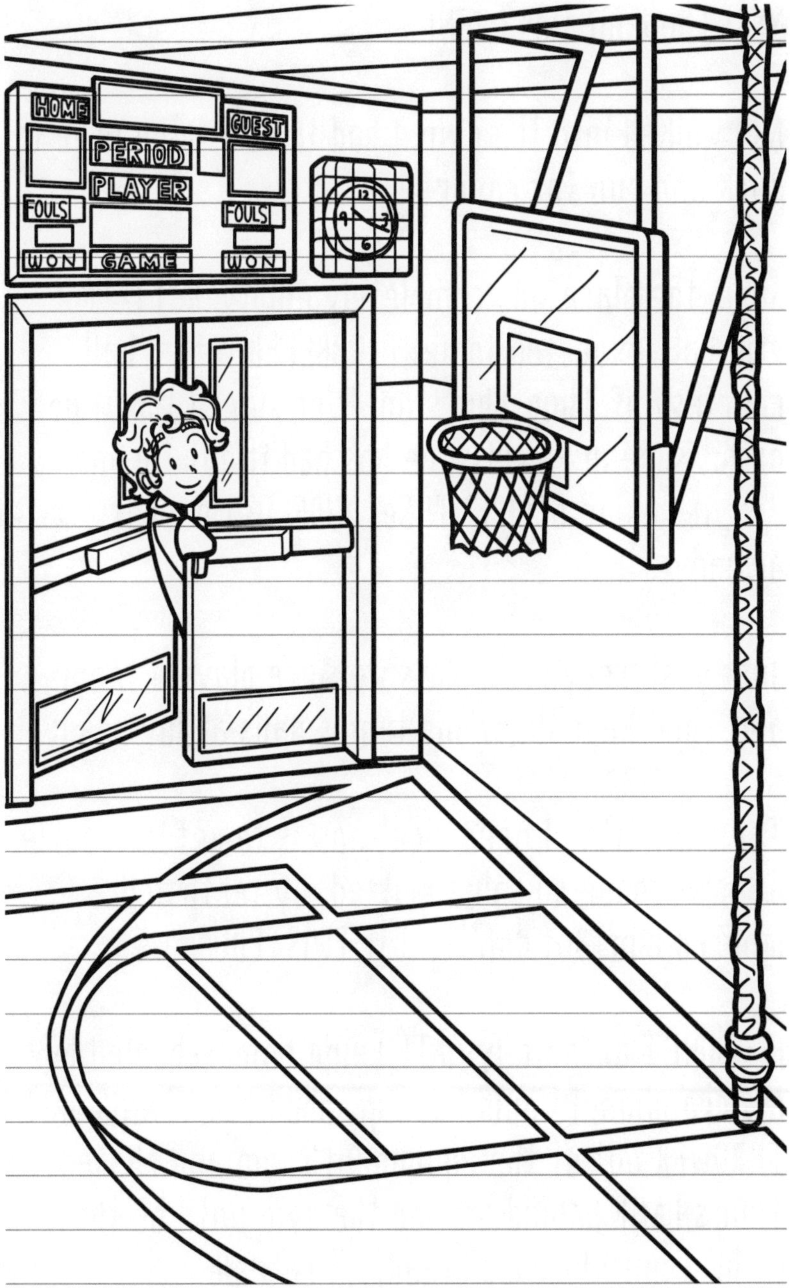
HOME
GUEST
PERIOD
PLAYER
FOULS
FOULS
WON
GAME
WON

YES! The door was OPEN!

As I walked into the gym, I had to resist the urge to duck and run for cover.

Sure, the place was completely empty. But I still half expected to get CLOBBERED with a ball, courtesy of Thug Thurston. Ever since I threw up on his shoe in PE class, he has had it out for me. Hey, it was an ACCIDENT! So, DUDE! Get over it, already!

Just yesterday in PE class we were playing tennis and Thug kept slamming tennis balls at my head.

The LAST thing I need right now is to get in trouble at this school, so I just gritted my teeth and ignored him. But don't get it TWISTED!

If I DIDN'T absolutely HATE being homeschooled by my grandma, I would have grabbed the TENNIS BALL THROWER out of the equipment room and chased Thug's LAME behind around the gym until he threw up his Fruity Pebbles breakfast cereal! . . .

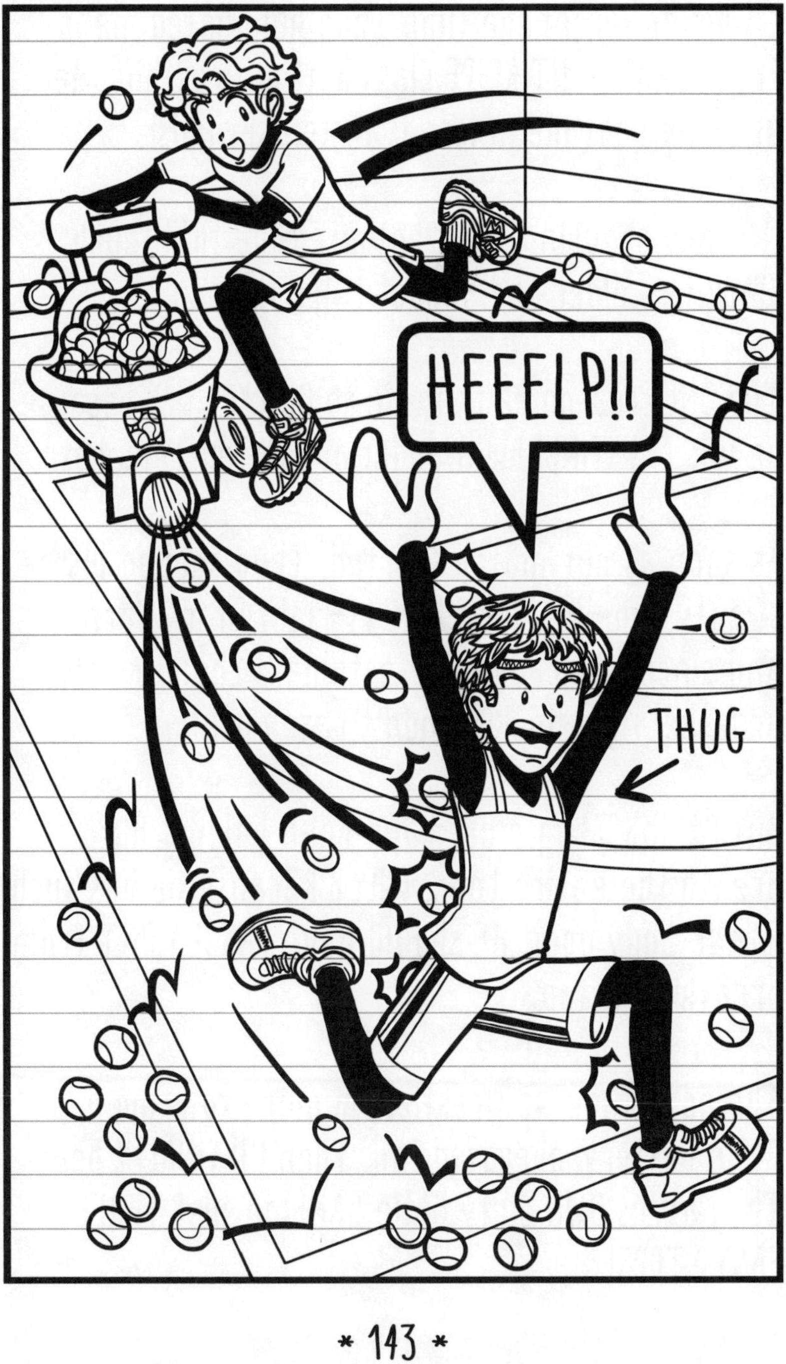
HEEELP!!
THUG

I'll never forget the time Thug humiliated me in front of the ENTIRE PE class during wrestling. He actually beat me in less than ten seconds!

It really shouldn't have bothered me that much since he's older and almost twice my size.

The ONLY reason he beat me so QUICKLY was because he was CHEATING! Right under our PE teacher's nose.

As soon as our match started, Thug shoved his sweaty, smelly, hairy ARMPIT right in my face! And since I already have asthma, I could barely breathe. I was lucky I didn't pass out!

But I think Thug must have been holding HIS breath the entire time. WHY? Because he has such STANK body odor, HE should have PASSED OUT from breathing it too.

The next time we wrestle, I'm going to bring a little battery-operated fan. Then I'll FINALLY beat Thug at his OWN dirty little GAME! In just THREE EASY STEPS! . . .

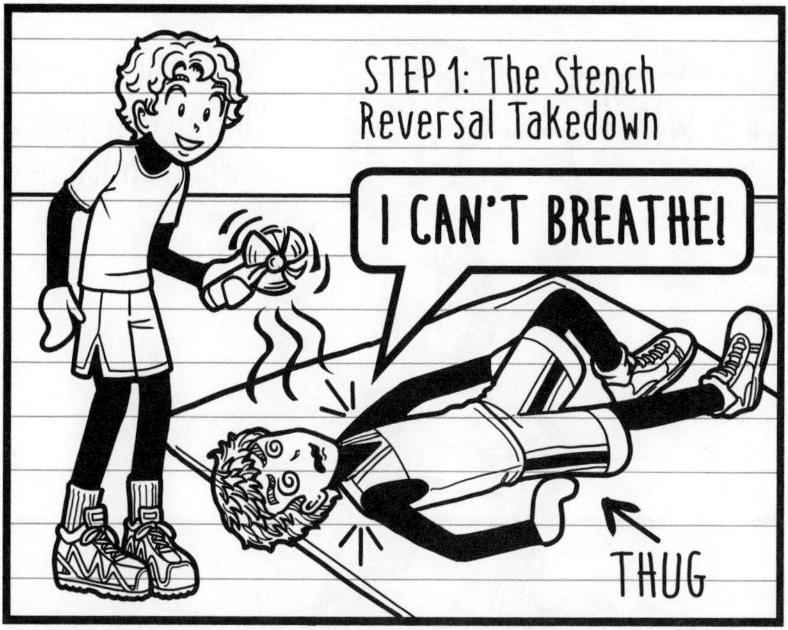
STEP 1: The Stench Reversal Takedown
I CAN'T BREATHE!
THUG

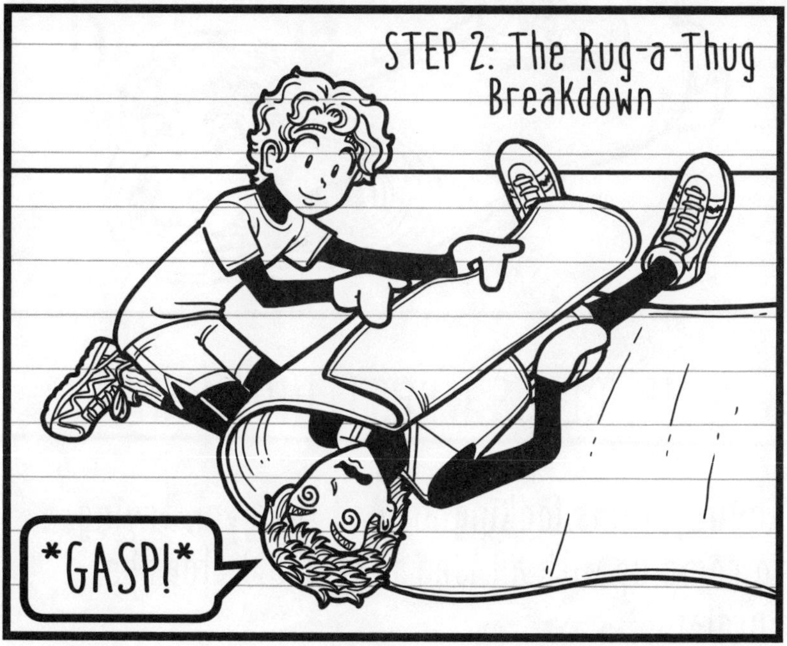
STEP 2: The Rug-a-Thug Breakdown
GASP!

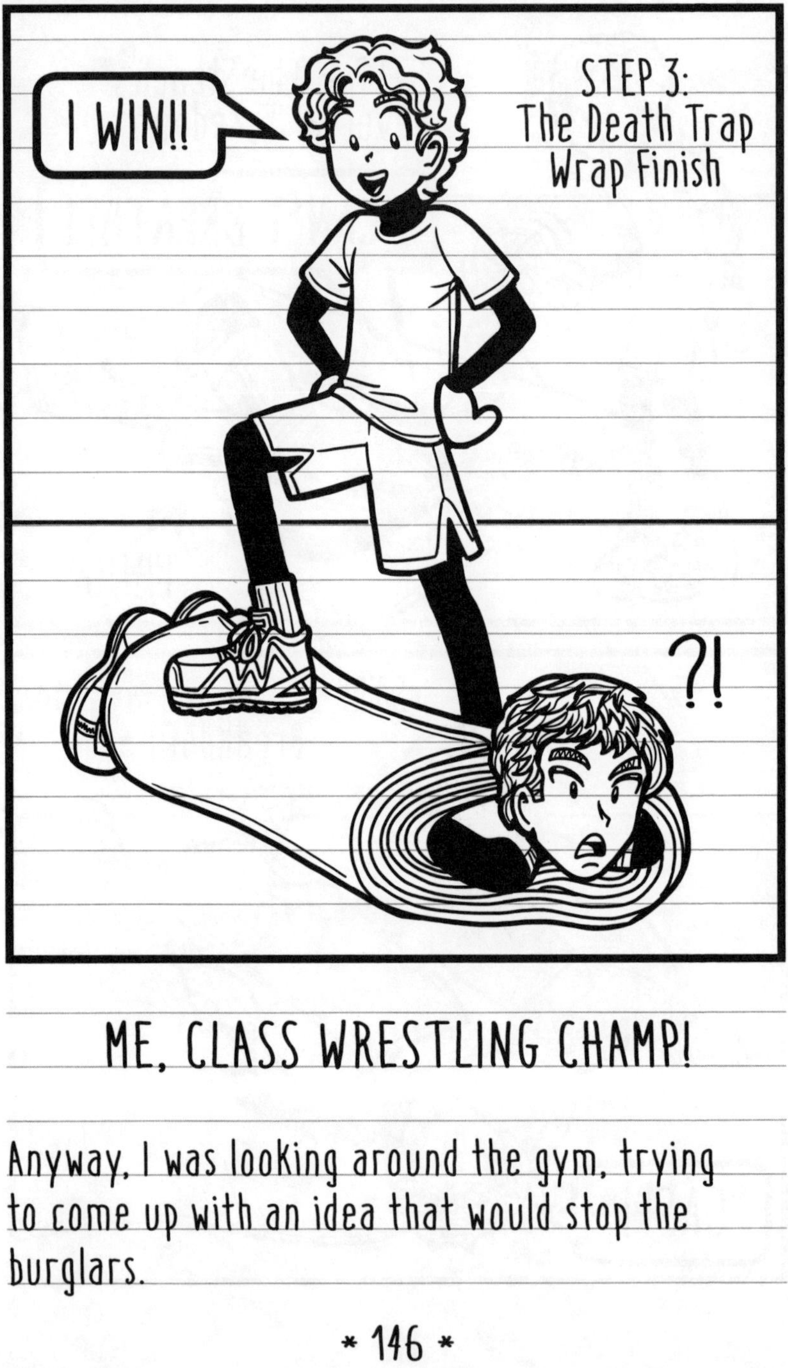
I WIN!!
STEP 3:
The Death Trap
Wrap Finish
?!

ME, CLASS WRESTLING CHAMP!

Anyway, I was looking around the gym, trying to come up with an idea that would stop the burglars.

"Erin, what in the gym can you control on your computer?" I asked.

"Let's see. Actually, quite a bit. The game clock, scoreboard, buzzer, ceiling fan, and basketball backboard and net. I also see some audio files and Internet radio. Would you like to hear our school song, 'Go, Green Gators'? Or how about 'Lego Luv: The Remix'?" she snorted.

"No! Just . . . NO! BOTH of those songs are so CRAPPY, I'll need a roll of toilet paper to wipe my ears!" I joked.

I was walking past the climbing rope when I suddenly got a really WACKY idea!

But I was worried it would probably be too complicated and difficult to pull off.

I decided to check out the equipment room, and I hit the jackpot! I found items I could use, like an old soccer goalie net, bungee cords, jump ropes, and an expandable pole with a hook on the end.

Erin and I had a quick brainstorming session and came up with a brilliant plan to take out Tucker.

I grabbed the expandable pole, and after a few tries I managed to unhook the rope and move it to a new location inside the gym.

I placed the soccer net and other items on the floor near the rope. Erin lowered the basketball hoop to within my reach, and FINALLY everything was ready. The ONLY thing missing was a burglar.

"So, HOW are we going to lure Tucker down here?" I asked Erin.

"Simple! Let's just send him an invitation," she answered.

"That's the STUPIDEST idea EVER!" I exclaimed.

But after Erin explained all the details, I had to admit her idea was AWESOME! I grabbed my pen and ripped a blank page out of my journal. Then, in my neatest handwriting, I wrote the note that Erin dictated.

My heart was pounding as I headed to the classroom where the two crooks were hanging out. Luckily, Ralph was distracted with his phone call.

I knocked on the door loudly and then quickly stuck my note on the window of the door using a melted chocolate chip (sorry, I didn't have any tape!) . . .

Hey Tucker,

Want a snack? I found some cookies! I left a box for you in the gym.

But please don't tell Ralph, because he'll just get mad at us and throw them away. I'll be back in 10 minutes.

MOOSE

16. HOW TO ROPE A DOPE!

I didn't wait around to see if Tucker actually answered the door or read my letter.

Instead, I sprinted back to the gym and hid out in the equipment room. Then I cautiously peeked out of a small window in the door to see if Tucker had taken the bait.

"Do you think he's going to come?" I asked Erin.

But before she could answer, Tucker came jogging into the gym.

"Hey, Moose! What's taking you so long with those office computers? Ralph is getting really MAD! And where are the cookies?! Is this some kind of a joke?! Because I don't see . . . ! What the . . . ?! Moose?! WHY did you put my cookies up there?!"

WORDS cannot BEGIN to describe the PURE INSANITY that occurred inside that gym. So I won't bother to use any. A picture is worth a thousand words, right? . . .

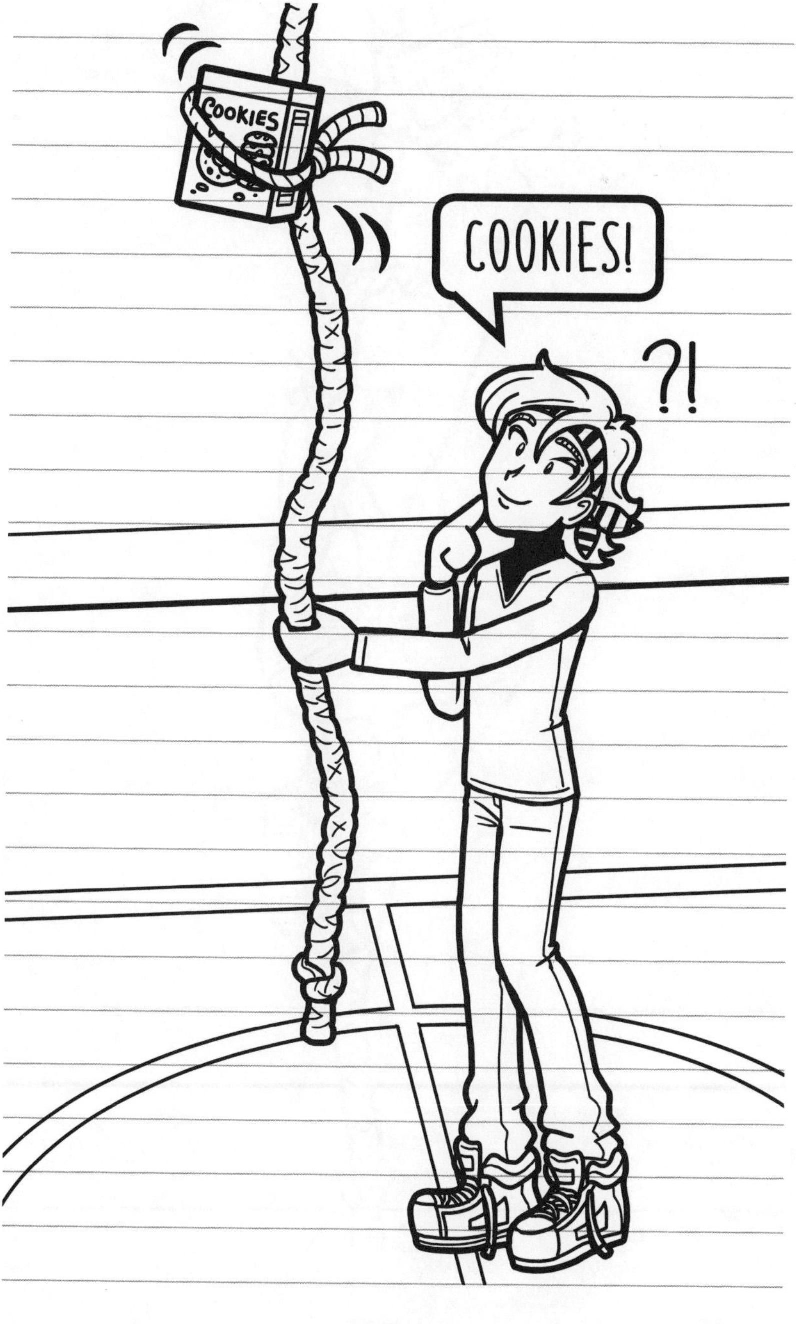
COOKIES
COOKIES!
?!

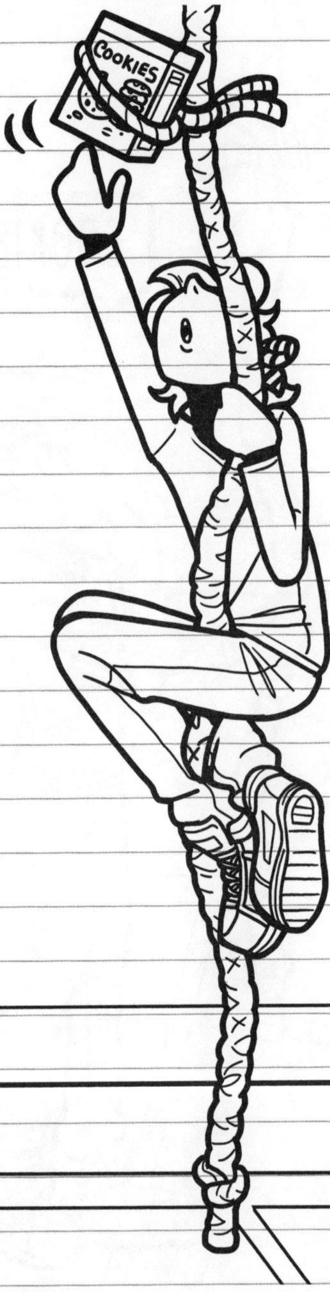
COOKIES

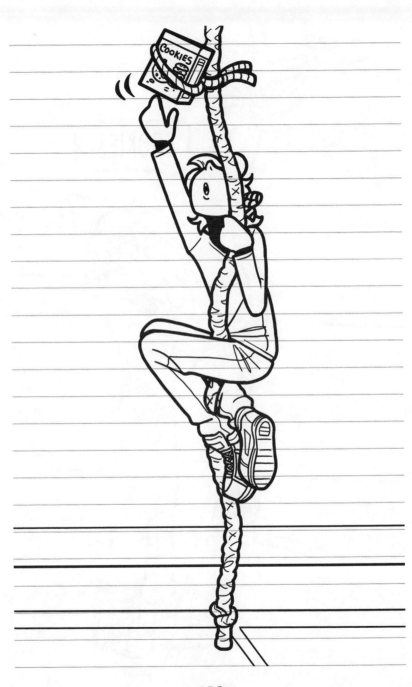

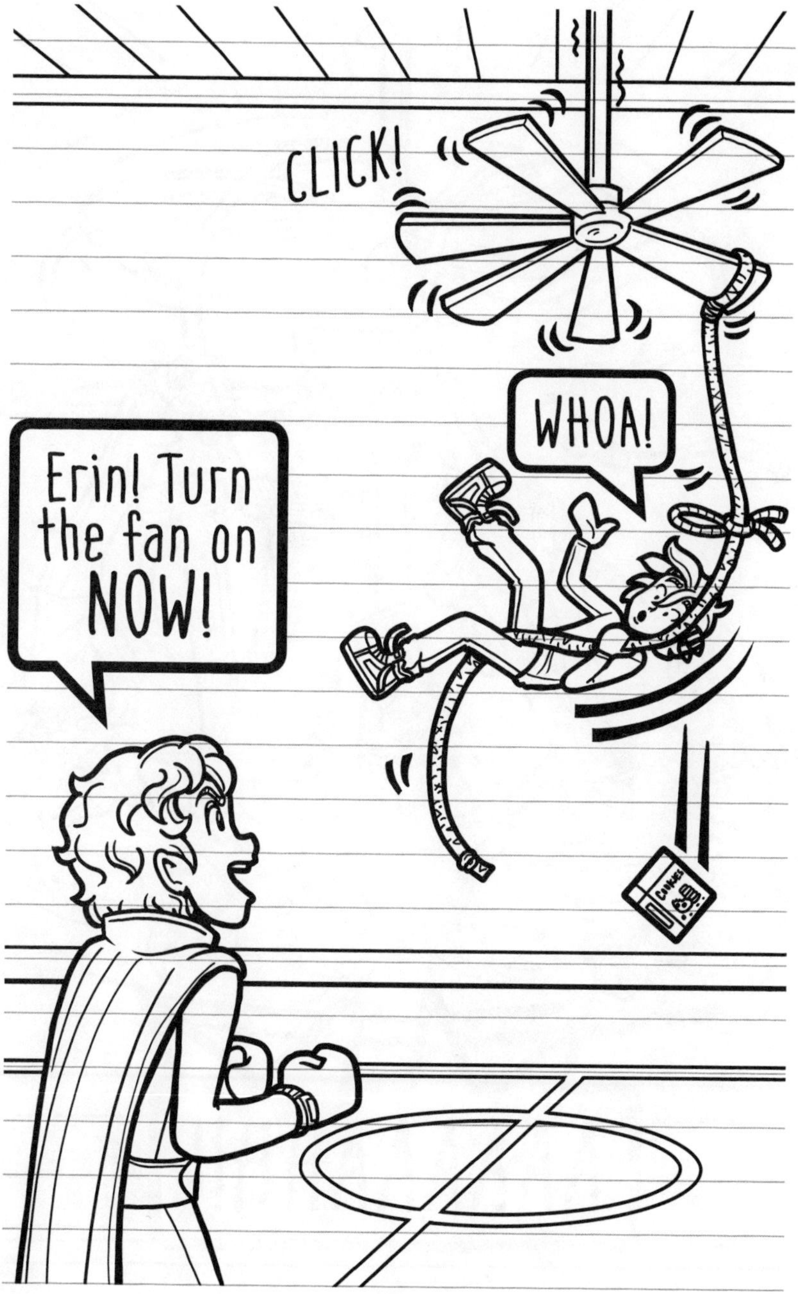
CLICK!
WHOA!
Erin! Turn the fan on NOW!

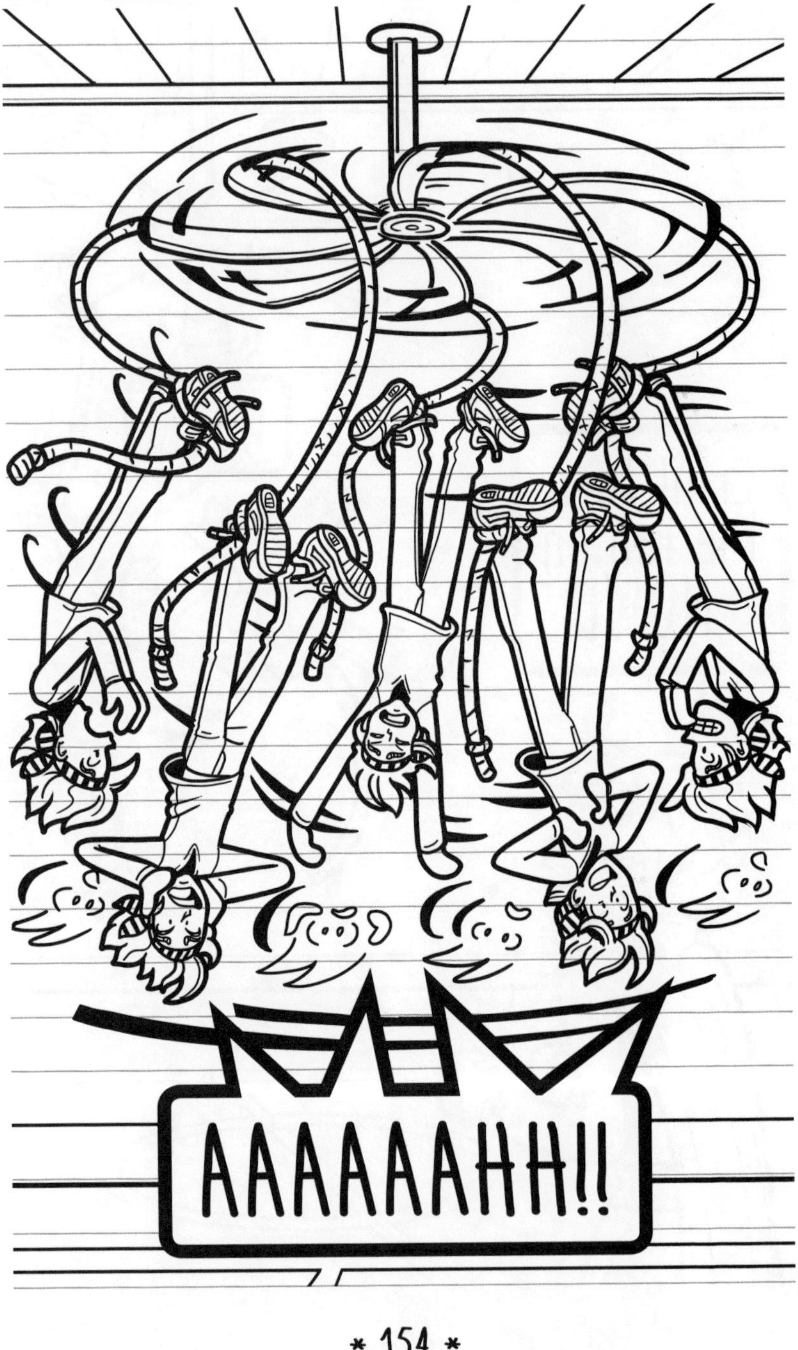
AAAAAAHH!!

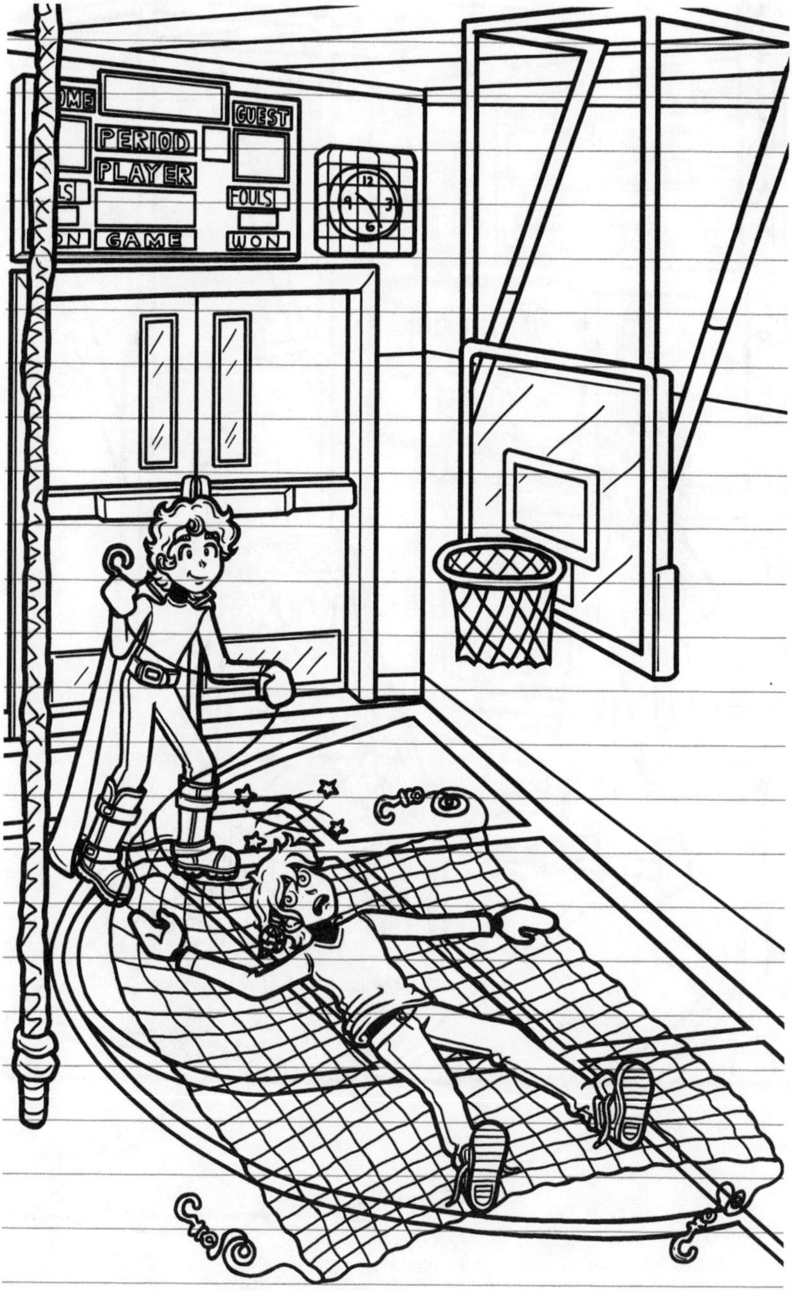
GUEST
PERIOD
PLAYER
FOULS
GAME
WON

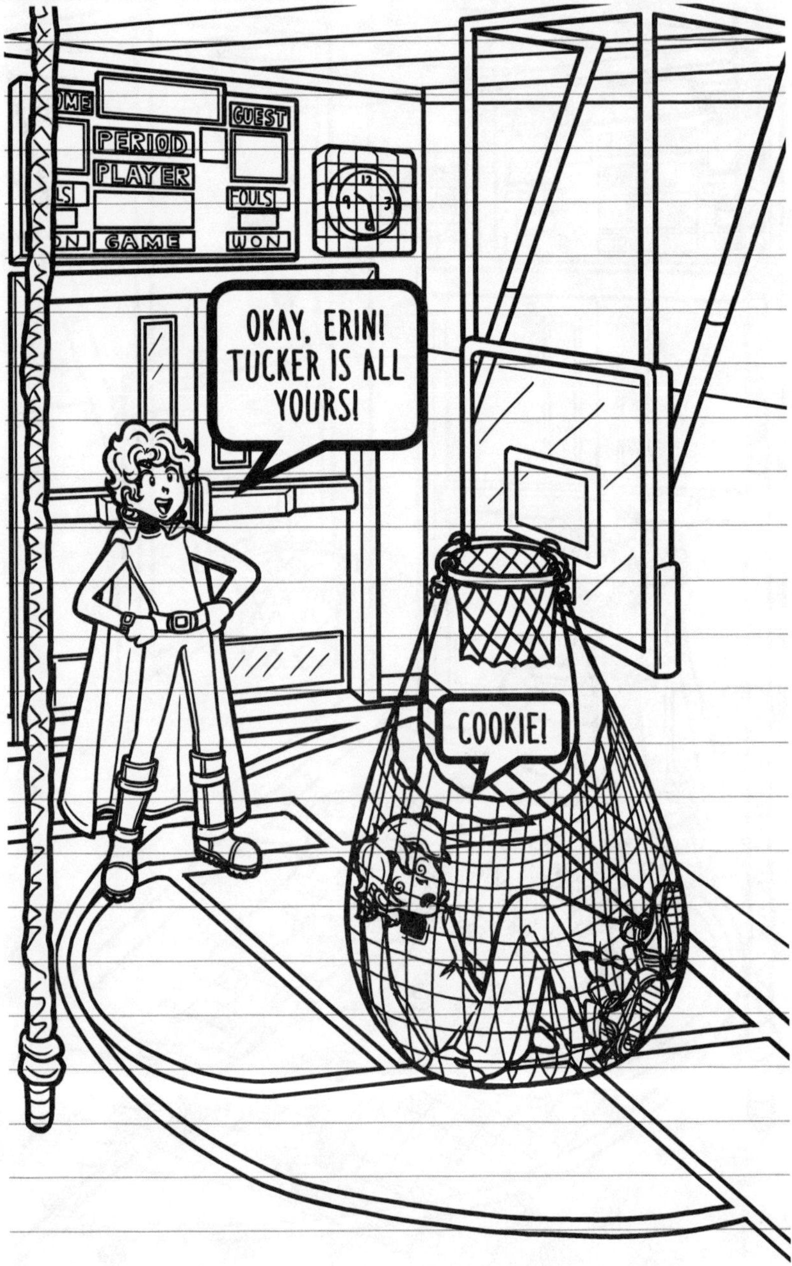
HOME
GUEST
PERIOD
PLAYER
FOULS
FOULS
WON
GAME
WON
OKAY, ERIN! TUCKER IS ALL YOURS!
COOKIE!

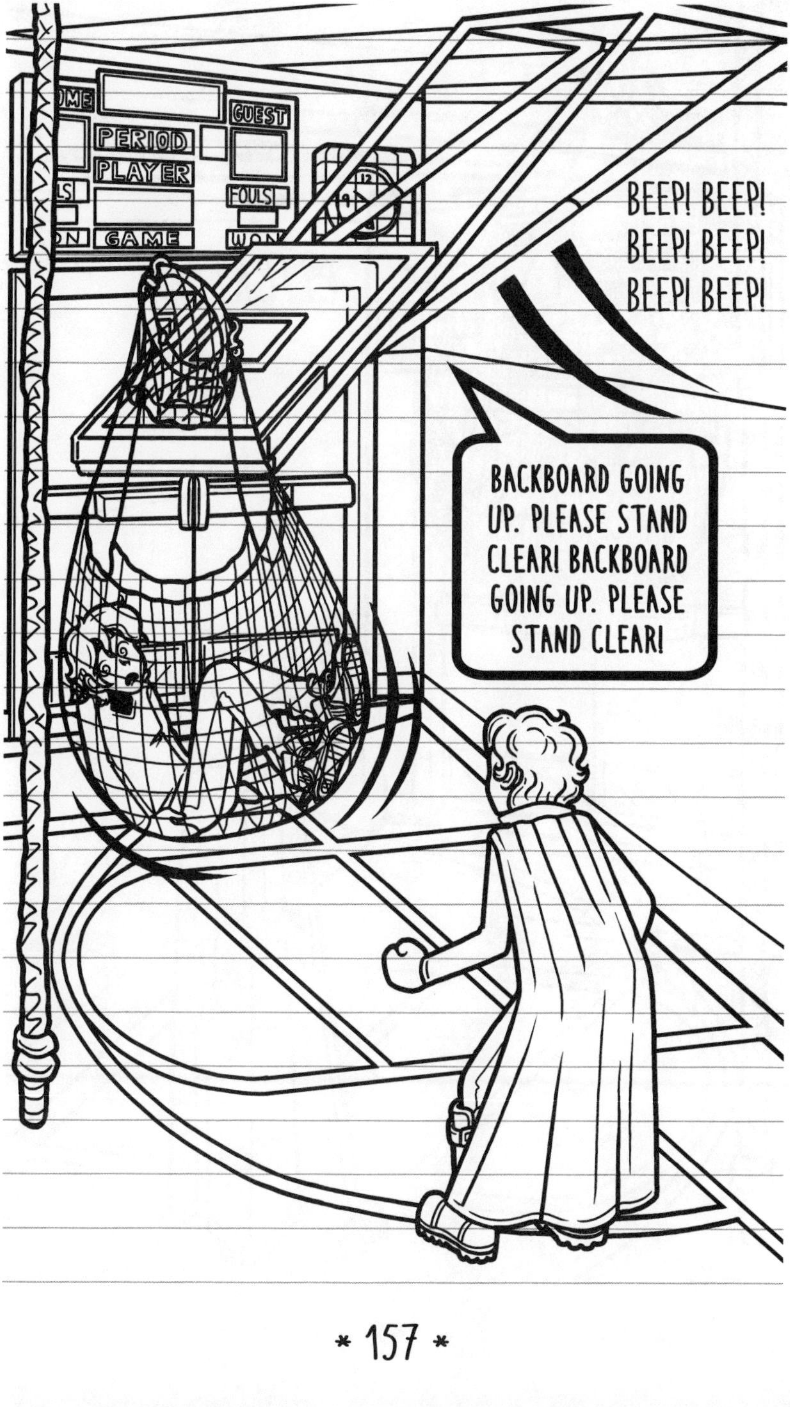

HOME
GUEST
PERIOD
PLAYER
FOULS
GAME
WON
BEEP! BEEP! BEEP! BEEP! BEEP! BEEP!
BACKBOARD GOING UP. PLEASE STAND CLEAR! BACKBOARD GOING UP. PLEASE STAND CLEAR!

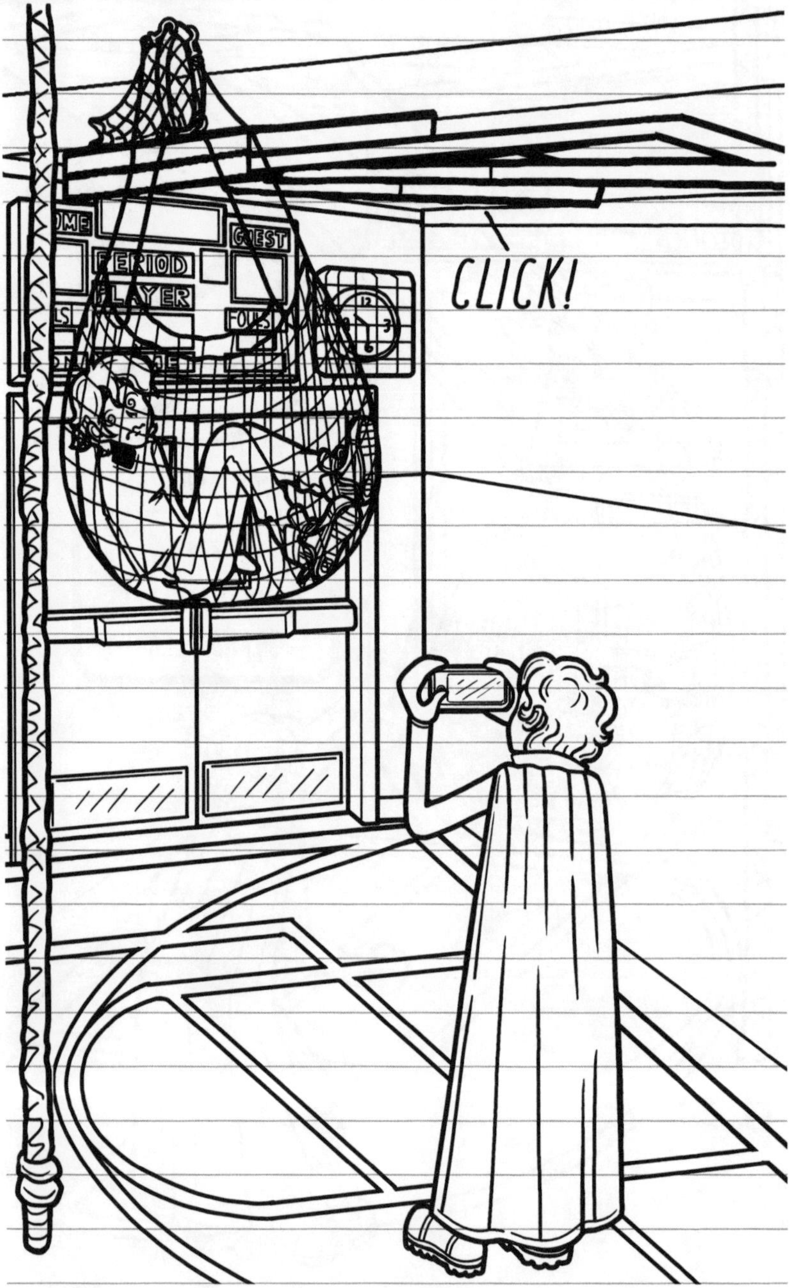
GUEST
PERIOD
PLAYER
FOULS
CLICK!

Hey, I **WARNED** you!

This stuff is enough to make your head **EXPLODE!**

I held up my phone so Erin could see what we had caught in our net. . . .

GUEST
PERIOD
PLAYER
GAM

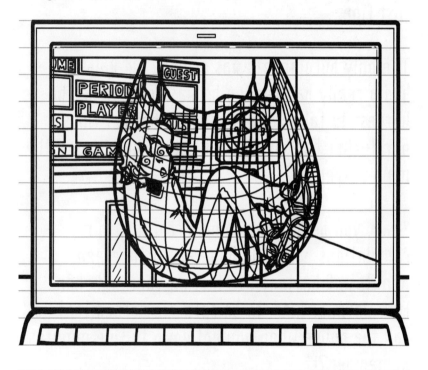

OUR MUG SHOT OF TUCKER

"OMG! This is CRAZY! I can't believe our plan actually worked," Erin uttered in disbelief.

After Tucker's little ride on that fan, he was still a bit disoriented and kept mumbling, "Cookie! Bad cookie!"

But once he was able to chill out for a while up in that net, I was pretty sure he was going to be just fine.

The only burglar left was grumpy old Ralph. I had a really bad feeling he was going to be the hardest to take down. And since neither Moose nor Tucker had my comic book, Ralph was now the main suspect.

"Max, you better get going! According to my calculations, you only have about fourteen minutes of battery life left on your cell phone!" Erin warned. "And, to be safe, we agreed that I'd call the police when you got down to five minutes. Remember?!"

"Yes, Erin, I remember! Actually, how could I FORGET?!" I muttered. "Just stop worrying, okay?! I GOT this!"

I sighed and stuck my phone back in my pocket.
Then I immediately started to panic.

My situation looked HOPELESS!

I STILL had to take out Ralph AND find that comic
book, and I ONLY had NINE minutes left to do it!

NINE MINUTES?! That was IMPOSSIBLE!

I was also sick and tired of fighting—fighting
Thug, fighting to escape from my locker, fighting
the burglars, fighting my fears, fighting so other
kids like me would have a chance.

I didn't have a choice but to ask myself a very
difficult question. . . . Was it finally time to
accept defeat and KISS South Ridge Middle School
good-bye?!

NO. FREAKING. WAY!

Sorry, but Max Crumbly was NOT going down
like that!

17. HOW TO GET GROUNDED UNTIL YOUR TWENTY-FIRST BIRTHDAY!

Just the thought of dealing with Ralph again totally FREAKED me out! I didn't know where to begin.

"So, Erin, do you have any ideas for Ralph?" I asked, trying not to panic.

"That guy is going to be tough! So I suggest we use my eighth-grade honors biology classroom. It's super close to the stairwell to the south exit, and there's lots of cool stuff in there that we can use. Including a biofuel rocket that I built. Did I mention I got an A+ on it?" she bragged.

"No! Actually, you didn't," I answered.

"Guess what, Max? I got an A+ on my rocket!"

"Very funny, Erin. I'm impressed!"

That's when I heard a sudden commotion. At first I thought it was coming from the hall.

But then I took out my phone and saw this....

"ERIN MADISON! Are you still awake at this hour?
I thought I heard voices in here! WHO are you
talking to?!" her mom scolded.

"How many times have we told you no social media,
texting friends, or cell phone calls AFTER nine p.m.?
Erin, this has gotten completely out of hand!" her
dad lectured.

"MOM?! DAD?! You didn't KNOCK!! You both agreed NOT to just barge into my room like this! I'm entitled to my PRIVACY!" Erin complained.

"NOT when you're breaking the rules, young lady!!" her mother shot back.

"Erin, you're grounded for one week, and I'm confiscating your laptop. Hand it over NOW!" her dad demanded.

"NO! I CAN'T! THIS IS SUPER IMPORTANT! I'M TALKING TO . . . I MEAN, I'M WORKING ON . . . A REALLY BIG . . . UM, SCHOOL PROJECT?!" Erin protested.

"Well, I'm sure your little project can wait until tomorrow! NOW GO. TO. SLEEP!" her dad scolded.

"DAD! NO!! PLEASE, GIVE ME BACK MY—"

CLICK! Then there was dead silence.

I just stared at my phone in complete shock.

18. HAVE A HAPPY BIRTHDAY! NOT!!

Suddenly I felt really sick.

Like I was actually going to throw up.

It was one thing for ME to get MYSELF in trouble.

But I felt horrible knowing that I had gotten Erin in big trouble.

All because she was trying to help ME!

That's when I decided it was GAME OVER! It was finally time to give up and go home.

Tomorrow morning I planned to go straight to Erin's house and explain everything to her parents and apologize.

I didn't really care what happened to me anymore.

My actions had hurt a person I really cared about, and that made me a total LOSER!

As I was leaving I couldn't help but hear Ralph's voice echoing through the hall.

He was talking on his cell phone. I crept up to the classroom door and eavesdropped. . . .

"Listen, Tina! I'm REALLY sorry I missed your mother's birthday dinner. I'll make it up to both of you, I promise. I'll take her to Queasy Cheesy or someplace fancy like that, okay? But right now I'm busy WORKING! I gotta WORK to pay the bills and BUY you nice things, sweetie pie. What? Did I BUY your mother a birthday present? Um . . . Actually, I don't remember if I— Huh? NO, Tina! You DON'T need to put your mother on the phone so I can APOLOGIZE to her for missing her birthday and not buying her a gift. I don't have time to talk to her right now. I'm WORKING! Tina! Tina, stop SCREAMING at me! PLEASE! . . ."

I peeked through the window to see if I could spot my comic book.

It just HAD to be in there SOMEWHERE. . . .

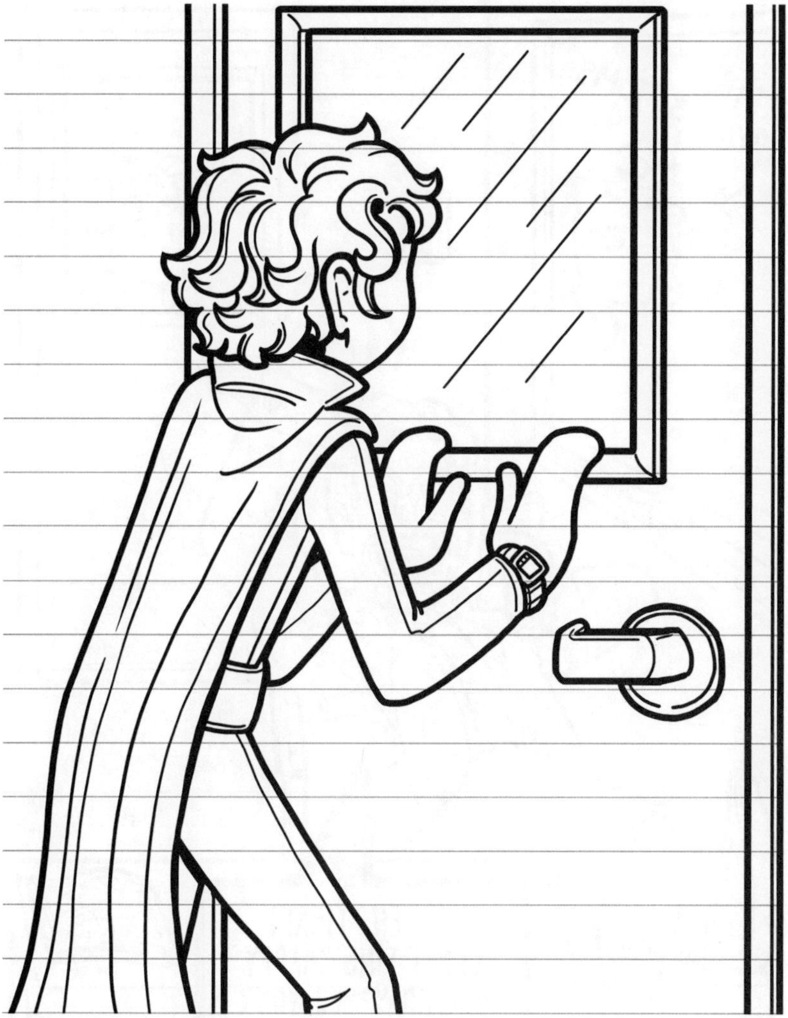

And my gut instinct was correct!

I was beyond desperate! So I took a huge risk to try to pull off the CRAZIEST stunt EVER!! . . .

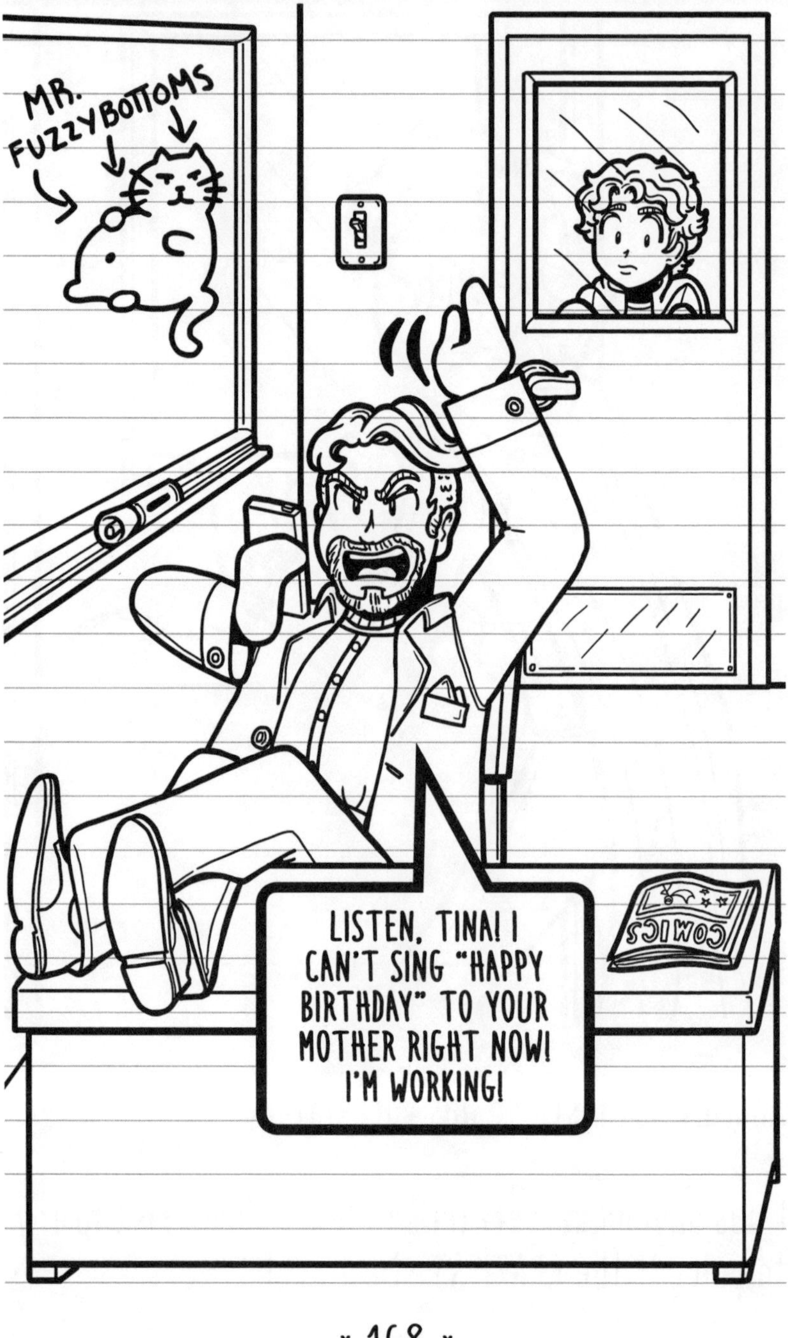
MR. FUZZYBOTTOMS
LISTEN, TINA! I CAN'T SING "HAPPY BIRTHDAY" TO YOUR MOTHER RIGHT NOW! I'M WORKING!
COMICS

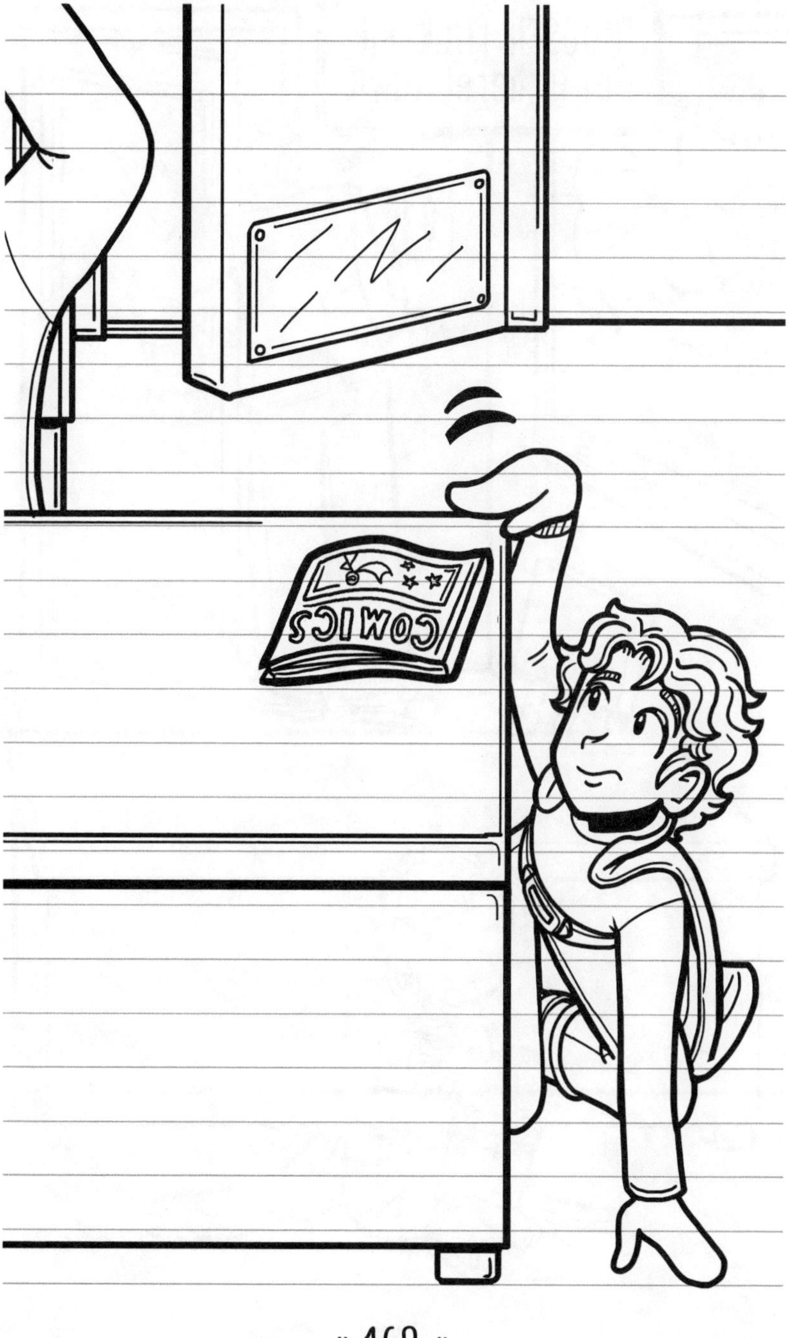
COMICS

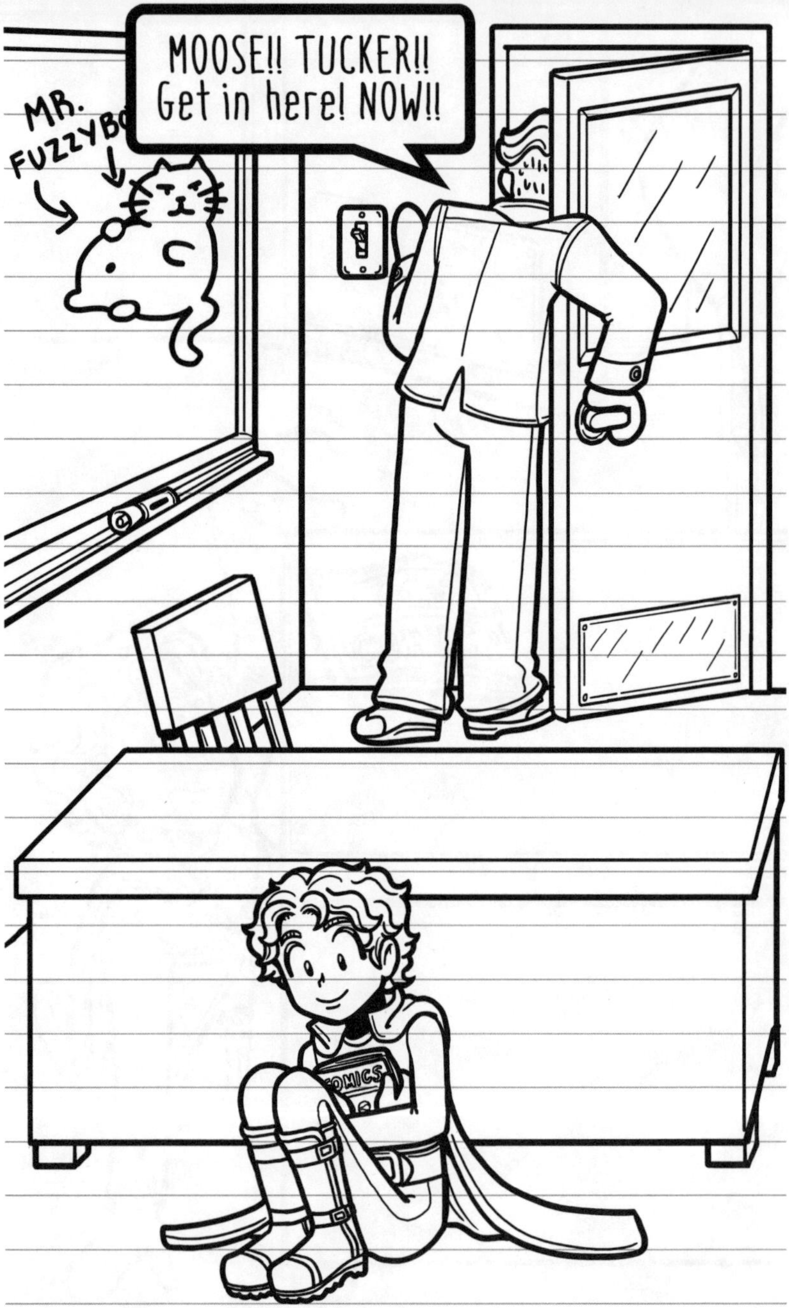
MOOSE!! TUCKER!!
Get in here! NOW!!
MR. FUZZYBO
COMICS

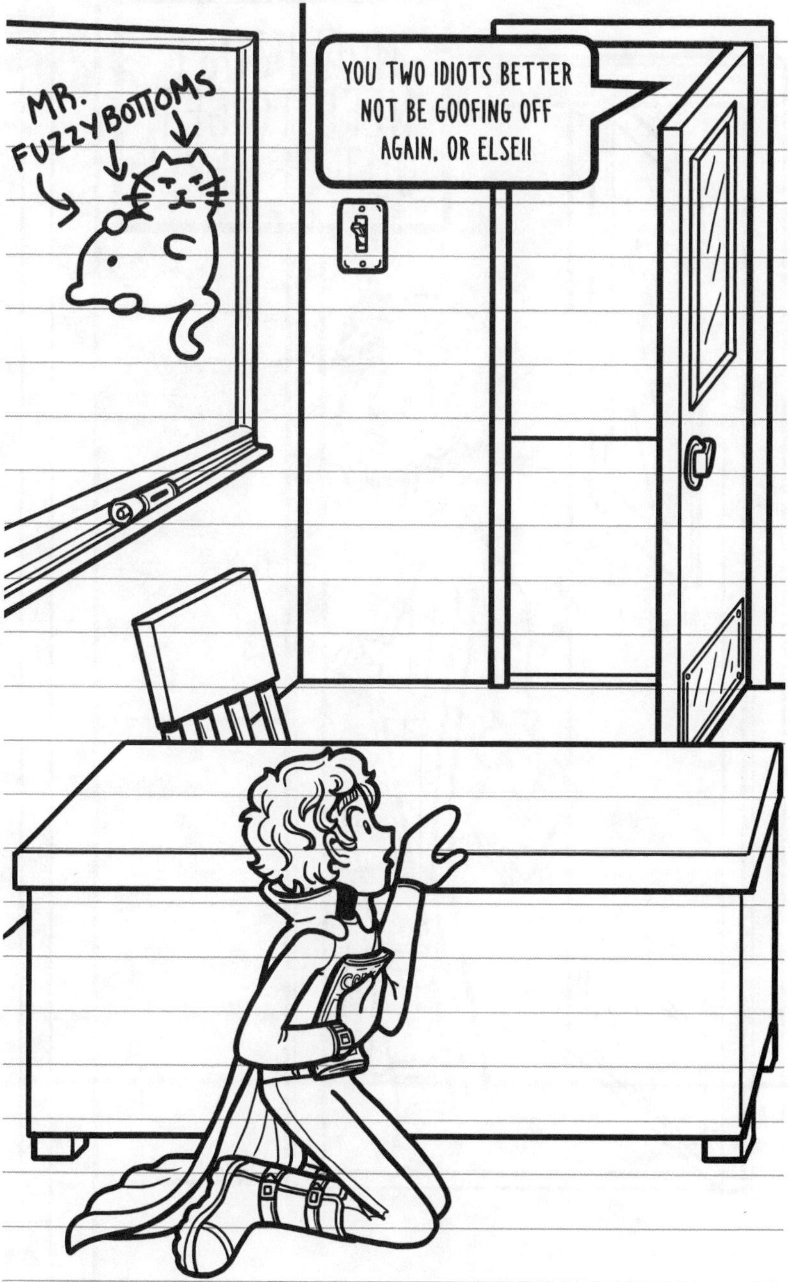
MR. FUZZYBOTTOMS
YOU TWO IDIOTS BETTER NOT BE GOOFING OFF AGAIN, OR ELSE!!

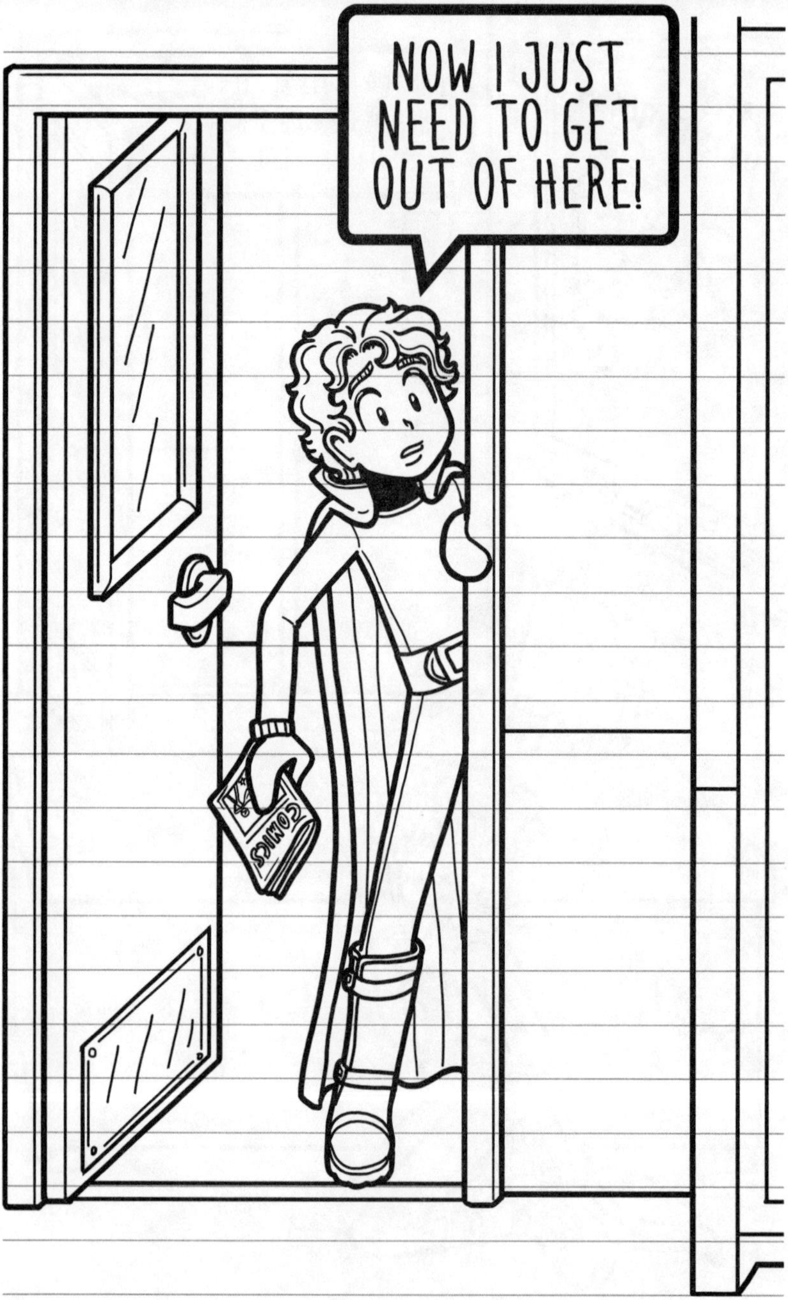
NOW I JUST NEED TO GET OUT OF HERE!
COMICS

19. I MAKE MY GREAT ESCAPE!

Yes, I know! I KNOW! The STUNT that I'd just pulled off was CRAZY DANGEROUS!

WARNING!: KIDS, DO NOT TRY THIS AT HOME!!

I realize I was VERY lucky to have made it out of that room alive. But I HAD to get my dad's comic book back ~~or HE was going to KILL ME~~!

Thank goodness Ralph was totally distracted by that phone call from his lovely wife, Tina.

~~Just between you and me, I was personally very SHOCKED by Ralph's OUTRAGEOUS behavior. I know he is a lowlife, two-bit CROOK!~~

~~But what kind of person DITCHES his mother-in-law's BIRTHDAY dinner, FORGETS to buy her a present, and then REFUSES to sing "Happy Birthday" to her?!~~

~~There is no doubt in my mind. RALPH IS A HEARTLESS MONSTER!!~~

I stood frozen there in the doorway, trying to figure out what to do next.

If Ralph went to the kitchen for a late-night snack and found Moose . . . I was DEAD!

If Ralph went to the gym for a quick workout and found Tucker . . . I was DEAD!

If Ralph came back to the room to get the comic book and found ME with it . . . I was DEAD!

It was quite obvious to me that my work here was DONE! Finally! It was time to get the HECK out of South Ridge Middle School. And as soon as I made it safely out of the building, I was going to call the police.

Then I was going to text Erin to make sure she was okay. I felt pretty awful that she had gotten in trouble with her parents while trying to help ME.

Anyway, Ralph had completely disappeared! As soon as I hit that EXIT door at the end of the hall, this NIGHTMARE was going to be OVER. . . .

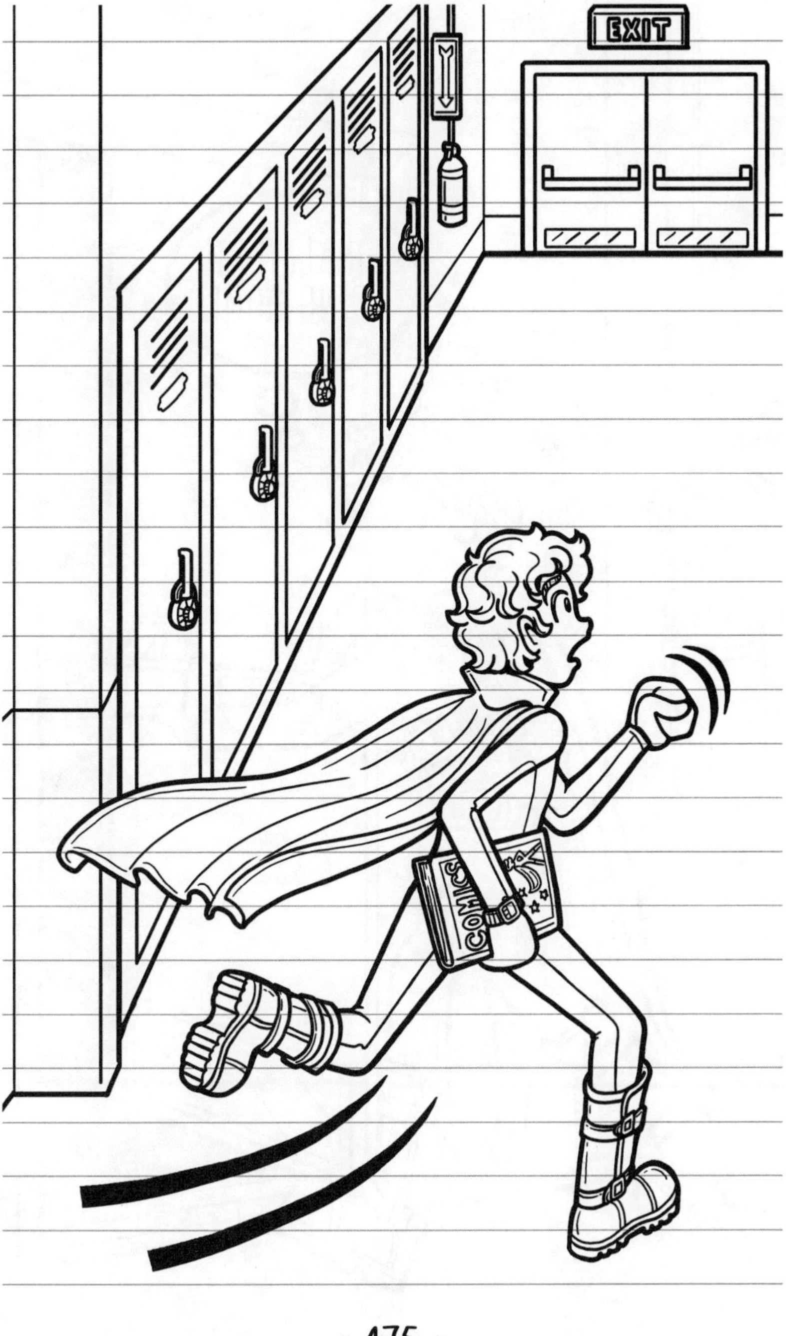
EXIT
COMICS

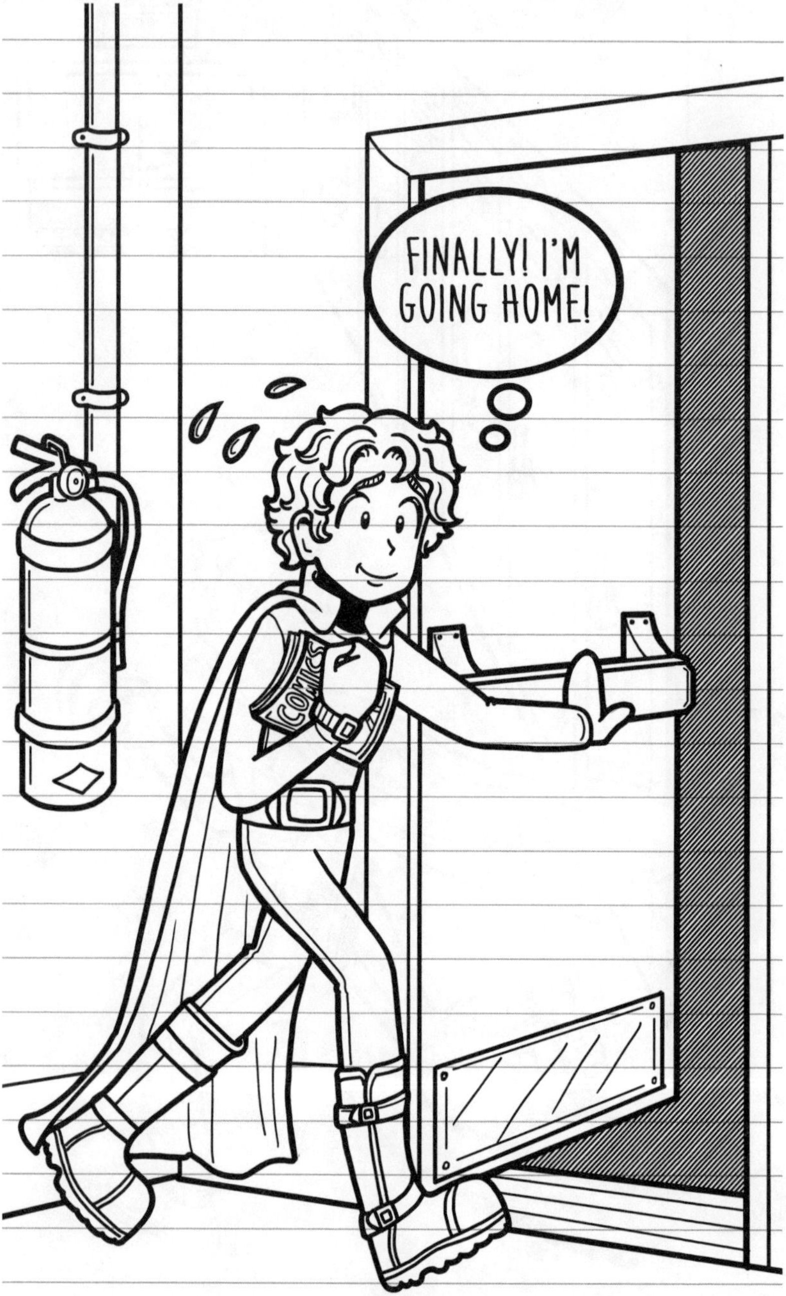
FINALLY! I'M GOING HOME!
COMICS

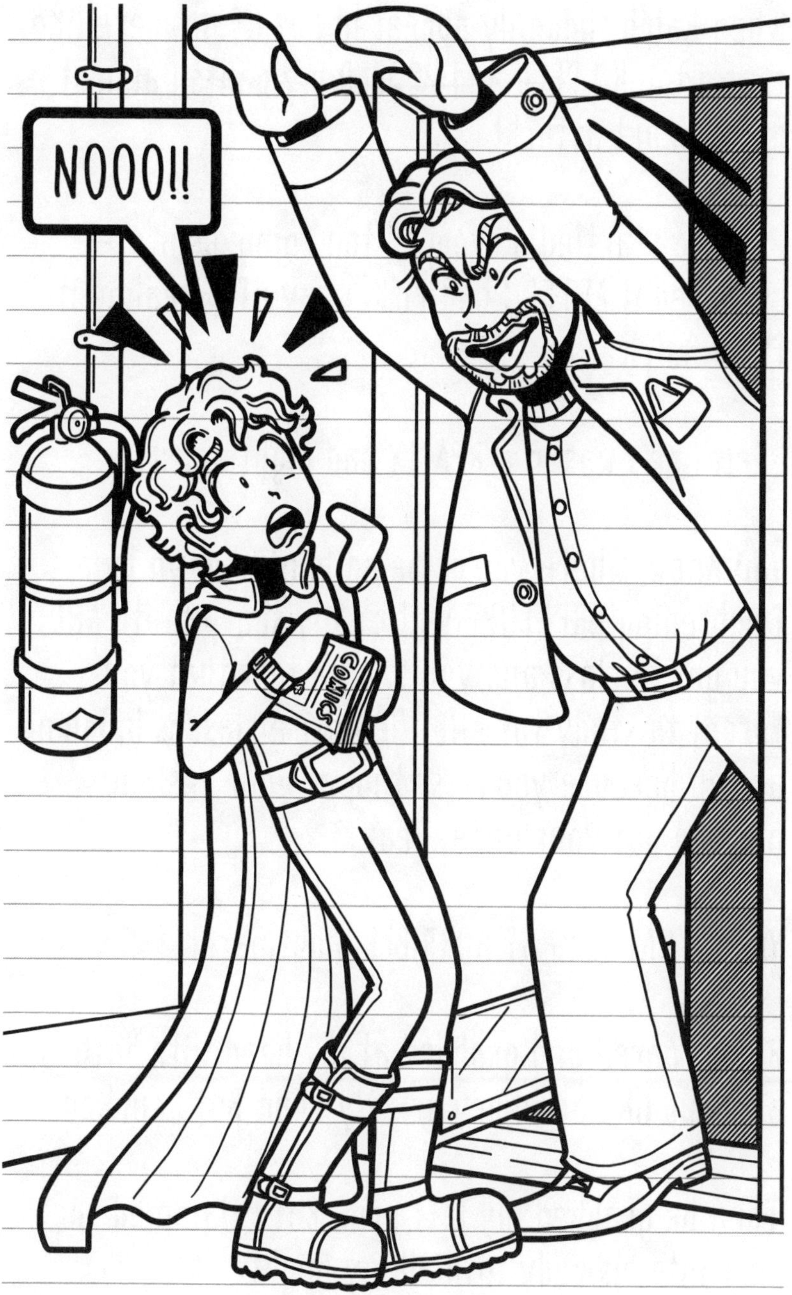
NOOO!!
COMICS

When Ralph suddenly appeared out of nowhere like that, I think ~~I PEED and POOPED my pants~~ I almost had a heart attack!

I was so startled, I dropped the comic book. Yes, I dropped it AFTER I had risked my life stealing it from Ralph.

I felt like I was in a REALLY bad nightmare!

You know, where you're being hunted down by a frightening CREATURE with really sharp teeth AND you get to class and you have a test that you forgot to study for AND the entire class is laughing at you because you're sitting at your desk in nothing but your underwear.

Yeah, THAT kind of HORRIBLE nightmare!

Ralph roared and grabbed at my head with both arms up like an angry grizzly bear. But I ducked.

Then he grabbed my left arm. But I slammed the door into his body with all my might.

It stunned him and knocked him off-balance just long enough for me to pry my arm out of his grip.

I took off running down the hall. And when I glanced over my shoulder, he was picking up the comic book.

He scowled, shoved it inside his jacket, and came barreling down the hall after me.

My lungs felt tight and it was hard to breathe. But I didn't know if it was because I was RUNNING or merely FREAKING OUT over the fact that I was out of asthma medication.

One thing was very clear. Anywhere I went in the entire school, Ralph was going to FOLLOW me like a raging, charging bull.

CORRECTION! . . .

Ralph could follow me ANYWHERE in the school EXCEPT for ONE place. . . .

The ventilation system!

20. ATTACK OF THE KILLER TOILET!— PART 2

At the next hallway I hung a right.

The boys' bathroom on the south end was the closest entry point back into the vents. It was STILL a stinky mess from the little accident I'd had in there earlier.

Come on, people! It wasn't THAT kind of accident!! Your snarky comment was NOT even funny.

I'd learned the hard way never to ignore a sign in a bathroom that says "VERY Out of Order!" And in spite of everything that had been drilled into me since potty training, there comes a time in life when it is better NOT to FLUSH.

I carefully climbed over the toilet like I was navigating a minefield and somehow made it safely up into the vent.

I felt really SAD about what happened to Ralph. . . .

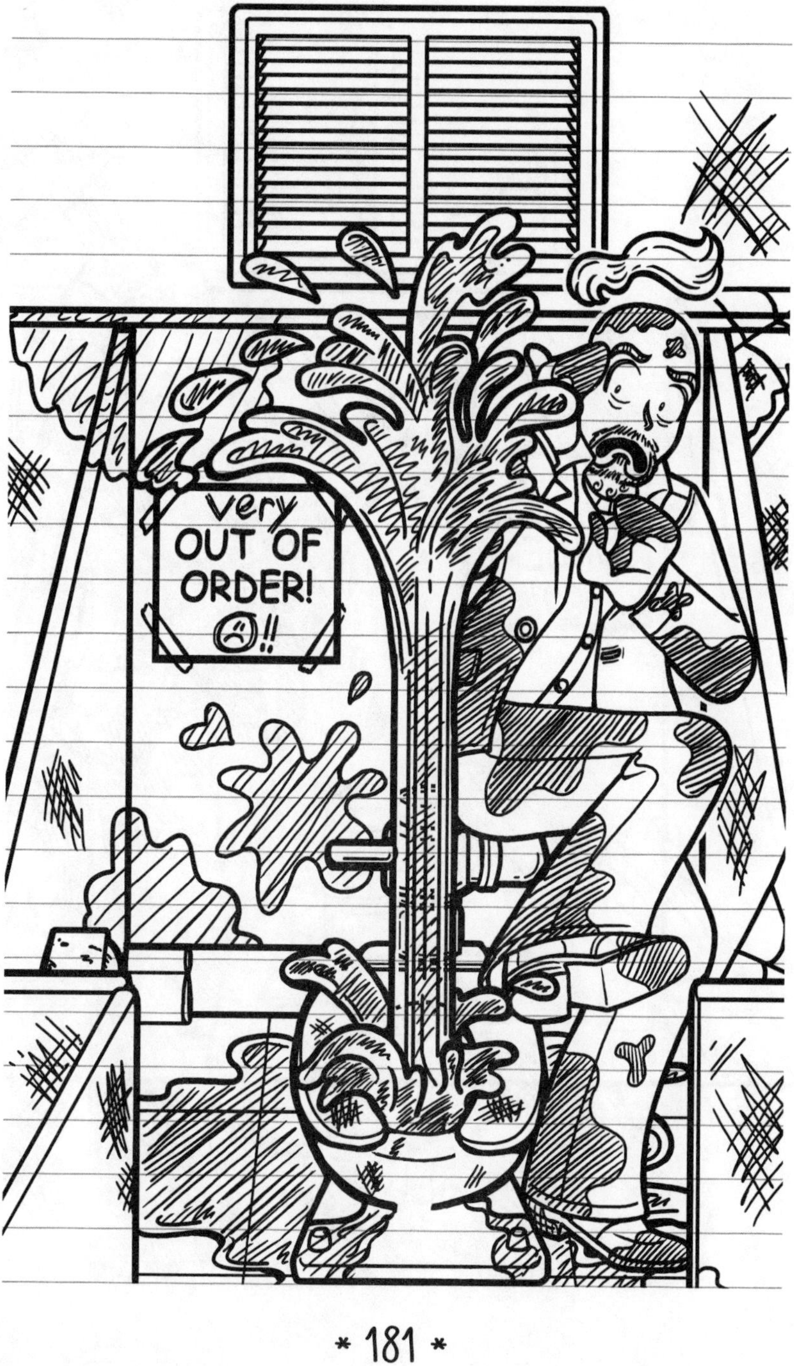
very
OUT OF
ORDER!
☹!!

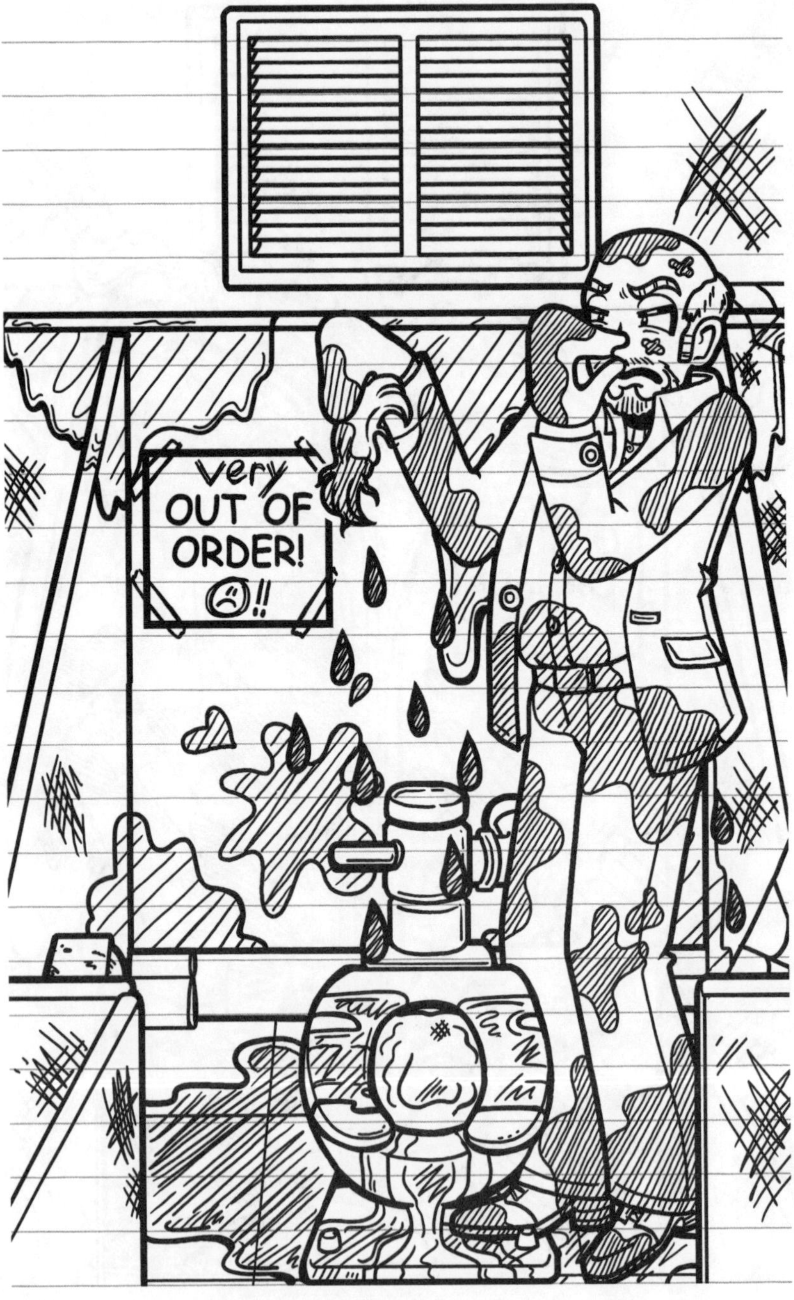
Very
OUT OF
ORDER!
!!

NOT!!!

Ralph was SO angry, he started yelling not-so-nice things at me as he kicked the gushing toilet. . . .

"LISTEN, KID! WAIT UNTIL I GET MY HANDS ON YOU!! I'M GONNA HUNT YOU DOWN AND RIP YOUR FACE OFF! YOU'RE NEVER GONNA MAKE IT OUT OF HERE ALIVE! THAT'S A PROMISE! DO YOU HEAR ME? DOOO YOOOU HEEEEAR MEEEEEE?!"

It was quite obvious that Ralph was having a complete nervous breakdown.

But a cold shower in stinky black muck that looked and smelled like elephant diarrhea would probably make most people have a meltdown.

I was exhausted and just wanted to go home.

The comic book was a lost cause.

At this point there was no chance WHATSOEVER that I'd get it back from Ralph.

And when my parents found out about all of the trouble I'd caused, I'd be back homeschooling with my grandma by Tuesday.

But the worst part was that I'd probably NEVER see Erin again.

EVER!!

I was sure she probably HATED me by now.

I guess it was nice while it lasted.

Whatever "it" was!

If I was going to make it out of this school alive, I needed to get to an exit ASAP.

That's when I suddenly remembered that Erin had said her honors biology class had stuff I could use to trap Ralph and was close to the south exit stairwell. So that was exactly where I was headed. . . .

I could hardly wait for this FIASCO to finally be OVER!

21. HOW MY DREAMS WENT RIGHT OUT THE WINDOW

Erin's biology classroom looked almost identical to my physical science classroom.

However, the biology room had aquariums filled with fish, tanks filled with reptiles, and cages filled with mammals.

There was also an area for insects and arachnids, which contained several huge tarantulas and a half dozen ant farms.

If only Erin hadn't gotten grounded by her parents! We could have had a BLAST in this room with Ralph!

I was in such a big hurry that I had an accident while I was coming down from the vent.

I could NOT believe I knocked over a half dozen test tubes and glass beakers that were on a nearby shelf. . . .

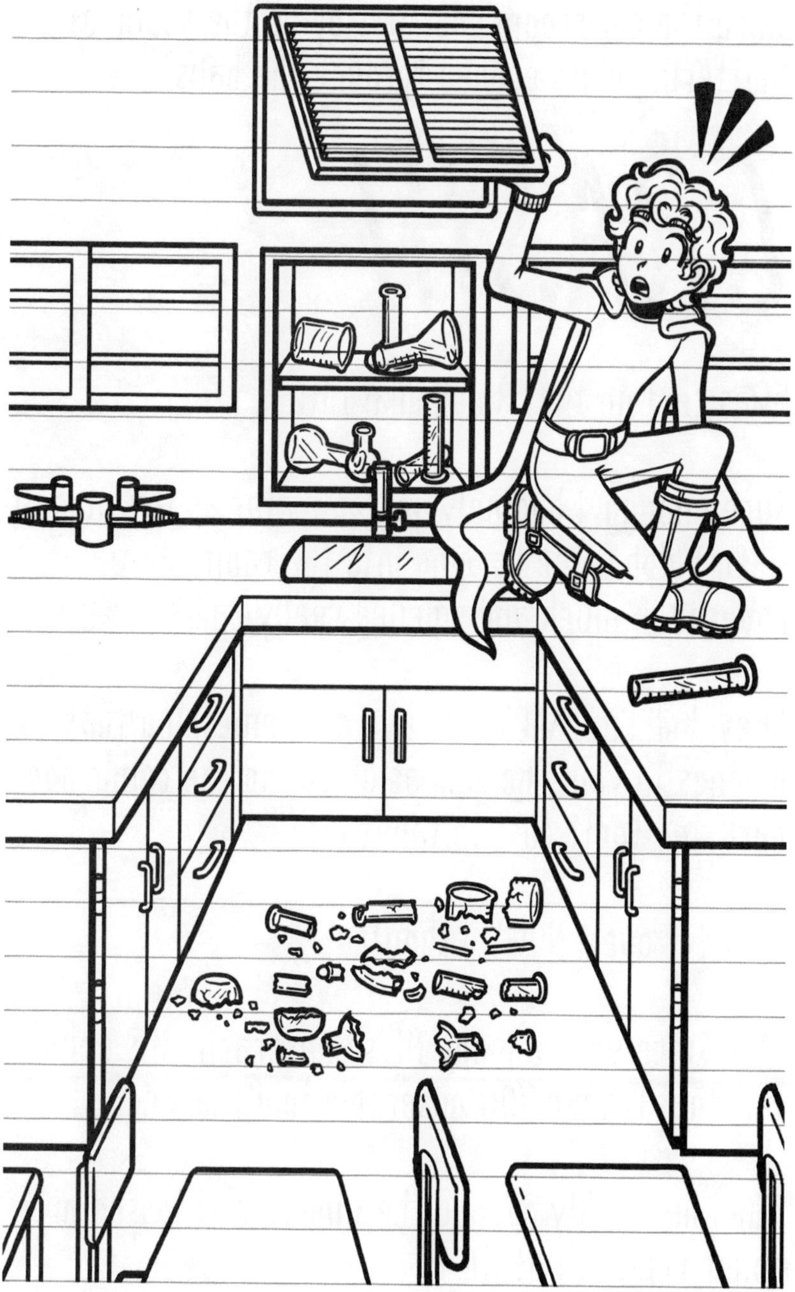

Since the classroom door was open, the sound of shattering glass echoed through the halls. . . .

CRASH!

I was certain that Ralph heard it!

Sure enough, I had only gotten as far as the window when Ralph came barging into the room. He was covered in muck and smelled really bad.

"Hey, kid! I'm BAACK! And I've got something that belongs to you!" he said as he swung the comic book back and forth just to taunt me.

"Hand it over! NOW!" I shouted.

"NO! Since you've made ME so miserable, it's only fair that I make YOU miserable too!" he said.

Then he quickly opened the window and tossed my comic right out of it!

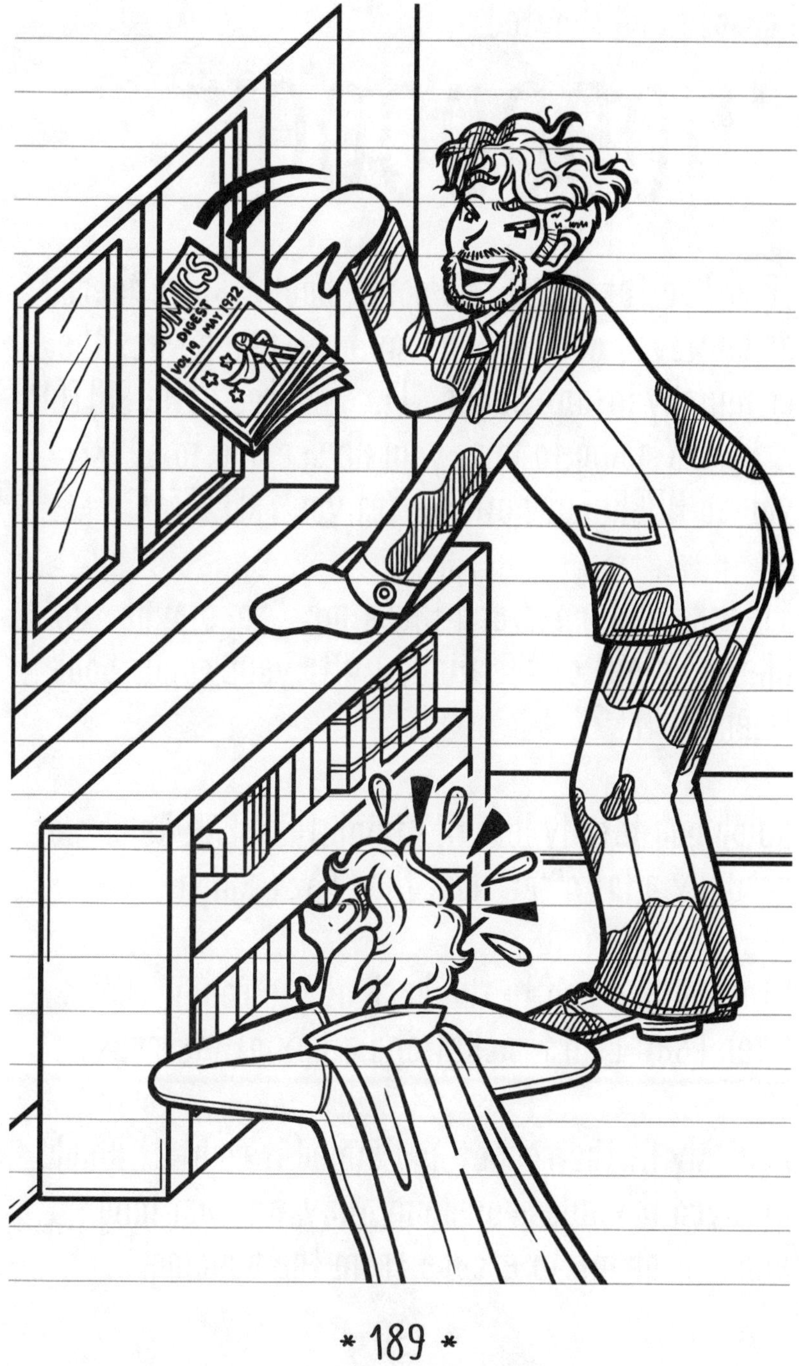
OMICS
DIGEST
VOL 19 MAY 1972

I gasped and shouted . . .

"NOOOOOOO!"

"Bye-bye forever, little comic book!" Ralph jeered as he waved good-bye at my book like he was the criminally insane Joker. "I'm sure the little SNITCH is REALLY going to miss you! He seemed to ADORE you so MUCH! But now I've set you FREEEEEE!"

Then Ralph turned and faced me. "So, maybe YOU'D like to go out of the window with your comic book friend?! YES?"

Ralph had totally lost it! I think the MEAN Ralph was actually a lot nicer than the CRAZY Ralph.

I turned and ran to the back of the room. That's when I saw Erin's rocket and a box of matches.

I quickly lit the rocket and aimed it right at Ralph. I prayed it would scare him away, at least long enough for me to escape from the building! . . .

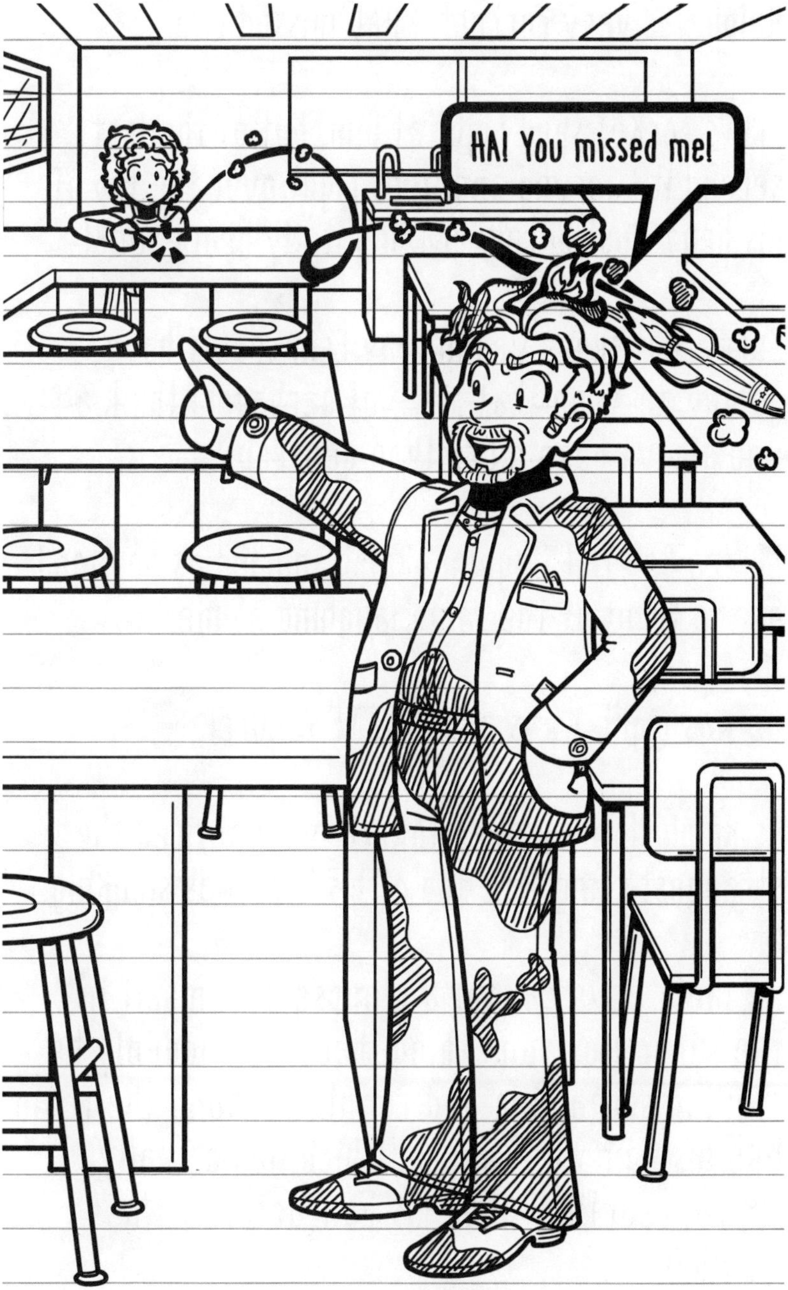
HA! You missed me!

Ralph was very correct. I HAD missed him.

Erin's rocket sped right at him, but at the last second it swerved and went right over the top of his head, just barely grazing it. My heart sank!

~~Sorry, but there was no way Erin should have gotten an A+ on that piece of garbage! I think a D would have been more than generous.~~

"Pizza Boy FAILS again!" Ralph snarled as he stood at the front of the room laughing at me.

He was right. I was a COMPLETE failure!

As Ralph slowly walked toward me, I noticed the strangest thing. The top of his head was smoking.

He must have caught a glimpse of himself in the window or something, because suddenly he started screaming and running around the room like his hair was on fire. Which was a really logical reaction since his hair actually WAS on FIRE! . . .

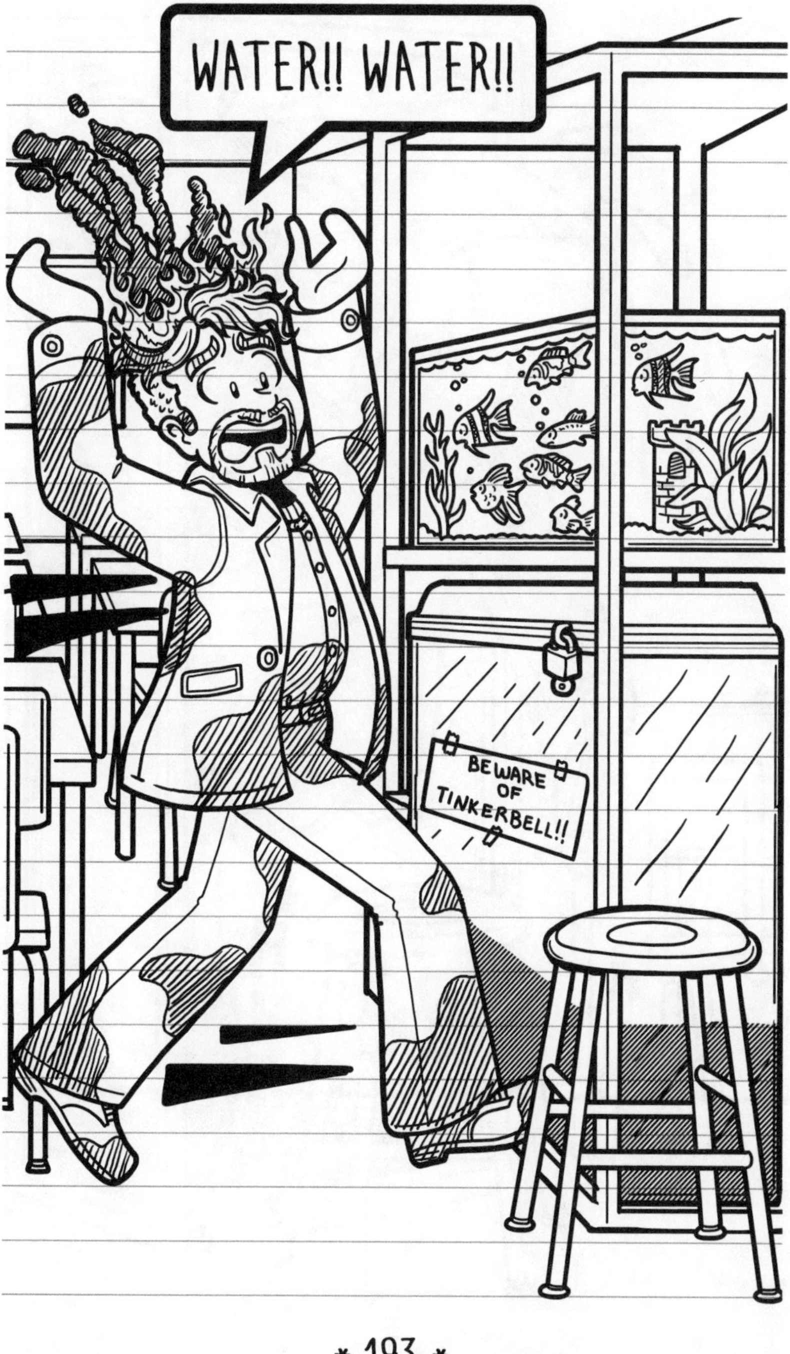
WATER!! WATER!!
BEWARE OF TINKERBELL!!

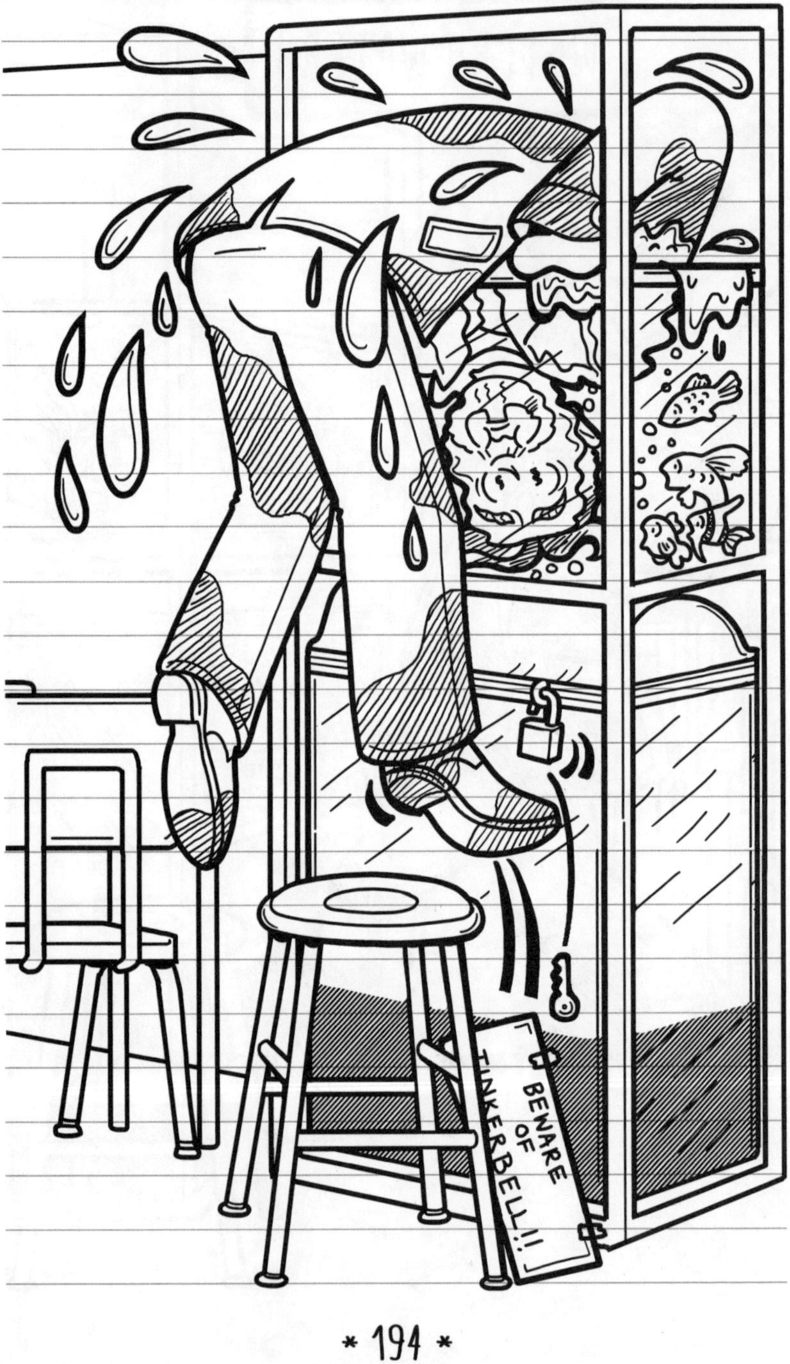
BEWARE
OF
TINKERBELL!!

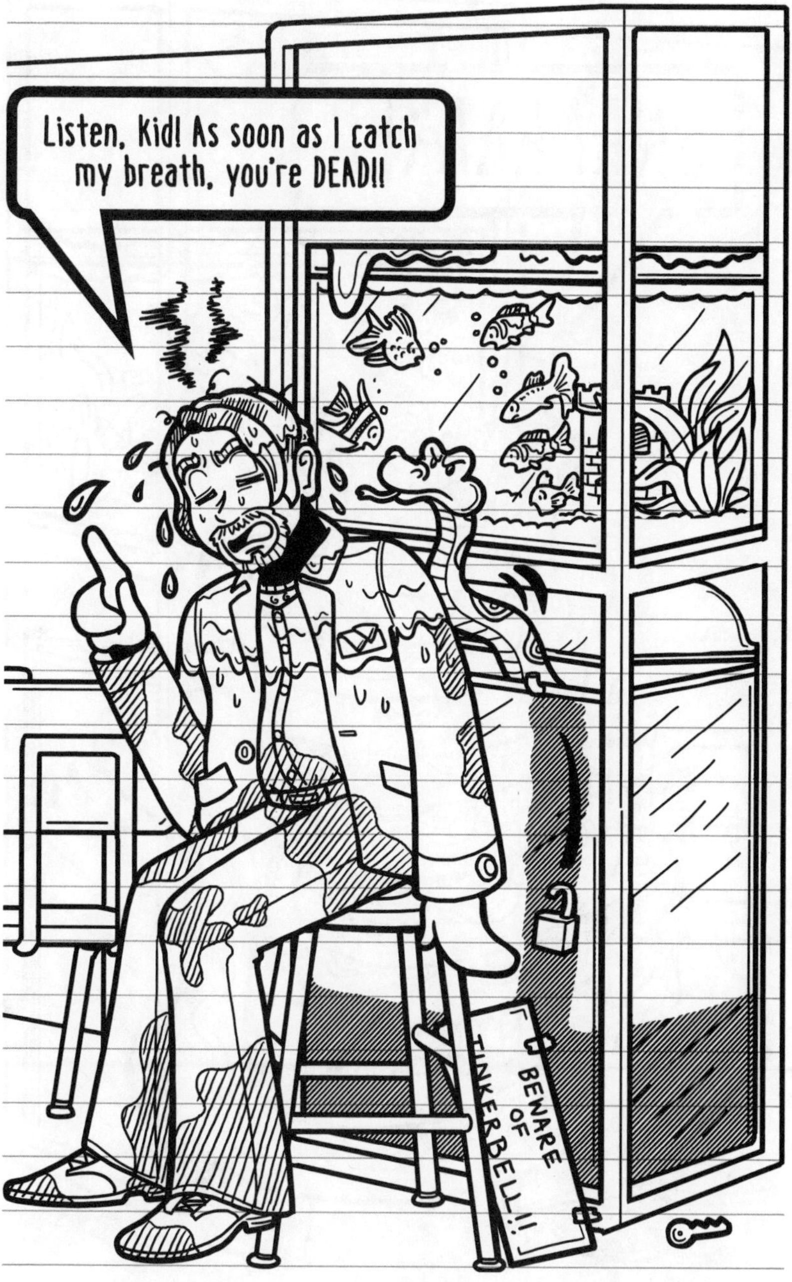
Listen, Kid! As soon as I catch my breath, you're DEAD!!
BEWARE OF TINKERBELL!!!

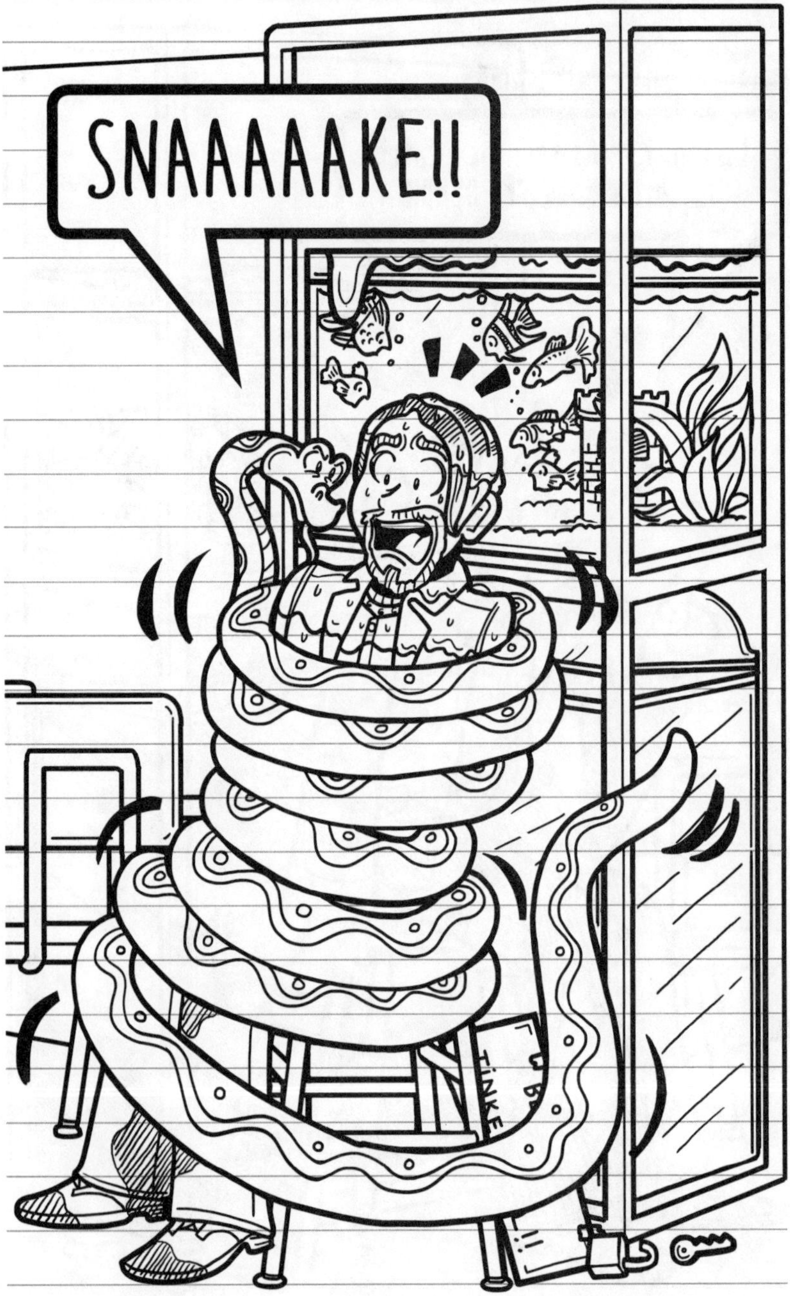
SNAAAAAKE!!

At first I was a little worried about leaving Ralph with Tinkerbell like that.

But she actually seemed to like him, because she kept licking his face and trying to play with him. Like a giant ten-foot-long, one-hundred-and-fifty-pound, um . . . PUPPY?

I think it's safe to assume that Tinkerbell is a very tame animal since she's a SCHOOL PET.

I had never seen her slithering through the halls SWALLOWING random students and teachers WHOLE!

Come on! HALF of our school population would have been eaten by now. So Tinkerbell HAS to be HARMLESS, right?!

But, of course, I could also be very WRONG about that.

JUST KIDDING!

NOT!!

I took out my cell phone and shot a photo of Ralph. Now I had MUG SHOTS of all THREE burglars!

I thought about sending it to Erin. But she probably wouldn't see it right away since her parents had confiscated her computer. . . .

OUR MUG SHOT OF RALPH

Erin hadn't even been gone for an hour yet, and I was ALREADY starting to miss her. FOR REAL!

22. DUMPSTER-DIVING DUDE

I could NOT believe Ralph had actually thrown away my dad's comic book by tossing it out of a window like that.

That whole fiasco brought back some very TRAUMATIC memories from my childhood. When I was younger, I was totally obsessed with Superman.

And when I found out that his parents had sent him to Earth in a spaceship, I decided to build one too. Right in my bedroom. It took weeks to collect all the supplies and finally finish it.

My plan was for Superman and me to pay a surprise visit to his parents. And while I was hanging out on his home planet, I would acquire superhuman powers TOO!

But my little brother, Oliver, ruined everything when he started WHINING about my very authentic-looking glass SPACE HELMET. . . .

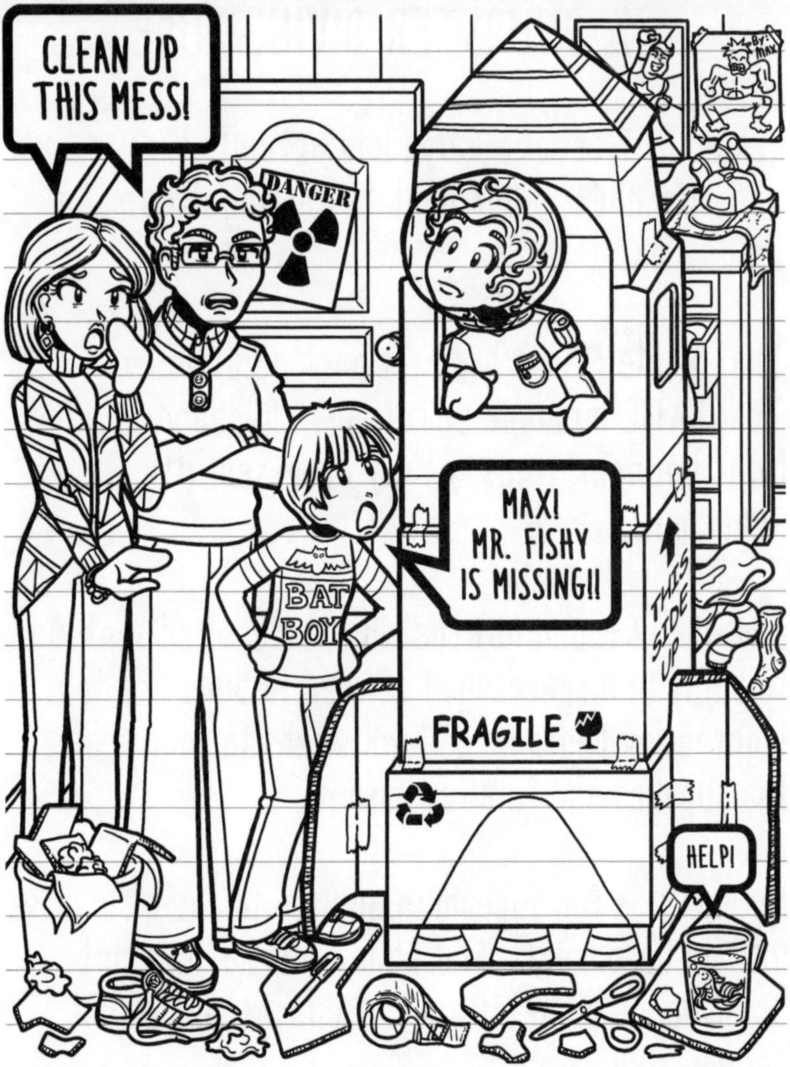
CLEAN UP THIS MESS!
DANGER
MAX! MR. FISHY IS MISSING!!
BAT BOY
THIS SIDE UP
FRAGILE
HELP!

Of course, my parents got an attitude about the whole thing and took Oliver's side like they always do. Instead of appreciating all of my hard work, they told me to clean up my messy room.

And when I came home from Boy Scouts later that day, I found my wonderful spaceship in the TRASH! I just HATE it when people throw away really important stuff that belongs to me! . . .

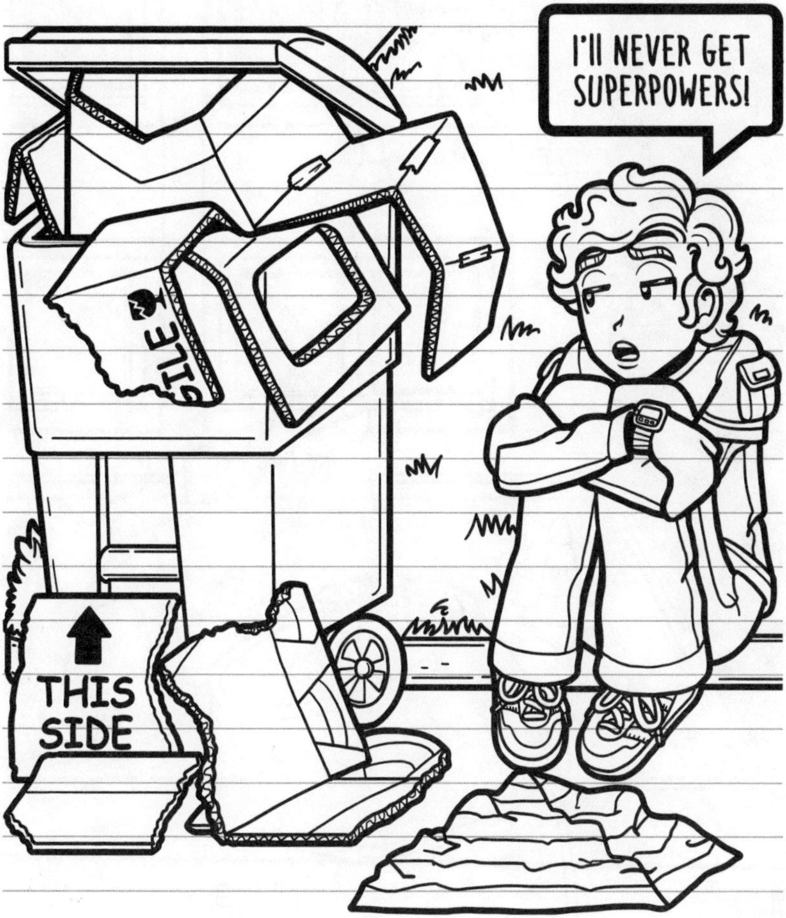
I'LL NEVER GET SUPERPOWERS!
FRAGILE
THIS SIDE

Anyway, now that Ralph was out of the way, I rushed over to the window and looked out. . . .

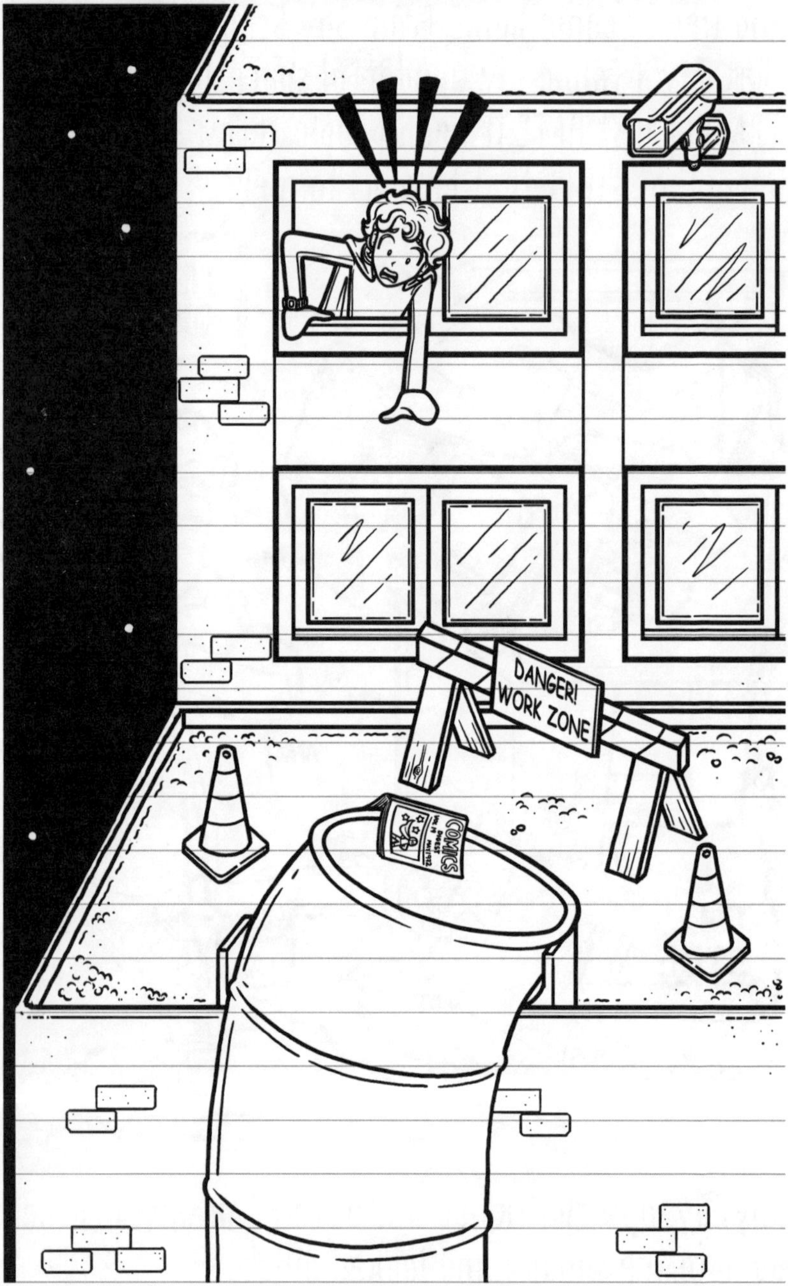
DANGER!
WORK ZONE
COMICS

I couldn't believe my eyes! My comic book had actually landed right on top of a strange-looking tube-shaped structure that was attached to the school building.

It also looked like workers were putting a new roof on that section of the school building.

I saw cones, a barricade, and a sign that said "DANGER! WORK ZONE," which meant no one was allowed in that area. But I had an EMERGENCY!

So I carefully climbed out of the window, hung from the windowsill, and lowered myself down onto the roof.

It was pretty dark outside, but the roof was lit up by a light that was attached to a security camera.

I ran over, dropped to my knees, and reached for the comic book. But it slipped down into the giant tube.

I lunged after it and completely lost my balance. Suddenly I was falling! And I kept falling . . .

And falling! . . .

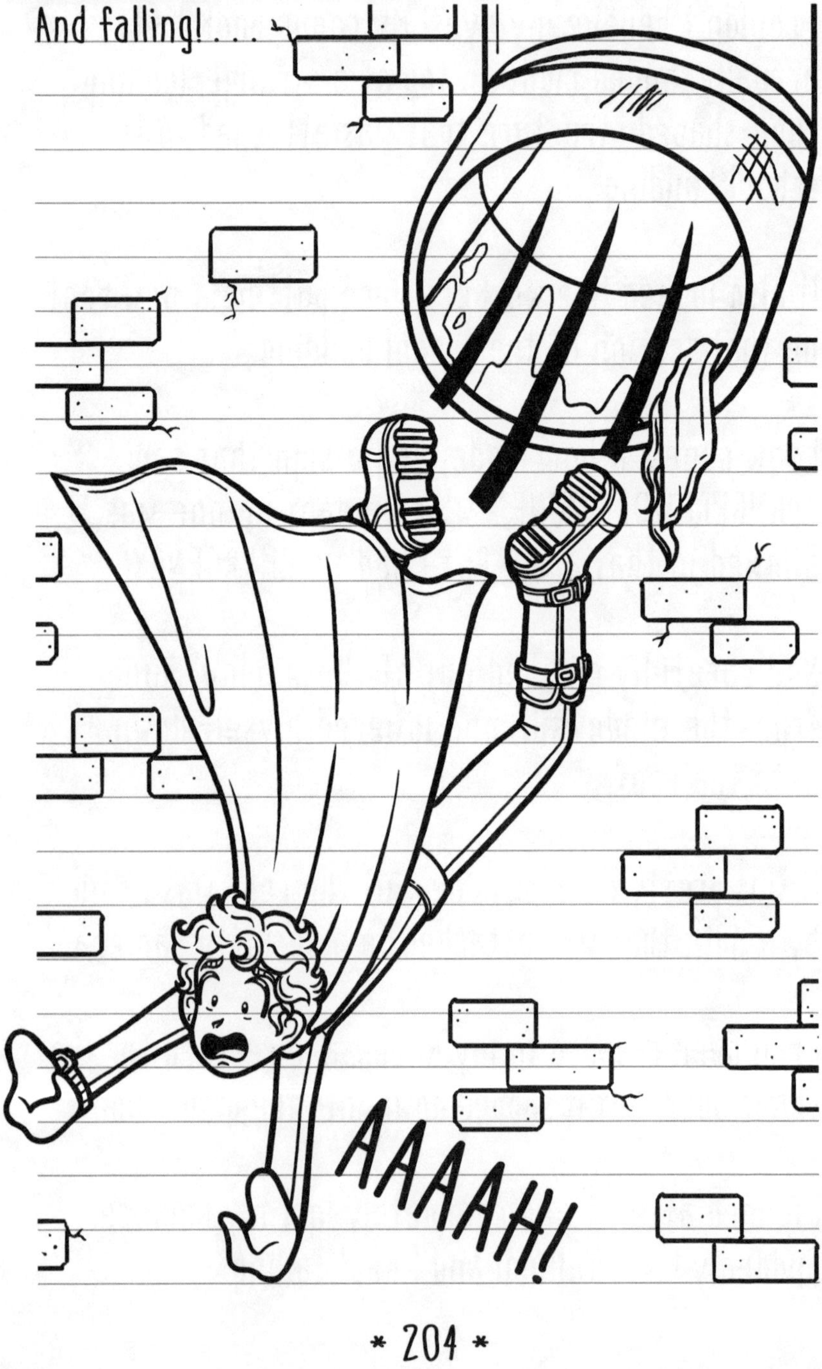
AAAAAH!

Until . . .

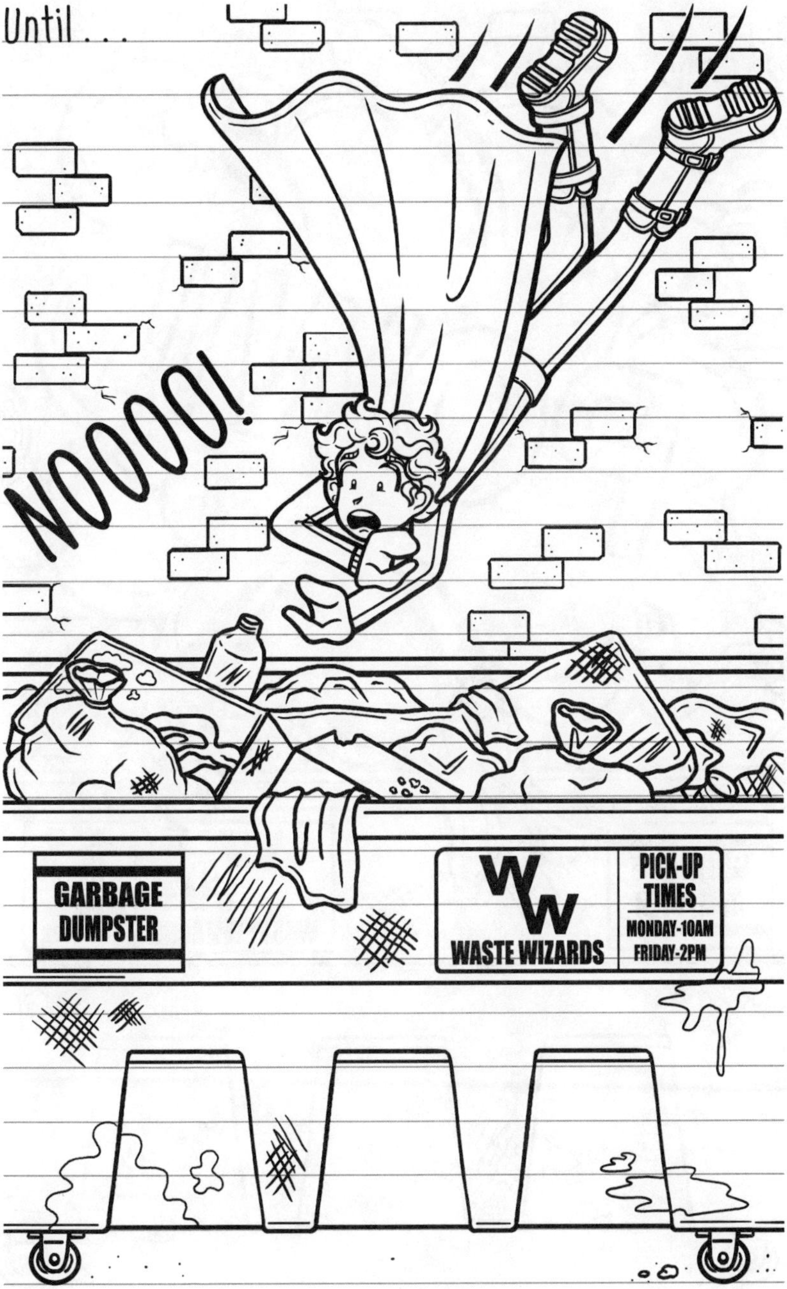

NOOOO!
GARBAGE DUMPSTER
WW
WASTE WIZARDS
PICK-UP TIMES
MONDAY-10AM
FRIDAY-2PM

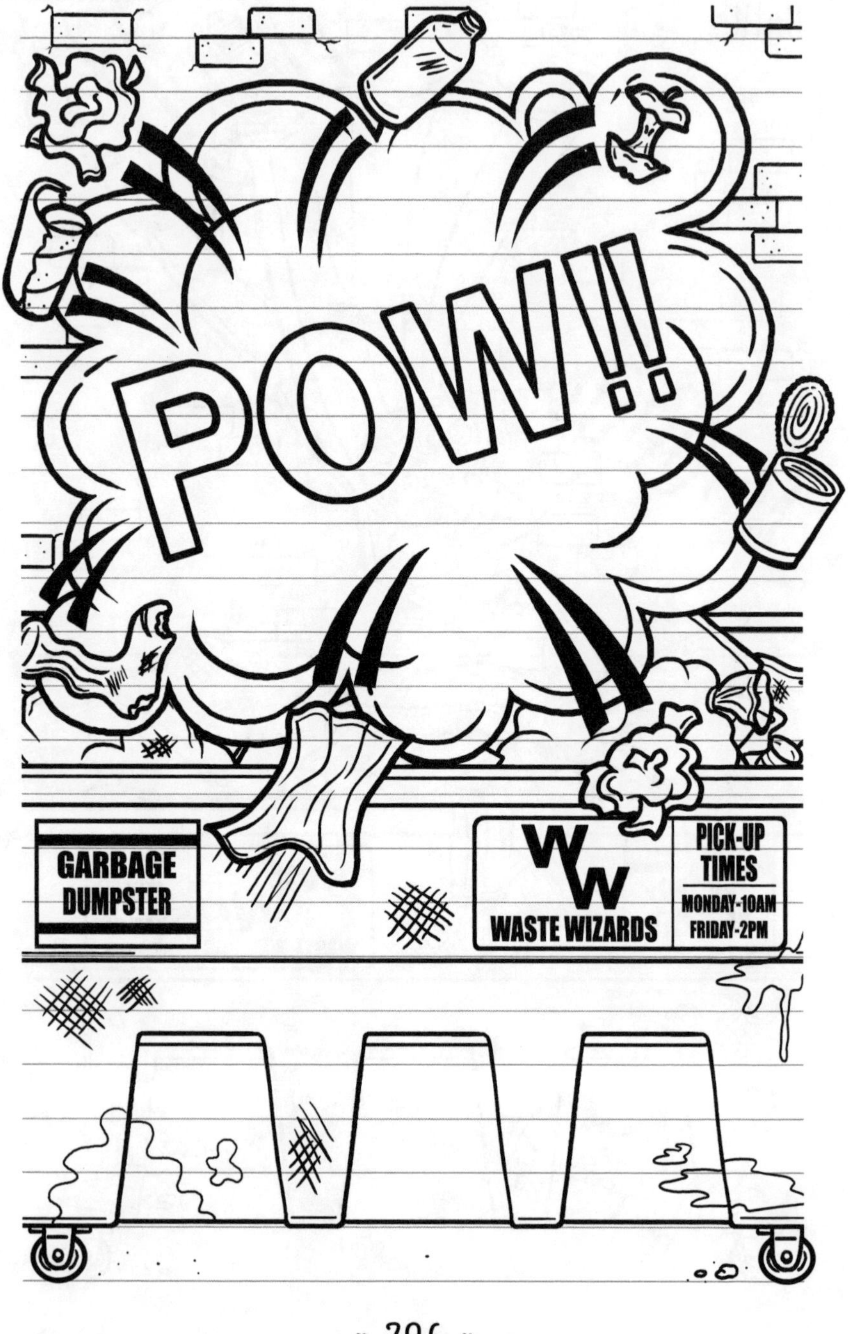
POW!!
GARBAGE
DUMPSTER
WW
WASTE WIZARDS
PICK-UP
TIMES
MONDAY-10AM
FRIDAY-2PM

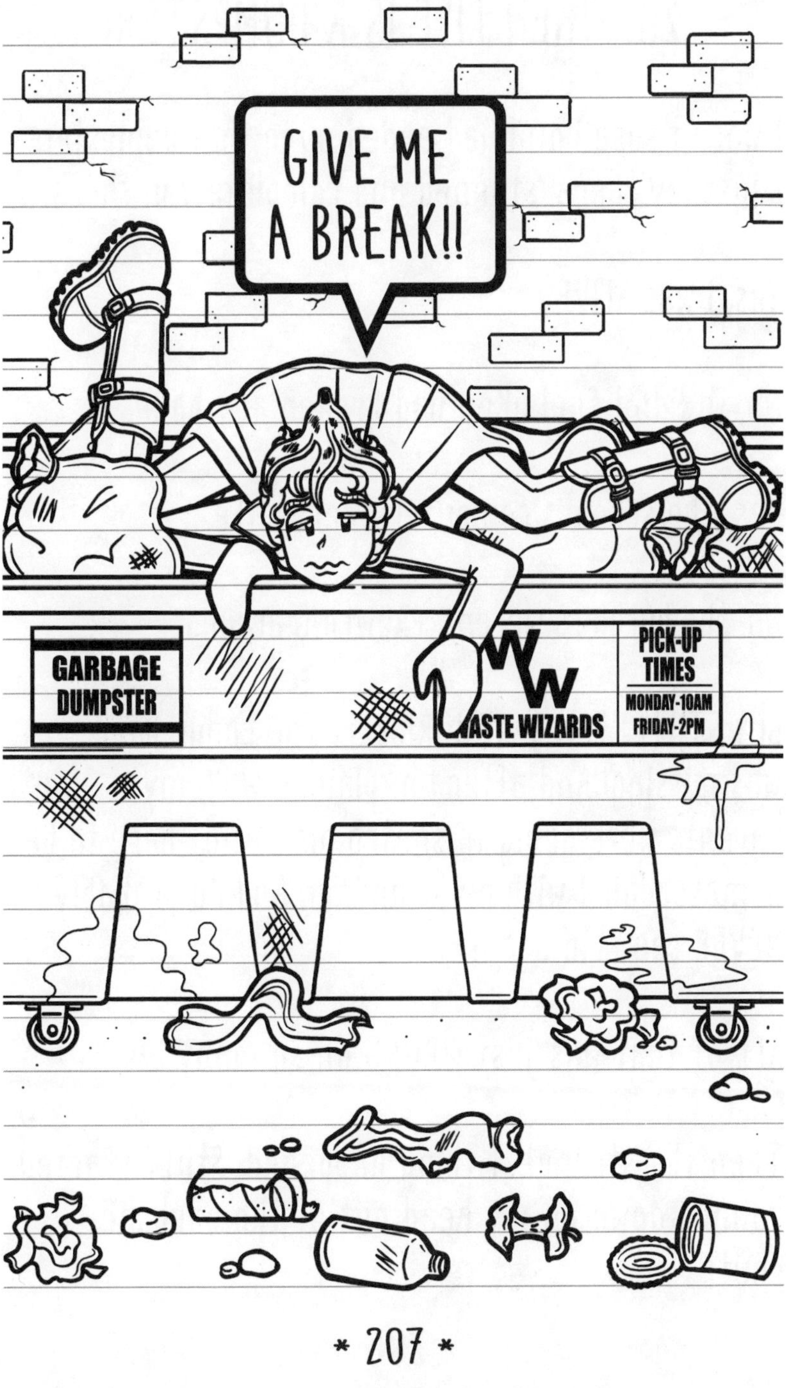
GIVE ME A BREAK!!
GARBAGE DUMPSTER
WASTE WIZARDS
PICK-UP TIMES
MONDAY-10AM
FRIDAY-2PM

23. WHEN LIFE IS A DUMPSTER!

I wasn't sure how I had ended up in that Dumpster. I just lay there, stunned and completely in shock.

Yes, I was ALIVE.

No, it didn't feel like I had broken any bones.

Yes, the school's computers were safe.

No, the burglars weren't PROWLING around.

But STILL! I felt just HORRIBLE! The comic book was missing! And after I explained WHY, my parents were going to snatch me out of here to be homeschooled with my grandma. And I'd probably NEVER see Erin again.

ALL of that was just WRONG on so many levels!

Then the strangest thing happened. Stuff started raining down on my head out of the garbage chute. . . .

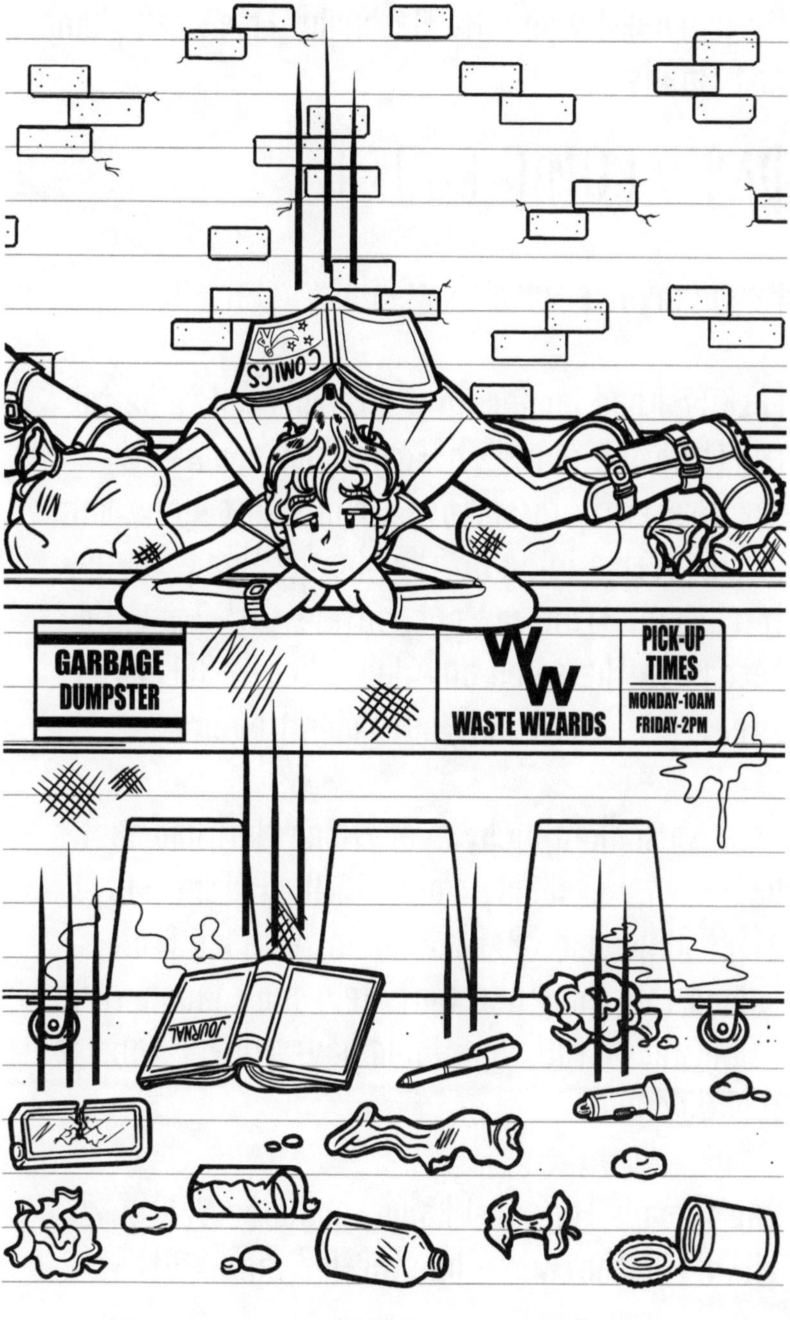
COMICS
GARBAGE
DUMPSTER
WW
WASTE WIZARDS
PICK-UP
TIMES
MONDAY-10AM
FRIDAY-2PM
JOURNAL

My journal. My pen. My flashlight. Erin's cell phone. And finally . . .

DAD'S COMIC BOOK!!

Maybe my life wasn't so CRUDDY after all.

Luckily, I had landed on what appeared to be the cot from the nurse's office, which apparently she'd recently tossed out. I had spent many hours in her office lying on that lumpy thing, trying to recover from my encounters with Thug. I'd recognize the smell anywhere. Yes, it REEKED of sweat, pee, and vomit, but I didn't even care.

I was so shaken up by everything that had just happened, I probably smelled WORSE! Especially after Ralph had GRABBED me in the dark from behind that door like that. Hey, don't laugh. If he had grabbed YOU, you would have POOPED your pants too! No doubt.

One thing is for sure! Ralph should be VERY THANKFUL that when he startled me like that, I

didn't go into NINJA mode and give him a good
BEATDOWN! No joke.

I was totally bummed when I discovered that the
cell phone was completely BUSTED. But the battery
was probably DEAD by now anyway. So I wouldn't be
calling the police (or anyone else, for that matter)
anytime soon.

But at least I had my dad's COMIC BOOK back! And,
miraculously, it didn't even look like it had just
been through World War III.

SWEET!!

I suddenly felt inspired to write a rap. . . .

TOSS THE BAD!
(A RAP WRITTEN BY COOL MAX C.)

This might look like
a bunch of TRASH!
But call it ANTIQUE
and it's COLD, HARD CASH!

I've got a G.I. Joe
with a missing head.
Three busted iPods,
the batteries dead.

Eighty-nine pounds
of mystery meat.
Forty gym socks that
STINK like feet.

Five broken skateboards,
not a thrill!
Moldy baloney
that'll make you ILL!

A rusted lock.
Old Lego blocks.
A busted clock.
A gray pet rock.

A dirty pink hat.
A dead brown rat.
A fat stuffed cat.
An old cracked bat.

Odds were against me.
I thought I'd fail!
Now three crooks
are going to jail!

I was down in the dumps,
now I'm riding HIGH!
My lyrics are grungy,
but my style is FLY!

One dude's trash
is another dude's treasure!
YOUR inner WORTH
no one can measure!

When life is a DUMPSTER,
don't get MAD!
EMBRACE the good,
and TOSS the BAD!

24. BLINDED BY THE LIGHT

Overall, I was feeling pretty good. I couldn't wait to tell Erin everything that had happened.

If I hadn't been sitting on top of a giant pile of trash in a Dumpster, I would have broken into my victory dance.

So I just did it inside my HEAD instead. But only for about fourteen seconds.

WHY?!

Because that's how long it took me to figure out I was NOW completely trapped inside a fifteen-foot-tall brick enclosure.

A LOCKED fifteen-foot-tall brick enclosure!

Even standing on the top of the Dumpster on my tippy toes, I STILL came up short from the top of the wall.

Which meant there was no way out. . . .

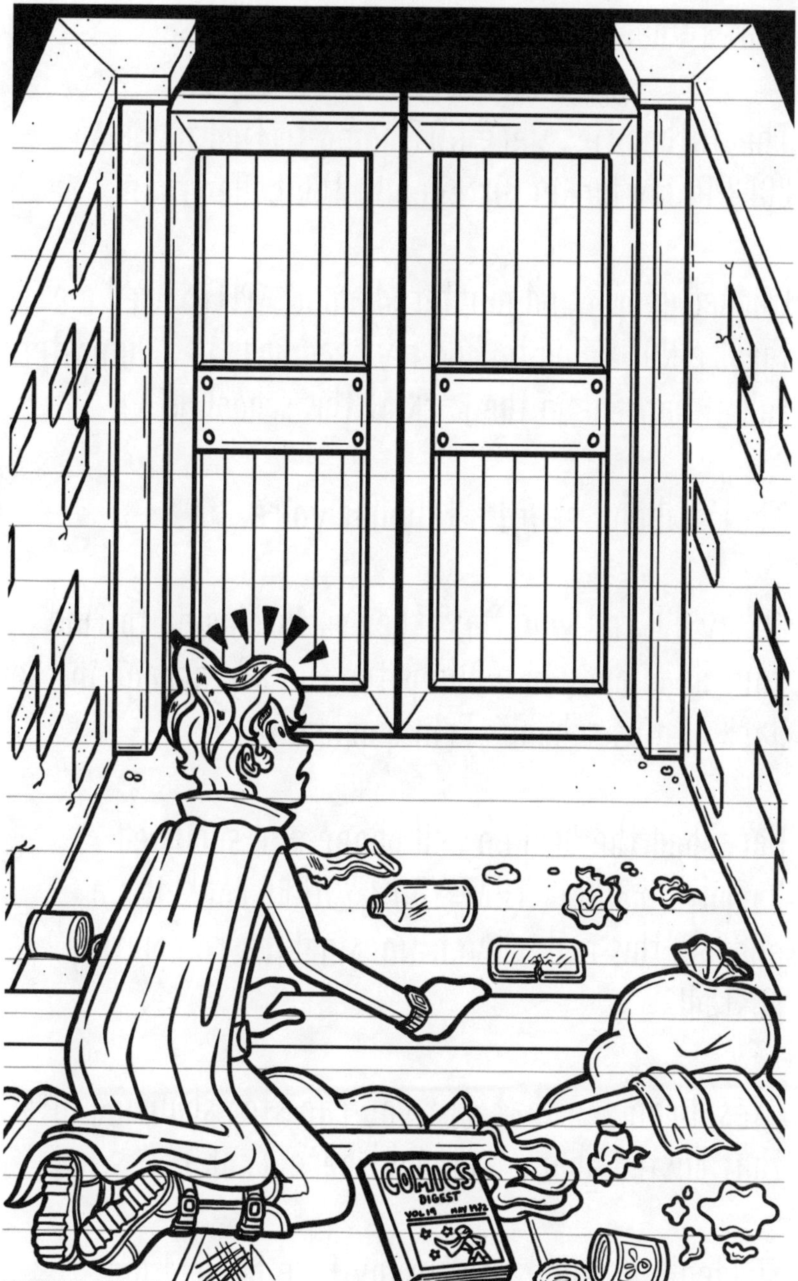
COMICS
DIGEST
VOL. 19

That's when it hit me like a ton of bricks!

The authorities were NOT going to find my DEAD BODY in my locker. Or even in the boiler room.

I sighed deeply and muttered aloud, "PLEASE tell me they're NOT going to find my dead body in a Dumpster full of garbage in the back of this school?!!"

That's when I heard a familiar voice.

"Okay, I'll tell you. Max, they're NOT going to find your dead body in a Dumpster full of garbage in the back of this school!" Erin giggled.

I grabbed the broken cell phone and shrieked happily, "ERIN! IS THAT YOU? YOU'RE BACK! It's a miracle this cell is even working! It's completely busted!"

"Yes, I can see that. But you can stop shouting into that busted phone. I'm right here. Look up!"

Suddenly a bright light in my face blinded me. . . .

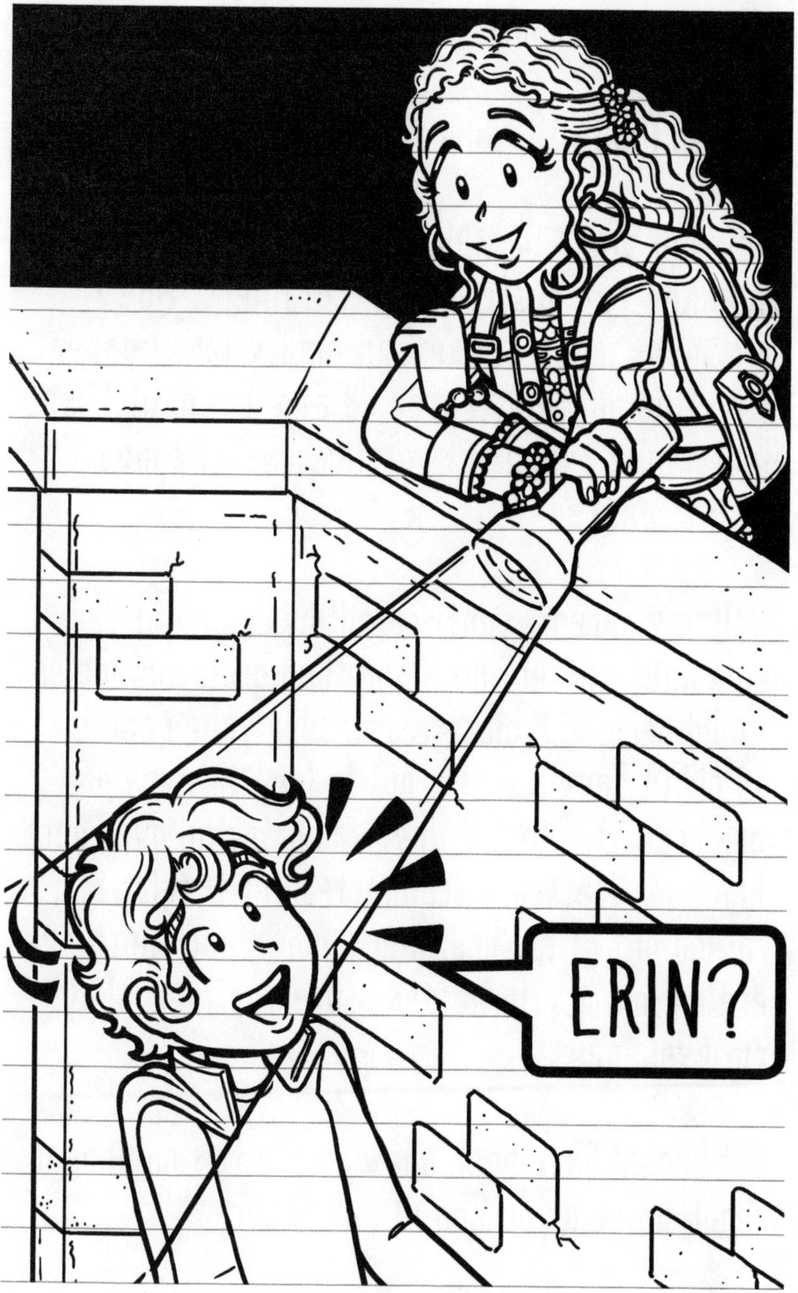
ERIN?

"What are YOU doing here?!" I gasped.

"Well, actually, it's kind of a long story."

"Hey, I'm stuck in a Dumpster. All I've GOT is time! And two busted ortho retainers, forty dirty gym socks, seventeen empty toilet paper rolls, five partially eaten PB and J sandwiches, eighty-nine pounds of rotting mystery meat, etc.," I snarked.

"Well, my parents confiscated my computer for being online after hours and then grounded me so I would become a more responsible young adult. So I didn't have a choice but to hack into my dad's work computer to see what was going on over here. Then I got dressed, disconnected our burglar alarm, crawled out of my bedroom window, and snuck over here on my bicycle to make sure you were okay," Erin explained.

"But I could have been anywhere in this humongous school. How did you know I was in here?"

Erin leaned back and shined her flashlight on the security camera at the top of the building. "When I saw your comic book fly out of that window, I knew it was just a matter of time before YOU'D be flying out of that window after it. That's when I knew I had to get over here. And FAST!"

Suddenly Erin turned serious. "So, are you okay?"

"I'm FINE!" I muttered. "But thank you! For coming over here to check on me. Especially after all of the drama with your parents. I just, um . . . really appreciate it," I gushed.

"Well, let's get you out of here! I called the cops a minute ago, so they'll be arriving soon."

That's when Erin moved her flashlight, and suddenly my whole outfit was in the spotlight. "MAX CRUMBLY! WHY ARE YOU WEARING MY ICE PRINCESS COSTUME?!"

I stared right into her eyes and waved my hands slowly in front of her face. . . .

"Max, are you INSANE?! Or maybe you hit your head when you fell into that Dumpster, because now you are acting CRAZY, dude!"

"Um, actually, that was my attempt at a Jedi mind trick!" I grinned sheepishly.

"Well, your Jedi mind trick obviously DIDN'T work! Now, WHY are you wearing my ice princess costume?!"

"You do NOT see an ice princess—"

"Cut it out, Max, that's not funny!"

"No, I'm very serious. It just might work!"

Suddenly Erin's eyes glazed over, and she gave me a blank stare.

"I. Do. NOT. See. An. Ice. Princess. Costume," she muttered in a trance-like state.

Of course that freaked me out.

"Erin, I was just kidding. Come on, snap out of it! Please!" I pleaded.

Finally she couldn't keep a straight face any longer and burst into laughter. I did too. I mean, it WAS funny. Kind of.

"Come on, Erin, seriously. Don't you think I have a cool superhero vibe going on? I actually like it!" I said, striking a macho Batman pose.

"Do you really want to know what I think, Max? I think you'd make a really great understudy for Elsa the Snow Queen in the next blockbuster *Frozen* movie!" she giggled.

I rolled my eyes at that girl.

THAT was just WRONG on so many levels!

For real!!

25. YET ANOTHER MORTIFYING MISADVENTURE OF MAX CRUMBLY

"Here, grab ahold of my backpack and I'll pull you up," Erin said as she dangled it within my reach.

"Are you SURE you can pull me up?" I asked. "And that backpack of yours is cute, but will it hold my weight?"

That's when we suddenly heard sirens wailing in the distance. The police were on their way to the school.

"Hurry up, Max! We need to get out of here before the police arrive! If my parents find out I snuck out of the house, instead of one week, they're going to ground me until my twenty-first birthday," Erin complained.

I took a running jump and grabbed Erin's backpack.

After that everything seemed to move in slow motion.

First Erin screamed in shock and surprise.

Then she toppled headfirst over the brick wall.

Finally she landed on the cot, right next to me in the DUMPSTER, with a loud . . .

THUMP!

"EW! OMG! What's that horrible smell?!" she shrieked.

"Come on, Erin! We're sitting in a DUMPSTER. Remember?! That SMELL could be anything! Rotting food, moldy books, even a dead animal," I teased.

Of course, I very conveniently left out the part that it could also possibly be . . . ME.

"So, how are we going to get out of here?! We BOTH could get kicked out of school!" Erin panicked.

"I don't know! But we'll figure it out, okay?" I exclaimed. "Just CHILLAX!" We sat there awhile. Then Erin started to bug me. . . .

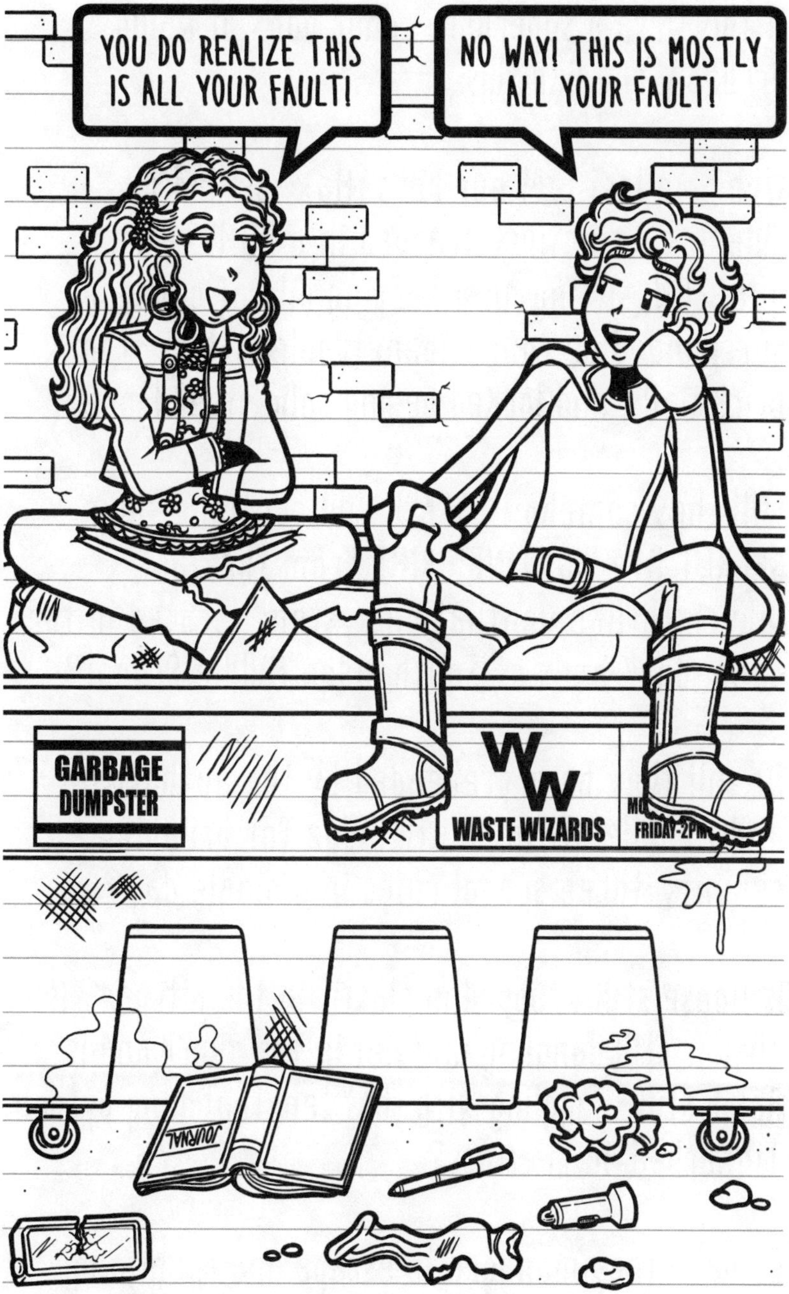
YOU DO REALIZE THIS IS ALL YOUR FAULT!
NO WAY! THIS IS MOSTLY ALL YOUR FAULT!
GARBAGE DUMPSTER
WW
WASTE WIZARDS
FRIDAY-2PM
JOURNAL

If this were a superhero comic book, it would probably end like this:

When we last left our hero, Max, he and his sidekick, Erin, were trapped in a DUMPSTER DUNGEON, sitting on a heaping pile of garbage, surrounded by four impenetrable fifteen-foot brick walls, and locked behind solid steel doors.

Will they somehow ESCAPE and continue their SECRET life FIGHTING CRIME from the vast, labyrinth-like ventilation system, located in the dank, dark halls of South Ridge Middle School?

Or will they be apprehended by the authorities and expelled from South Ridge for breaking seventy-three school rules in a single day?

Is Moose still wrapped in plastic in the kitchen? Is Tucker still dangling in a net in the gym? And is Ralph still snuggling with that ten-foot-long python, Tinkerbell, in bio class?

Or have they managed to escape and reunite in

a dark, twisted plot to seek their REVENGE?

Okay, people! You shouldn't be shocked or surprised that I'm leaving you hanging like this.

AGAIN!

I warned you this was possibly going to end in a cliffhanger just like a real comic book. Which means my journal is . . .

TO BE CONTINUED!

Now, listen to me VERY carefully. . . .

YOU ARE A HERO!

YOOOOOU ARE A HEEEEEERO!!

So go out and save the world!

WARNING! You have just become the unsuspecting victim of a Jedi mind trick.

Please be aware that becoming a SUPERHERO could result in mind-blowing adventures.

~~Including possible contact with garbage, slime, sewage, and other smelly substances. DON'T WORRY, I'M JUST KIDDING!~~

~~NOT!~~

If I can prevent what happened to ME from happening to YOU or another kid, then every second Erin and I spend suffering in that disgusting Dumpster dungeon will be worth it.

Because if WE can become heroes and make the world a better place . . .

YOU CAN TOO!!

FOR REAL!

ACKNOWLEDGMENTS

When we last left our superhero team, led by Batgirl (my editorial director, Liesa Abrams Mignogna), Liesa was busy orchestrating an ingenious master plan for getting my manuscript finalized, staying clear of booby traps and gridlocks. Using her supersonic listening skills and telepathic communication, she was able to literally edit manuscript pages before they were actually written. She's super creative, amazing, and can conquer anything with poise and a smile. Thank you, Batgirl, (and Bat Boy, too) for being my bat caped crusaders.

Using her magical powers to shape, shift, and manipulate illusions, Karin Paprocki, my gifted art director, was diligently creating a mind-blowing cover and fabulous layouts guaranteed to mesmerize kids across this universe. Thank you for your hard work and dedication.

My incredible managing editor, Katherine Devendorf, was busy using her powers of literary manipulation to edit words into thrilling sequences. With a stroke of her pen, she could thwart impending danger lurking on the pages of my manuscript, and for that I am grateful.

My fantastic superagent and ally, Daniel Lazar, was using his enhanced intellect and clairvoyance to transform a simple dream into reality. Thank you for your tireless and unwavering support and for being a true champion, advocate, and friend.

My league of superheroes at Aladdin/Simon & Schuster—Mara Anastas, Mary Marotta, Jon Anderson, Julie Doebler, Faye Bi, Carolyn Swerdloff, Matt Pantoliano, Catherine Hayden, Michelle Leo, Anthony Parisi, Christina Solazzo, Lauren Forte, Chelsea Morgan, Rebecca Vitkus, Crystal Velasquez, Jenn Rothkin, Ian Reilly, Christina Pecorale, Gary Urda, and the entire sales force—were collaborating, using their vast and unrivaled superpowers and abilities to make this series a huge success. Thanks for your fearlessness and commitment. You are the best team ever!

Torie Doherty-Munro at Writers House; my foreign rights agents Maja Nikolic, Cecilia de la Campa,

Angharad Kowal, and James Munro; and Zoé, Marie, and Joy were all busy using telepathic powers to translate Max's world into a universal language that everyone on this earth can enjoy. Thanks for all that you do!

My super-talented sidekick, Nikki, was busy creating new illustrated life forms. I'll always enjoy our day-to-day adventures and challenges in the publishing industry. I consider myself a very lucky mom to have the pleasure of working with you every day.

My other sidekicks, Kim, Doris, Don, and my entire family were protecting the home base and executing our mission. I could not do this without you. You are forever by my side no matter the quest or the escapade.

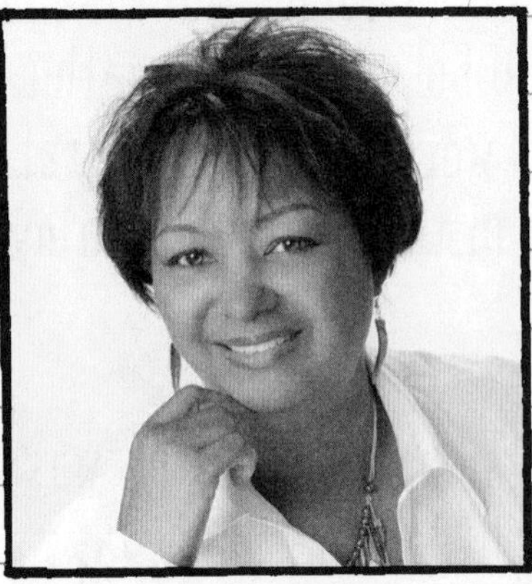

PHOTOGRAPH © BY SUNA LEE

RACHEL RENÉE RUSSELL

is the #1 *New York Times* bestselling author of the blockbuster book series Dork Diaries and the exciting new series The Misadventures of Max Crumbly.

There are more than thirty-five million copies of her books in print worldwide, and they have been translated into thirty-six languages.

She enjoys working with her daughter Nikki, who helps illustrate her books.

Rachel's message is "Become the hero you've always admired!"